BOUND

Samantha Wilde

Copyright

Bound © 2021 Samantha Wilde
Print Edition

ISBN: 978-1-7770799-6-3

Cover design by Covers by Combs
Formatting by BB eBooks

Table of Contents

Acknowledgements and Dedications

I'd like to dedicate this book to my wonderful daughters, Skylar and Isla. You're the reasons why I put my heart and soul into writing and I hope one day you have something you're passionate about. I want nothing more than to see you chase your dreams.

Jesse, thank you for being my greatest support in every area of our lives. You make writing possible on those days where I just need to plunk down and work. I'm so grateful to have you by my side while we both follow our ambitions.

Mom, thank you for reading all of my books. For supporting me in everything I do and never questioning my decisions. You're a great listening board, friend, and confidant. I love you.

Last but not least, I have some very special friends to thank! Rachel, thank you for your copyediting expertise. I'm so fortunate to have a wonderful editor in my corner. Doris and Britt, thank you for your excellent proofreading skills and valued input. Danielle, you've been there from the very first spark of inspiration for this book (well, all of them, haha) and I'm deeply grateful for our friendship and your opinions. Without all of you, this book would be a document shoved at the far corners of my laptop! I'm truly blessed to have you all in my life.

For my readers, who are probably annoyed by

the rambling of my dedications, this book is for you. You're the reason I write. It's my hope that somewhere I'm making a person smile while they read these words, or smacking their boyfriend with a "can't you be more like him?" comment lol. I hope you love Lexi and Nash's story. This couple is fierce and fiery and they light the pages.

All my best,
Samantha Wilde

CHAPTER 1

NASH'S DICK STRAINED under the restriction of his jeans. Lust burned through him, and he wanted nothing more than to lose himself in the sexy fucking thing pressed against him. Her scalding-hot tongue flicked over his bottom lip; her long, manicured fingernails curled into his shoulders.

"Jesus, Leah." Nash ground his face into her neck. Her warm vanilla scent was intoxicating.

She tossed her head back and settled against the wall, toying with the strap of her red dress. The neckline was cut down to her sternum, leaving less than two feet of material to the bottom of the dress. Her mussed red hair fell in a long curtain to her waist, and her cool, almost-turquoise blue eyes sparked.

His heart ached. His temples throbbed and his vision wavered. Shit, what was wrong with him?

He dropped his face to her shoulder and nipped her creamy flesh. His hand skimmed under her dress and rounded the soft corner of her hip. He

1

roamed his fingertips over the scant material of her panties before cupping her ass. Her body jolted, and her fingers channeled a wall of fire through his hair. Exploring between her cheeks, he brought his hand to the velvet skin on the inside of her thighs, reveling in how she arched sharply into his hand. He lifted the dainty lace and brushed his fingertip over her sex.

"Ah, my god," she panted.

He pulled away from the sweet skin at her neck and met her gaze. He pushed his middle finger deep inside her. Her mouth parted, revealing the ridges of her white teeth, and her fingers fisted his shirt. Her teeth nipped his earlobe, and a fog surfaced in front of his eyes. His stomach knotted with frustration.

Dammit, he'd only had two drinks all night. He'd never been so turned on in his life, but was he so damn horny that keeping his body vertical was a struggle? Once he lost himself inside her, the thick fog would surely pass.

He pulled away to meet her gaze again, waiting for the silent go-ahead. Her smoky eye makeup was a sharp contrast to her clear blue eyes and pale skin. She moved from the wall, and his hand fell away from her. Her fingernails pressed into his wrist as she led him to the bed.

The floor tilted, and his body threatened to meet it. He planted his feet in the soft carpet, but still his body wobbled. She stopped at the side of the bed, and the rustle of clothes hitting the floor brought his attention back to her. Black lace barely covered her full breasts, and a skimpy triangle of the same material rested between her thighs.

"Bend over," he urged. His voice shook and his knees wobbled.

She came closer. Her hand rested on his shoulder, and her lips moved over his ear, mumbling something about lying down. He tunneled his hand in his hair and fought another ripple of dizziness. This time it was too great. He staggered to his knees and shot his elbows out to catch himself on the mattress. His pulse raced ferociously through his veins and his skull threatened to burst with pressure.

"Come to the bed." Leah's voice was a distant whisper. She pulled on his bicep until he stood and dropped onto his back on the bed. She kneeled on the mattress, peering down at him, her vibrant red hair dangling onto his shoulder. She lifted a hand and tucked her hair behind her ear. Then she pressed her other palm into his chest, holding him down. He struggled to hold onto consciousness, but her soothing hand kept him from sitting. His eyes fluttered against the gravitational pull of sleep. He watched Leah's face through constant shuttering of his eyelids. No concern etched her smooth features, her face turned, scanning the bedroom.

She's looking for something.

He snapped his eyes open, this time fighting off the clutches of darkness. Rage pulsed through him. He circled her wrist with his hand and tightened his grip. "*You*," he hissed. "What did you do to me?"

She pulled against his grasp, amplifying his suspicion. Adrenaline shot through his veins. He bolted up, snagged her shoulders, and flipped her over, pinning her to the bed beneath him.

"What the fuck did you do to me?" His voice crackled in his ears and his fingers itched to wrap around her neck and strangle the truth out of her. Her satiny breasts rubbed against his forearm, and the heat between her legs radiated through his jeans. The strength in his hands ebbed away as numbness crept over his body. Sweat rolled down the back of his neck with the effort it took to hold himself up.

Her eyes narrowed into slits. She moved swiftly, shoving him to his back. Pain erupted through his chest with the force of her blow. Darkness closed in around him, eating away at his vision like a school of termites. The mattress dipped under him, and his eyes searched for her. Fear burned up his esophagus.

She's here to kill me. Who the fuck sent her?

She crossed the room to his dresser, her pert, round ass swaying in the black thong as she tossed his belongings to the floor.

She's looking for something.

He tried to form words, but only a low mumble came from his lips. She turned to face him. The world tilted on its axis, sending an earthquake of pain through his skull. She took a step toward him and her form swayed. He lunged off the bed, his hands outstretched. But the hard, unrelenting floor knocked the wind from his chest.

"God, you're dramatic." Her gentle voice rang with irritation. "It's a roofie. You'll be fine in the morning." She pressed her cool palm to the side of his head, lifted his cheek from the floor, and stuffed a pillow under it.

"What do you want?" His slack lips garbled the words. Silence ticked by, and the black oblivion that sucked at his consciousness pulled him deeper into its clutches. She stood, offering him a delicious view of her heart-shaped ass.

And damn if he still didn't want her.

"Revenge." The single word fell around him, drumming through his consciousness.

Revenge for what?

But his mouth wouldn't cooperate with his brain. She scooped up his iPad from the dresser and moved swiftly around the room. His body hummed and his eyelids drooped with the weight of anvils. He forced them open one last time and caught her rummaging in his closet. He scoffed, and the sound came out like a snort. She could take whatever the hell she wanted. Money and electronics could be replaced. *As long as she doesn't get her hands on the ledger.* Impossible. He'd hidden it well.

The ledger was irreplaceable. Having the contents in someone's hands outside of the organization would put the Grand Chancellor through the roof and Nash in the hot seat. A high-pitched ring reverberated through his ears and his face sunk deeper into the pillow, like a stone falling into the ocean. He lost the battle to open his eyes. Blackness closed in around him, and he slipped into sleep.

★　★　★

ALEXIS SHIMMIED BACK into her dress and swept her hair into a bun. She had to hurry. Nash was a damn ox. She'd given him two roofies and it had taken almost an hour for him to pass out. He'd fought it every second. The feel of his rock-hard dick against her leg had sent anticipation fluttering through her, and if he hadn't passed out when he had, she might not have been able to say no.

Bend over.

Good god, he would have taken her from behind and she wouldn't have minded one bit. She fisted her hand against her forehead and squeezed her eyes shut. She shouldn't be having these thoughts about Nash Holmes. He was a monster—or at least a monster by association—but god, could he kiss. She'd expected it would be a struggle not to vomit in his face, but from the moment she'd approached him in the hotel bar, her stomach had been tied in knots. Heat had spread through her belly and scorched her thighs. She sure as hell hadn't planned on letting him finger her either, but she'd quickly run out of ways to stall waiting for the drug to take over. She'd been seconds from coming, and it had taken all her self-control to stop him.

A little nudge of guilt gnawed at her. Had she given him too much of the drug? She pressed her lips together and shook her head. She couldn't concern herself with that. He was one of *them*. He was a murderer, a heartless bastard. Killing him wasn't on her agenda, but he deserved whatever came to him. She had to find the ledger and get the hell out of here.

She shifted her eyes to his unmoving body. She'd feel better if she checked on him first, as stupid as that was—the last thing she needed was to end up in jail for murder.

She huffed a sigh and dropped to her knees next to him. As she studied his full, slack mouth, apprehension erupted on the back of her neck. His breath came out in long, low puffs. His thick black finger-length hair barely reached the tops of his ears. A red tint covered his cheekbones and the straight bridge of his nose. Probably from the drug. And his arousal. Her lips twitched with amusement. He was going to wake up with some serious blue balls.

Her fingers itched to drag her hand over his jaw's dark stubble, which had abraded her lips only minutes ago. The top of a tattoo peeked out from the neckline of his shirt, and a jagged scar slashed through his eyebrow. It did nothing to take away from his good looks. Instead, it enhanced them, showing the edge and deadly side that lurked behind the now-closed steel-gray eyes.

She stretched her shaking hand out and pressed two fingers to the side of his throat. Her nerves twitched, expecting him to jolt at any second. He lay still. His pulse beat slowly against her fingers. Slowly, but strong. He'd be fine. She straightened away, scooped up her bag, and hurried to the safe she'd spotted in his walk-in closet.

He sure knew how to live. The massive, modern condo with warm neutral tones swallowed her. The bathroom sported a six-person walk-in glass shower and soaker tub, as well as a floor-to-ceiling two-sided gas fireplace. Lionsgate obviously paid him well to do their dirty work.

She stepped through the pocket door and made her way to the safe hidden behind a line of perfectly pressed dress shirts. She skimmed over the keypad looking for some telltale sign of the code, as if it would illuminate before her.

If she guessed wrong, it would lock her out and all of this would be for nothing. She had his tablet, but that too was password protected. She needed incriminating evidence—she needed inside information that only he possessed. Pushing her tongue over her lips, she took a deep breath through her nose. Then, turning on her heel, she marched back into the bedroom. Maybe he was as forgetful as she was with passwords and stored them in his phone. That too would likely be blocked with a code, but it was worth a try.

She dropped to her knees again and fished his phone out of his back pocket. The screen flashed at her. Password needed. *Shit.* She tossed the phone to the ground and let out a growl. What had she been thinking? She should have tried to get him to talk first, maybe threatened him to get the code. Not that he'd be intimidated by her. Her eyes drank in his six-foot-four-inch frame.

Then her gaze fell on the tattoo at his neck. She squinted and leaned closer. The gentle curve of the number three lay barely covered. She inched closer and tugged down the V-neck. Right beneath his collarbone, on the right side of his chest, was a six-digit number above the telltale Lionsgate emblem. She'd recognize the similar sequence anywhere. Lionsgate's membership number was given to each member once they passed a certain level of seniority in the organization, almost like a permanent medal. The members often tattooed the number on their person so they could easily prove their standing within the brotherhood.

But would Nash use it as a password to his safe? It was almost too stupid, but at the same time fit the cockiness of Lionsgate Kinship. They were untouchable.

Alexis leaped to her feet and raced back to the closet. Her fingers trembled as she punched in the number: 38-9432.

Please work.

A green light flashed, and the lock released with a soft click. *Yes!* She swung open the door and chewed the inside of her cheek. Her eyes widened. *Holy shit.* She lifted one of the many stacks of hundred-dollar bills. Her mouth went dry.

Blood money.

There had to be at least a hundred grand. She put the cash back in the safe and turned her attention to its other contents. A brown leather-bound book sat neatly on top of a few other books and a velvet case. She pulled out the leather book first—the ledger. She ran her fingertips over the emblem and goosebumps tickled over her skin. *Lionsgate Kinship* was scrawled beneath the group's emblem: a snarling lion's head.

Her hands burned to peel open the book, but she stopped herself. Once she opened it, she wouldn't be able to stop reading. She'd struck gold. This book held the power to incriminate a lot of people. First, she'd have to find the rest of the dirt on the organization.

She tucked the book into her bag and brought her gaze to the velvet case. She lifted it, and her arm buckled under its weight. Resting it on the edge of the shelf, she snapped it open. Twelve square gold medallions stared back at her. Roman numerals were etched in the top right corners, while the centers held various symbols. Her stomach twisted, and the cold finger of dread raked down her back. She slapped the lid closed and set the case back in the safe. She didn't need to take those. There was no way she'd make it through security, and stealing gold from a Lionsgate enforcer was as good as putting a bullseye on her back.

She certainly didn't need two.

She shut the safe and strode back into the bedroom. Nash's deep snores split the air. God, he looked uncomfortable, one leg twisted at an awkward angle, his ankle bent under the bed. One arm lay sprawled above his head, and his hand crumbled against the nightstand. Balancing on the balls of her feet, she crept toward him. She circled her fingers around his thick wrist and lowered it so that it lay flush on the ground.

A chill bit through the air. The windows were tightly closed, so it was evident he had the central air set to frigid, despite the already cool weather. Irritation fizzled inside her. Why the hell was she worried about this big ape? He didn't have a goddamn soul. If he did, he sure as hell wouldn't be with the organization. She grabbed the comforter off the bed and yanked it over his body before racing out of the room as if the hounds of hell were on her heels.

In a matter of hours, they would be.

She closed the front door behind her and hurried down the hall of his condo building. Had she forgotten anything? God, what if she'd left something incriminating, something that would lead him to her . . . No. She'd been extra careful before leaving for the bar. She hadn't even brought her real ID, in case he'd gotten suspicious. She stepped into the elevator and her stomach shot up to her throat as the cart dropped twenty-something stories.

She gripped the rail at her side and took a deep, shuddering breath. She'd done it. Now all she had to do was get the hell out of Seattle. She wouldn't feel safe until a sea of distance lay between her and Nash. She breezed through the marble foyer, passing the bubbling stone waterfall cascading from the ceiling. The concierge lifted his dark eyebrows at her. His bald head shone in the fluorescent light. She smiled and waved, but his brows pinched together.

Shit. Was he a friend of Nash's? Would he go upstairs and check on him?

Stop being paranoid.

Her heels scuffed over the pavement. At the curb, she stretched her hand in the air, over the moving wall of traffic. A few seconds later, a cab slowed, and she yanked open the back door and slid in.

"Seattle-Tacoma airport, please."

The cabbie nodded.

Her scalp itched beneath the red wig. God, she couldn't wait to get it off. Her fingers tingled with the need to loosen it from her skin, but she couldn't. Not until she landed safely.

Once the organization knew she'd stolen from Nash, they'd be on the hunt for her. The depth of their reach was bottomless. She was traveling with a fake identity and a disguise, but that would only protect her for so long.

If they found her, they would try to kill her.

Again.

CHAPTER 2

R AGE COURSED THROUGH Nash's veins like the thundering freight train of a migraine that split his skull. He took the stairs up two at a time and ran over in his mind what he'd say to Conrad. "I'm sorry, she was just so fucking hot" wouldn't cut it. He'd kill the slithering little bitch once he got his hands on her. She'd lied, drugged him, and stolen the fucking ledger. Guarding it had been his responsibility for the last eight years. Talk about a one-night stand gone wrong. The real kicker was that he'd acted out of the ordinary.

Hell, he'd had his fair share of one-nighters, but not once had he invited a woman to his downtown condo. She'd told him she was leaving on a red-eye flight and had already checked out of the hotel, and he hadn't been able to resist inviting her to his place. He'd just had to have her.

Was she working for someone? He ripped through every job in his mind Conrad had sent him on recently. It was possible they'd pissed someone off, a gang maybe. But why in the hell would they take the ledger?

He reached the top of the staircase, and the long hallway creaked beneath the weight of his steps. When he first started coming to the House, he'd tiptoed around, afraid of the telltale squeaks. Over time, it had become a second home to him.

Punching-bag chains rattled two stories below. The sound echoed off the walls. He should be in the basement training with the other enforcers, sweat rolling off his body, feeling the satisfying jolt of the punching bag as he delivered death shots.

Not today.

Right now, he had to face the only man who had stepped up into a father role for him. A memory of his real father flashed in front of his eyes.

"I'll pick you up in a few hours. Go play with your brothers."

An iron fist crushed his heart. He drew a breath through his nose and forced away the suffocating pressure on his lungs. He'd been only six years old at the time. A week later, he'd been separated from his three brothers. He'd lived in whatever foster homes would take him until finally ending up at the group home four years later—the group home that Lionsgate Kinship owned and ran as a nonprofit organization.

Conrad had visited every week and he and Nash had bonded. Five years later, Conrad adopted him, and Nash had been part of the organization ever since. Along with his brothers, Lionsgate was his family, his blood. He stopped at the large wooden door with Conrad's name scribed on it and lifted his knuckles.

"Come in." Conrad's voice boomed through the thick wood. Nash's stomach clenched, and he lowered his hand to the metal knob. He stepped into the office, which had always reminded him of a cave. Red drapes hung over the window, blocking out what little light leaked in over the other buildings around them. The office's gloom mirrored his mood.

Conrad stood from the green leather chair at his wide mahogany desk. Hundreds of books lined the wall behind him. At sixty-five, Conrad was in his prime. He was over six foot five and worked out every day. The results showed in his wide-shoulder custom suit.

"Hey, son. Everything okay?" At his temples, gray strands blended with his dark brown hair. His slanted cheekbones met his wide nose, and a deep frown line creased his forehead.

Nash nodded and closed his fists at his sides. He dropped into the seat in front of Conrad's desk. Many times during his adolescent years, he'd sat in the very same chair—or the one identical to it—in Conrad's mansion.

"No, it's not. I fucked up, Conrad." He'd never been able to call him Dad. Maybe it was because deep down he'd always expected the man to drop him, just as his parents had. But Conrad hadn't. He'd taken on the responsibility of a fifteen-year-old boy and helped shape him into the person he was today—a mean, pummeling motherfucker, but one who'd been taught loyalty and now offered it in return.

Conrad's brown eyes hardened, and he pressed his palms into the wooden desk. He sat, not taking his eyes off Nash. "What happened?"

Nash let out a long sigh and rested his elbows on his knees. "Someone robbed me last night. The ledger is gone—"

Conrad held up his hand. "You didn't have it locked up?" The corner of his mouth twitched, and a red streak spread across his forehead.

Nash had witnessed Conrad's temper on a number of occasions, but it had never been directed at him. He spun the gold emblem ring on his finger, the one he'd gotten after his third initiation. Now, he wasn't worthy of it. "I had everything locked up." He lifted his eyes to his father figure. "I don't know how she figured out the code—"

Conrad snapped up straighter in his chair, his spine stiffening. "*She?*"

Shame filled him. Hell, he'd let a woman seduce, date rape, and rob him. He flexed and unflexed his fingers. Conrad waited, his breath coming out in fast pants.

"Yes, a woman."

"Fuck!" Conrad slammed his hand against the desk. The thick wood shook beneath the force. Crimson colored his cheeks and sweat collected on his brow. "What did she say her name was? Not that it matters," he said with a scoff. "She would have used a fake one."

"Leah Jensen."

Conrad stood and paced behind the desk. He shoved his hand through his hair and his lips moved, mumbling something inaudible.

Apprehension tightened the cords in Nash's neck. Something wasn't right. Conrad never got rattled like this. He'd expected Conrad to be pissed at him for not safeguarding the ledger, but what exactly had him so tightly wound? He straightened in his seat. "She drugged me, and by the time I realized, it was too late."

Conrad slowed and met Nash's stare. He pressed his knuckles on the desk, his face tense. "Would you recognize her if you saw a picture?"

Without hesitation, Nash nodded. There was no way he'd forget her face. The clear blue eyes outlined in a rim of indigo, her full, fuckable mouth and creamy skin. Conrad turned to the bookcase and removed several thick tomes, revealing a safe.

"Six months ago, I asked you to hire Cole to take care of a couple people. Do you remember?" Conrad kept his back to Nash as he punched the code into the keypad.

On rare occasions, Conrad requested the services of Nash's older brother. Cole was as dangerous as they came. All his brothers had been deeply affected by their parents' abandonment, but Cole had taken it the hardest. Nash loved his brothers, even though they'd been separated for a large portion of their childhood. While they'd all made an effort to stay in touch, Nash had seen Cole the most. When Cole and his twin Dallas had turned eighteen, they'd taken custody of the second youngest brother, Dare.

Nash shook his head, trying to remember the specific occasion. "Is that when he was out of the country and had to refer you to someone else?"

"That's the one." He sifted through a folder in his hand. "Yuri Ivanov and his son Brooks were members of the House. They were traitors who sold our information. His daughter, Alexis," he said, slapping a picture on the desk between them, "is an investigative journalist. Is that her?"

Nash peeled up the edge of the glossy photo of a young woman. She sat in a coffee shop, a mug halfway to her full mouth. His blood oscillated against his throat. The woman in the picture had soft brown hair that waved over her breasts. Her blue eyes were slightly lowered, gazing at the laptop screen in front of her. Her perfectly shaped mouth was parted, and the two beauty marks he'd noted last night were accentuated in the sunlight— one on her cheekbone, the other on the column of her throat.

It was her all right.

He hesitated. Malik, the assassin Cole had referred, had set the Ivanov's residence on fire, and the inhabitants had supposedly died. The other details of the job evaded him. His eyes grazed over the smooth lines of the woman's cheeks, the gentle curve of her chin and delicate shoulders.

Revenge.

The last word she'd spoken to him echoed through his head. Revenge for her family? Lionsgate Kinship members weren't exactly the epitome of upstanding citizens. It was damn possible they could have pissed off the wrong people. Nash was well aware of some of their shady business activities, but at the end of the day, no one got hurt . . . at least no one innocent. If someone crossed them or fucked with one of their kin, that person would get a beatdown from one of the enforcers and scared into silence. If that didn't work, Cole or one of his associates would be contracted out. But those people were scum, assholes trying to sell inside information or blackmail them. If Conrad had killed Alexis's family, he wouldn't have done so without reason.

Lionsgate protected the innocent. Along with the Seattle House, other Houses across the country had group homes. They took adolescent kids off the streets and gave them an alternative to foster homes.

If it weren't for Lionsgate Youth Center, Nash wouldn't be where he was. He never would have been adopted by Conrad. Though living with his older brothers would have been okay, it wouldn't have given him the stability he'd needed. And Cole had had one less mouth to feed.

Nash lowered the photo. His loyalty was to Lionsgate. Alexis had screwed the wrong people and now, they needed to get back what she'd stolen. "It's her. Her hair is different. It was red last night, but it's definitely her."

Conrad clenched one hand into a fist and pinched the bridge of his nose with the other. "If that was Alexis Ivanov, this is worse than we ever could have imagined." He lowered his hand. Ice passed over his brown eyes, turning them almost black. The whites of his eyes were bloodshot. The plains of his face hardened and his brow twitched.

"Why?" Nash's fingers bit into the corner of the picture, creasing the edge.

Conrad drummed his fingertips on the edge of the desk. His gaze never faltered from Cole's. "Her father was a traitor, as was her brother. They tried to sell our secrets to the papers, mostly half-truths and fabricated bullshit to ruin our reputation."

More questions burned on the tip of Nash's tongue, but he forced them down his throat. Conrad wasn't a monster. He was fair and just, and if Alexis's family had been marked, it was because Conrad was telling the truth.

"Kill her." Conrad's words came out deep and raspy.

Nash's body tensed and his pulse slowed. Conrad wasn't just agitated—he was fucking scared. Who the hell did Alexis Ivanov think she was and what dirt was she trying to dig up? It didn't matter. She'd made a fool of him and had threatened his family.

That didn't mean she deserved to die. Nash pinched his lips together. She'd pay for what she'd done, but putting a bullet in her head went against his grain. Fuck, maybe he was getting soft. Had a guy done what she had, Nash wouldn't even have second thoughts about terminating him.

"I'll find her," Nash promised. He tucked the picture back in the envelope and held it tightly as he turned away. Conviction arced through him. Damn right he would find her. What he'd do with her was something he'd figure out later.

"Nash," Conrad called, and walked toward him. Nash paused and turned to face him.

"She'll have fled far. I think you should take backup."

The muscles around his shoulders contracted. Backup? Because of a woman? He let the insinuation fall between them. They were in this position because he hadn't been on his toes around her. That wouldn't happen again.

Nash shook his head sharply. "No. I have a very personal interest in this. I'll call Dare. He should be able to locate her by the end of the day."

The corner of Conrad's lip turned up. "Get even, son. She fucked with the wrong family." His hand landed on Nash's shoulder, and fire scorched through his skin. Nash shrugged, making Conrad's hand drop.

"I'll keep you posted." He left the room, closing the door behind him and immediately pulling out his phone. At thirty-five, Dare was two years older than Nash and the third oldest of the Holmes brothers. As a very skilled hacker, club owner, and black market dealer, there was nothing Dare couldn't do. Nash's computer skills were more than mediocre, but Dare was a wiz. If anyone could locate Alexis, it was him.

"I need a big favor." Nash spoke low into the phone. He didn't need anyone else knowing about this, though the House was mostly empty at this time of day. He moved swiftly through the halls.

"What's up?" Dare said.

Dare would be be intrigued by the challenge of the task. Nash exited the House and strode to the vine-covered gate.

"I need you to use your facial recognition software. I'm going to drop off a picture, and then I'm heading home to pack. I'm leaving for the airport in a couple hours, and I hope to hell you can tell me where I'm going by then."

Nash disconnected and climbed into his car. Images raced through his mind. Alexis's face, her soul-sucking blue orbs . . . and then the thought of Conrad's bone-chilling order to kill her.

Nash had never disobeyed a request.

★ ★ ★

INSIDE THE ONE-BEDROOM hotel suite, Alexis let the door slam shut behind her and dropped her carry-on. Immediately she yanked off the bleached-blonde wig. Twenty-five hours of traveling had drained the strength from her bones and the moisture from her eyes. But the real torture was not being able to pore over the ledger. It hadn't moved from the tight pocket of her purse, though she'd checked to make sure it was still there a zillion times.

Lionsgate members were everywhere. Nearly every major city in the world held a House. And since no women were permitted in the organization, it would be an enormous red flag for her to be seen with one of their very recognizable books.

She dropped into the living room chair by the window and dragged her oversized purse onto her lap. She'd requested a room on the twentieth floor, but height wouldn't keep her safe. In two days, she'd change hotels, possibly locations. If she wanted to live, she'd have to change them almost as often as she'd changed planes, IDs, and wigs on her journey.

The bed's plush white duvet called to her, but she couldn't pass out yet. She'd probably sleep for two days. First, she had to look at the ledger. Fatigue made her muscles tingle and her movements clumsy. She opened the zipper in her purse and pulled out the leather-bound book.

She'd finally have the name of who killed her family. The police report from that night had described three bodies burned to death in the fire—her father's, mother's, and brother's. Only her brother hadn't died, of that she was certain. He'd called her from an encrypted phone with the intention to drop something off to her at her parents' house and then the fire had broken out. He'd also mentioned his plan to snoop through one of the House's elite member's homes, and he'd refused to tell her whose. They must have caught him. It was the only explanation for his disappearance. They could have killed him by other means, but until she had answers, she had to assume he was alive. Brooks was a fighter.

Her eyes snapped to the open window next to her. Her heart clamored against her ribcage. God, she was careless. She tucked the book under the cushion against her hip and leaped out of the seat. She grabbed the heavy gold drapes and closed them tightly, sealing out the darkness.

She picked up the phone on the desk in the corner and called room service. Shoveling food in her face would hopefully keep her alert enough to do what she needed to. She ordered a salad and fries and then crossed the suite to the bathroom.

Her bones ached to climb into the glass shower, but that would have to wait until just before she went to bed. It was seven p.m. where she was, hours before her normal bedtime. Not that her body cared.

The bathroom was lavish, and complimentary Russian soaps decorated the marble countertop. She grabbed a pristine white washcloth and removed her makeup. After smoothing coconut oil on her face, she frowned at the sallow tone of her skin and dark circles under her eyes. Lord, she looked like something out of a zombie movie. She brushed out the rat's nest on her head and changed into comfy clothes then set out her toiletries on the bathroom counter.

Bang, bang, bang.

She jolted, dropping a jar. It fell to the floor with a sharp clatter. Damn, she was jumpy. She drifted through the suite and pressed her eye to the peephole. A man wearing a chef's coat stood at the door, a silver platter in his hand.

She opened the door, accepted the food, and handed him a tip. The hot, salty aroma of French fries hit her nostrils, making her stomach growl. She closed and locked the door before pressing her free palm to her flatter-than-usual stomach. She sank back into the room's most comfortable chair and opened the serving dish. She stuffed a few fries in her mouth and then pulled the ledger out of its hiding spot.

The book was thick—more like an encyclopedia than a book. The spine crackled softly as she peeled the ledger open. She wet her lips. The answers finally lay right in her hands. With this book, she'd begin her takedown of Lionsgate. Having been passed down through the organization, the ledger held the name of every person who had ever been a member of the Seattle House. The original date it was created was inscribed on the inside of the cover: 1917.

Her pulse barreled through her veins. No one outside Lionsgate had ever held this book. Its knowledge would be the organization's undoing. She'd nail its members to the damn wall if it robbed her of her last breath. There was a lot of information to digest. For now, she needed to know one thing. She stopped at the most recent membership update.

Conrad Hornick – Grand Chancellor
Allan Thompson – Grand Chancellor
George Herman – Grand Chancellor

Six names followed under *Ambassadors*, five under *Advocates*, three under *Treasurers*, about twenty-five under *Enforcers*, fifteen under *Watchers*, and fifty under *Porters*. The rest fell under first, second, and third ranks, yet to be assigned to a higher position.

Nash Holmes's name leaped off the page,

stalling her breath. She fought back the pressing images of his hands up her dress, his mouth wet and slick on hers. He would want the ledger back. She had no doubt he was looking for her by now. But he'd have a hell of a time locating her.

Before the night of the fire, Brooks hadn't disclosed to her what he suspected Lionsgate was up to. She'd tried to get him to talk, but he'd only say that the less she knew, the safer she'd be. But his last phone call had sent her in the right direction.

"If anything happens to me, go to the place that was our favorite when we were kids. I left something for you that will explain everything. Hand it over to the authorities and get the hell out of the country. I don't want you anywhere near this."

A French fry turned soggy in her mouth, and she forced it down with a gulp of water. Memories of that night and what she'd found out in the days after always made her stomach weak. It had been six months since her family died, and she didn't have a shred of closure.

Now, it was only a matter of time before she exposed Lionsgate and they crumbled.

A soft click at her door snapped up her attention. A dark shadow lingered under the door. Electric currents of panic jolted through her veins. She leaped to her feet and clutched the ledger to her chest.

No! They've found me.

CHAPTER 3

S WEAT COLLECTED AT the collar of Nash's T-shirt. He was dirty, tired, pissed the fuck off, and in Russia, of all fucking places. His shoulder blades bunched. He blinked against the brightness of the long hallway, but closing his eyes was like rubbing two pieces of sandpaper together. He was running on next to zero sleep and had had to cancel his plans with Gage, the teenage boy he mentored through Lionsgate Youth Center. Gage had of course understood that an emergency came up, but as someone who'd always been shuffled around and let down by parental figures, Nash felt really fucking shitty bailing on him.

She was here. The little fucking heathen had changed planes five times. One hell of a wild-goose chase. Thank god for Dare. Normally, his brother could locate someone in minutes, but it had taken him almost two hours to follow the breadcrumbs to Moscow. Alexis had changed disguises several times. Unfortunately for her, she couldn't change her face. If it weren't for Dare's facial recognition program, she would have succeeded in losing him. As it stood, they'd been able to locate her in her hotel, thanks to its security cameras. Nash had arrived in Moscow not long after she had, due to her six-hour layover in London and him having two less plane changes he'd been able to catch up to her.

He approached her door, pulled a credit card from his pocket, and rested his shoulder against the solid wood. Would she be asleep? He pressed his cheek to the smooth surface, but no sounds reached his ears. He slipped the short edge of the card between the door and the jamb, moving more carefully than he normally would. A metallic click sounded. He pulled out his gun and eased the door open a crack.

He leaned close, peeking into the room, being careful not to let too much light from the hall spill in. The living area was dark. He entered and closed the door softly behind him. His feet sunk into the carpet, cushioning his weight.

He wet his dry lips with his tongue. She was here . . . with his ledger. Satisfaction built in his spine, lengthening his height. Time to take back what was his.

He dropped the credit card into his back pocket and pulled his Beretta from the waistband of his pants. His pulse bounced against his throat as he scanned the dark room. Dammit, she'd even closed the curtains. He might as well be fucking blind.

He blinked quickly, clearing the shadows from his vision. His eyes landed on the open bedroom door behind the couch. He could just make out a rounded form in the center of the white-covered bed. She must not have closed the bedroom drapes, otherwise he wouldn't have been able to see a damn thing.

He sucked a breath through his nose, easing some of the constriction in his lungs. He shouldn't be on edge. He never was. But Conrad's order twisted his stomach. He'd make her talk and then decide what to do with her.

He stepped over the threshold of the bedroom, and the floor creaked beneath his weight. He winced and froze. A dark shadow leaped in front of him, and his feet left the carpet as his heart slammed into his throat.

"Jes—"

"Ahhh!" A female roar reverberated his eardrums and a small frame landed in front of him. A loud whir sounded inches from his face, and he was blasted with a cold, sticky mist.

Fire coated his eyeballs and pain exploded through his temples. He gasped, sucking in the smelly fumes, coating his already dry mouth in the rancid spray. He coughed and fell to his knees. He waved the air in front of him, trying desperately to clear away the suffocating gas. His taste buds tingled with chemicals, and he retched.

Hairspray?

A slim foot rushed into his hazy vision and connected with his jaw. His face went slack and his cheek throbbed. Rage blazed through him. He dove through the cloud in front of his eyes, and his shoulder connected with a slight, toned abdomen.

She hit the ground and he climbed on top of her, but for fuck's sake he couldn't focus his hairspray-glazed eyeballs on her arms.

Her fist crushed his throat and the air left his lungs. As she bucked free, he dropped his hands to the carpet, his gun still clutched in his grasp.

She was going to pay. He rubbed his eyes with the back of his hands and scanned the room. Thankfully, his half-dead form blocked the only way out. She stood against the far wall, her chest rising and falling in the moonlight, her eyes and mouth wide in her pale, oval face.

Enough of this shit.

He got to his feet and flicked the light switch beside him. The air left his lungs a second time. She was wearing short purple pajama bottoms and a tight white tank top. Her nipples pressed sharply against the thin material. Christ, he could even see their soft pink tint. His dick grew three inches and the muscles in his face locked. A glance at the bed revealed that she'd shoved pillows under the sheets to make it look as if a person were under them.

He closed the distance between them, stopping several inches from her toes. If she came at him again, he'd toss her little ass on the bed and tan her lush cheeks.

Her small pink tongue jetted out to wet her bottom lip. She tilted her head back and searched his face with her blue eyes. A streak of fear dilated her pupils, but it was gone as fast as it had appeared. His breath whooshed through his nose, fluttering the strands of her soft brown hair. His fingers ached to touch her cheek and his tongue to lick her moist bottom lip. Desire stirred inside him and his vocabulary left his head as her warm scent surrounded him.

He rubbed his lips with the back of his wrist. The hairspray collected on his skin pulled at his arm hair. Irritation curled his lip.

"Hairspray?" he sputtered. "You doused me with fucking hairspray?"

The corners of her lips twitched, and her eyes sparked with amusement. "Sticky?"

His eyebrows snapped down, and he stepped closer to her. His sternum pressed against her chest, and he lowered his gaze.

"Where's the ledger?"

She snorted. And damn her, not an ounce of intimidation radiated from her sexy body. Her nipples pressed into his chest and he took a deep breath, filling his lungs with the intoxicating scent of vanilla.

She lifted one delicate shoulder. "It's gone. I took what I needed from it and burned it."

He snapped his head back.

No way in hell she'd burned it.

He slapped his palm on the wall beside her head. She tensed, and satisfaction coursed through him. "Don't fucking lie to me," he growled.

Her lips pursed and she lifted her chin. "I get the impression you're feeling a little emasculated. Is it because I slipped you a roofie?"

He pushed his fingertips into the unrelenting drywall. He had never hit a woman and he sure as hell wouldn't start now, but he itched to wipe the smug look from her pretty face.

He smiled. "Nah, that has nothing to do with it. Do you wanna know why?"

Her eyebrow bounced.

He lowered his lips to her ear. She didn't flinch. "Because," he said, "you were soaking wet in my palm the other night."

Her fists slammed against his chest, but he didn't budge. He laughed, the sound derisive and salacious. He watched as a red hue crept up her chest, coating her throat and tinting her cheeks. "You lied to me, drugged me, and robbed me," he said. "But you want me."

"Like hell!" Her balled hands pummeled against him, and one connected with his jaw, sending a shockwave of pain through his skull. He collected her wrists in his hand and lifted them above her head, pinning them to the wall.

Her hot breath blew through her perfectly full mouth. He'd spent two hours in that hotel bar with her, flirting, drinking, and talking, and he'd been a sucker from the moment she approached him, her brow creased. She'd inquired if he was her late blind date. Stupidly, he'd thought they'd hit it off.

"I wouldn't sleep with you if my life depended on it," she said, her eyes blazing.

He snickered, his thumb stroking the soft skin of her wrist. She had a tough front. He needed to push this, to scare the shit out of her. It was the only way to get the ledger back.

He brought his free hand to her shoulder, stroking his finger over the thin strap of her top. Her eyes darkened, and the smooth skin at the side of her throat jumped.

"I bet if I touched you right now, you'd be throbbing and wet." His voice had grown deep and husky, challenging.

Her lips moved into a snarl. "Not a chance."

He shook his head. "By the way," he continued, ignoring her, "Alexis is a sexy name." Her eyes singed his as she inhaled sharply. The insides of her thighs tightened against his legs, and his body hummed with need. Lust muddled his brain into a thick fog. The only way out was to fuck. But even if she was game, he couldn't fucking do it. She was an enemy. No one crossed him. Ever. The fact that she knew who he was, what he was capable of, and still had the nerve to steal from him . . . She was one ballsy woman.

Without the cloud of perfume that had clung to her like the red wig, her natural scent floated to his nostrils. Her skin carried hints of roses and lilies like a bouquet of flowers. He tightened his hold on her wrist and brought his nose to hers, pushing the buckling sensation of her softness away. Not a single sliver of panic flickered in her turquoise eyes. Instead, she let out a wail of unspent outrage. He wouldn't assault her, but goddammit, he needed her to fear him.

"Deny it all you want, honey. Your pussy doesn't lie."

"Fuck you," she breathed. Her lip crimped into a snarl, and she jerked her knee between his legs. He blocked her blow with his hand, but his hold on her wrists faltered. She yanked one hand free, and jammed her knuckles into his jaw. Their proximity prevented the blow from gaining momentum, but pain throbbed through his mouth.

His blood bubbled beneath his skin. Inch by inch, he brought his gaze closer to hers. He lifted his fists to rest on either side of her head, trapping her in the cage of his ire. His knuckles dug into the drywall.

"I'm only going to say this once, so listen up." He lowered his lips to her ear again. Her soft, sweet breath invaded his senses. "Give me the ledger, Alexis. Life will be a hell of a lot easier for you."

★　★　★

ANGER RIPPLED THROUGH Alexis with the force of a tidal wave. Punching Nash in the face had done nothing to diminish it.

He was rough and hard—a killer and god only knew what else. If he touched her, she'd cut his fingers off. She searched his dark face. Was he involved in the ring Brooks's information had revealed? Of course he was. How could he be at the level in the organization he was and not know what was going on? If she laid out the evidence, would he crumble? Had he any remorse?

He was trying to rattle her and doing a damn good job. But he hadn't hurt her . . . yet. She wasn't stupid. As long as she held the ledger, she'd live. The only reason she was still breathing right now was because the book was in her possession.

She couldn't lose that book. It was the only way to connect the allegations to the members. It was her starting point for part two of her investigation. She folded her arms in front of her chest, shielding her traitorous nipples, which had grown hard the minute he'd zeroed in on them.

She lifted her chin. "You're not getting the ledger. You can threaten whatever you want, but you'll have to kill me first."

A muscle in his jaw jumped beneath two days' worth of stubble. This close, she could examine his face. The scar through his eyebrow stopped millimeters above his eyelid; its shiny texture indicated it was fairly new. His muscles bulged beneath his shirt and his throat looked as thick as a tree stump. The faint hint of his aftershave or soap struck her senses. Saliva swarmed her mouth.

His gray eyes turned deadly. "If you hand it over now, you can walk away from this." His voice was now gravelly, almost pleading.

She snorted. "Do you really think I'd fall for that? Why do you think I'm here?" She waved her arms in the air around her. "Lionsgate will kill me the first chance they get."

The corner of his mouth tucked in. In one swift move, he bent and snagged her legs, tossing her over his shoulder.

"Put me down," she hissed. She kicked wildly, but his hold on her thighs tightened. His shoulder dug into her abdomen, and she winced. "I'm not going to let you manhandle me, you sonofa—"

He sent her barreling through the air, and her ass bounced off the mattress at the end of the bed.

He knelt in front of her, his hands pressed firmly on the tops of her knees, preventing her from kicking him in the teeth.

"You're going to tell me where it is. But first, I want to know why you took it in the first place." One stony eye narrowed.

She leaned in, not taking the bait. "Figure it out. You know everything about me, I would imagine. I'm an investigative journalist, and let's not forget my family?"

He kept his expression blank, his mouth in a crooked line. His eyes were as solid as granite, and their color rivaled slate.

"You had a hand in killing them, didn't you?" No way in hell she'd let on that Brooks might still be alive.

He scraped his knuckles over his dark five-o'clock shadow, keeping one hand on her knees. At the bar he'd sported a slick do, but now his jet-black hair was mussed. A long day of travel had roughened his edges even more.

"I'll answer your question, but I want an answer to mine in return." His voice was gruff and reluctant. He pulled the chair from the corner by the window close and sat across from her.

Her mouth went dry. Had he killed her parents? Would he really tell her that? She nodded sharply, ready to agree to anything to get even a shred of information about that night.

"I was asked to hire an assassin to kill your father and whoever was in the house. I called one, but he was out of the country. He referred a colleague, who completed the job." He spoke carefully, never taking his eyes away from her face.

She swallowed. The motion took every effort. Tears burned her eyes and emptiness spread through her chest. She'd be damned if she let a single drop spill onto her cheek. Her throat constricted, but she forced down the overwhelming wave of emotion that threatened to strangle her.

Disgust engrained itself firmly in her stomach.

"So, in other words, you did have a hand in their death."

Something flashed across his eyes, but she couldn't put her finger on it. It didn't seem like regret, exactly, but it wasn't as cold and determined as the rest of his expression. The corners of his eyes creased, and he leaned forward, resting his elbows on his knees and invading her space. Cold sweat collected at the back of her neck. She leaped to her feet, but he snagged her wrist and pushed her back to the bed.

She glared daggers at him and yanked her wrist out of his hold. He was a murderer, a damn savage, and she'd do everything in her power to destroy him.

"Why did you take it?"

Every muscle in her body tensed. There was no way in hell she'd tell him what she knew. She lifted her eyebrow at him.

"After what they did to my family, I want Lionsgate to crumble. I will expose any dirt I find on them—and I guarantee you, I will find some." It was a half-truth, and all he was going to get.

He tented his fingers beneath his chin and tapped his thumbs together. His eyes bore into hers, dark embers that burned through her skin. He was weighing her, trying to find the easiest way to get her to crack, since she wasn't afraid of him.

"I'm responsible for the ledger," he said. "It's

my duty to get it back and eliminate the threat of who took it. I had the option for backup, or an assassin, but I opted out of that."

Her eyebrows lifted. "You wanted the honors to yourself?"

He let out a hiss of frustration. "Look, I'm pissed as hell you stole from me. But I can't wrap my head around what happened with your family. We aren't cold-blooded killers, despite what you think. If someone threatens our brotherhood or crosses us, then we rough them up. Murder is a rare last resort."

Her fingers tightened on her crossed forearms, and she pressed her knees together to keep from bouncing them. She watched his squinted eyes, and for a flicker of a second, she saw sincerity. A muscle jumped at her temple. She couldn't be dumb enough to believe him. He was using her weak spot as a way to get in her head and fuck with her so he could get his damn ledger.

"Well, that's reassuring." She dropped her back an inch and crossed one leg over the other. Her knee brushed against his, bringing his gaze down to her bare skin. His eyes trailed back up, and the moisture left her mouth.

He didn't move. "Humor me."

She snorted. "What do you think I've been doing?"

A mean glint crossed his eyes. "What exactly do you expect to find through your investigation, hmm? A list of fucking names and rituals? Secret handshakes and our code of ethics? You're going to take us down with that?"

Her lips twisted into a smirk and she leaned forward, resting her hands gently on her knee. "The ledger is a means to an end. The last piece of the puzzle I need. I've built my investigation without it."

His hands tightened into fists. "You're going to hand it over, Alexis. I'm not going anywhere without it. And if I have to, I can bring in more people. People who will make you talk." He leaned forward, matching her stance. "But I don't want to do that. Let's keep this simple. Hand it over and you walk free. That's a deal you'll never get again, I can promise you that."

The cold, heavy blanket of fear wrapped itself around her bones. She rolled her lips in and got to her feet. He could call whoever the hell he wanted. Tomorrow, she'd have her own backup.

"You expect me to believe that you're going to let me walk away? C'mon, Mr. Enforcer. You were given orders to kill me. I know how this works."

He rose as well and took a step toward her, the veins in his neck growing prominent with his frustration.

"You're damn right I was. But that doesn't mean I'm going to. You won't be able to return to the US, at least not for a long time, but—"

She laughed, a full-blown belly laugh that

shook her shoulders. "You're hilarious. You think I'm going to give up my life, my career?" She jabbed her index finger into his chest. It didn't give under the pressure. Rock-hard muscle tensed beneath her fingernail. "I won't let them win. You want to kill me? Go for it. Your ledger will die with me because you'll never find it." Her voice rang with such conviction that her body shook.

He looped his large fist around her hand, not crushing her, but not letting her move either. "It's a hotel room, Alexis. I'm pretty sure I can manage."

She lifted her eyebrows. "It's not here, Einstein. I gave it to someone for safekeeping. If anything happens to me, the ledger's contents will be breaking news tomorrow morning."

His hand turned ice cold over hers and gripped harder, making her tendons ache. Her blood pumped with violent speed through her body, making her heart thump against her chest.

"I'm going to blame your lack of common sense on fatigue. You have until the morning to change your mind." He let go of her hand and strode to the bedroom door. "I'll be on the couch."

Her face twisted, and she folded her arms over her chest. "You're not staying here! I'll call security. There's—"

He turned around then trudged to the small desk in the corner of the room and yanked the phone from the wall. "Good luck with that. And if you scream, I'll duct-tape your mouth shut."

Rage vibrated through her as he closed the door behind him. She let out a screech and hurled a pillow at the door.

He would pay. He'd be the first sonofabitch she took down.

CHAPTER 4

NASH PACED THE living room. A ball of lead settled in the base of his stomach. Sonofabitch, he'd underestimated her. He hadn't thought for one minute that she had contacts in Moscow and would hand the ledger off to another journalist.

But had she? Goddammit, he had no way of knowing. She had him by the balls. He needed to think quickly, to get her to reconsider. If he had to tell Conrad that he'd found her and couldn't retrieve the ledger, Conrad would send an assassin after her and make her talk.

He hadn't been lying about that.

Until now, he'd been one of Conrad's most utilized men. But as much as Alexis got under his skin, he didn't want to see her killed. If only she'd pull the stick out of her ass and hand over the ledger. He snorted. She wouldn't do that. She wanted revenge, and the unflinching blaze in her eyes confirmed that she'd get it at all costs.

She'd have to go through him first. He'd come

too damn far to have his reputation undermined by some headstrong journalist. One thing was for sure—even if he let her walk away, she wouldn't survive long. Conrad had likely already alerted all the other Houses. He'd have sent out her picture, and it'd be circling the vast, borderless community. And he would have placed a hefty bounty on her head, too. When Conrad wanted someone dead, he only had to breathe the words and every member would fight to carry out the order.

Tomorrow he'd call his friends inside Lionsgate and see what had been done. For now, he needed to sleep. Going head-to-head with Alexis had sucked all the energy he had left.

He made his way to the bathroom and stopped. He ground his palm into his eye socket and let a low curse fall from his lips. His carry-on was in his rental car in the parking lot. He eyed a tall-backed chair at the small dinette table. He'd have to lock her in.

He secured the chair beneath the bedroom door handle and then turned on the TV. Slipping out the hotel door, he flipped the bar lock between the door and the jamb, leaving it slightly ajar so he could get back in easily.

He strode to the elevator, his fingertips digging into his palms. He'd expected to be in and out of her room, ledger in hand, in fifteen minutes. Instead, he'd been greeted with a fucking attack. He jabbed his thumb into the Lobby button and the elevator soared down twenty stories. In less than five minutes, he was on his way back up. He stepped far enough into the living room to see that the bedroom door was still tightly closed. Relief washed over him, and he headed to the bathroom with his toiletry bag.

His eyes slid longingly to the tall shower. A deep ache for scalding-hot water and steam set into his joints, stiff from the day-long flight. But there wasn't a chance in hell he'd be able to relax long enough to even undress. He had no doubt that if Alexis heard the shower and knew he wasn't feet from her door, she'd get out of that room with skills that would rival Houdini's.

He'd tie her to the fucking chair tomorrow in order to get the shower he badly deserved.

He brushed his teeth and then stripped off his clothes on the way to the living room, leaving his boxers intact. He tugged on the bar of the pullout bed, which filled most of the room. Then he sent a quick text to Gage, letting him know he'd landed safely and would contact him as soon as he got back to Seattle. He switched off the lights, dropped onto the thin mattress, and stared at the ceiling until the sweet clutches of sleep sucked him under.

"Nash! Nash!"

He bolted clumsily from his bed and tumbled to the floor in his tangled sheets. His breath came out in fast, sharp puffs, and he pushed away from the narrow single bed pressed against the wall. For once, he had the room to himself. Two kids had been adopted. He wiped his forehead with his arm and charged for the bedroom door. The high-pitched scream still rang in his ears; the raw fear in the voice gripped his heart. There was no way that'd been a dream.

He raced down the hall for the front door, the floorboards groaning beneath his feet. Outside, warm, sticky air invaded his lungs, further heating his already burning skin. His bare feet slapped against the still-hot walkway as he darted toward the street. A rusted brown van sat at the curb a hundred feet down the road. A flash of blonde hair in the window caught his eye.

Summer!

★   ★   ★

ALEXIS'S HANDS SHOOK. The thick blanket scratched her skin as she tucked it into the crack under the door. Kramer's high-pitched voice cackled through the air. Nash was watching *Seinfeld*. One thing was for sure—if the enforcer heard her on her cell phone, her plan would be blown to pieces. She'd waited more than an hour, hopefully he was asleep now.

She pulled her phone out of the nightstand drawer. Unfortunately, all she could do with it was call her contacts. She'd left the Wi-Fi password in the living room and had no clue what the 9-1-1 equivalent was in Moscow. It had been fifteen years since her last visit.

She glided her fingers over the screen and selected a name from her contact list. Crossing to the farthest corner of the room, she crouched against the wall near the window. The line rang in her ear.

"Hello," a young male voice barked in Russian. She tightened her grip on the phone and sucked a deep breath through her nose.

Dmitry. Why the hell was he answering his father's phone?

"Dmitry, it's Alexis. I need to speak with Uncle Pavel. It's urgent." Deliberately, she spoke in English, knowing it would displease her cousin. He *tsk*ed disapprovingly.

"Ah, my dear cousin. Tell me, what is so urgent that you need to speak to my father and not to me?"

Her nerves grated together like nails on a chalkboard. She should have hung up when he answered. If Dmitry sensed she needed Pavel's help, he'd do everything possible to keep her from speaking with him. Another male voice sounded in the background, this one older and vicious. A scuffle rasped through the phone, followed by Dmitry's curses.

"Alexis." A long slew of Russian flowed quickly through the phone. Her uncle's voice was low and berating. He spoke so quickly that she picked up only a handful of words: *How could you be so stupid?*

"Uncle Pavel," she said firmly, cutting him off. He'd always been good to her. Despite the fact that he'd spawned her ruthless cousin Dmitry, she'd always been close with Pavel, his wife, Olga, and their daughter, Alina. "I need to speak with you about something urgent. Are you alone?" She kept her voice low.

More Russian words dripped angrily off his tongue, but the background noise fell away, followed by the soft click of a door. "*Dorogoy*—"

"English, please."

He huffed. "What the hell have you done? You're going to get yourself killed. You're fucking with the wrong people."

She drew her knees in tighter to her chest and lowered her chin. She wasn't going to take this shit. "No, Uncle Pavel," she said, her voice barely above a whisper. "They fucked with the wrong family. Look," she said, rubbing the pad of her thumb between her eyes, "I know I'm in danger. That's why I'm here. I came for your help. Lionsgate is evil. If you can meet me somewhere tomorrow, I can explain everything. We have to stop them."

The soft click of a lighter followed her plea, and then a long, low inhale—he was always smoking cigars. He had to help her, to at least listen. She had no one else.

"My dear, I know you're struggling with your

family's deaths, especially since you know for certain who's behind them." He paused and took another drag. The paper crackled in her ear. "But I'm sixty-three years old. I've been with the House for more than half my life. I can't, and won't, risk my family. Lionsgate is my blood. They're my brothers. The best thing I can do is advise you to get the hell away from here."

Her fingernails dug into the thin skin at her forehead and her teeth cut into the sides of her tongue. Her own blood would turn their backs on her. All because of Lionsgate.

Because they fear them.

It was next to impossible to sit quietly. All she wanted to do was scream.

"If you need money, we'll help," her uncle said. "But stay the fuck away from the brotherhood."

She tore the phone from her ear and disconnected the call. She wouldn't take a damn cent from him, not when his loyalty was to her enemy. She'd expose every member for every illegal act they'd ever committed, starting with the hulking asshole outside her bedroom door.

She crawled into bed and pulled the covers to her chin. Her senses stayed on high alert all night, but the enforcer never returned to her room.

When sunlight finally streamed through the window, she squinted against the throbbing at the back of her eyes. She flipped the covers off and looked at the clock: 7:01. She tugged on a fresh pair of jeans and a long-sleeved shirt. The last thing she wanted to do was face Nash Holmes, but he was the only thing that stood between her and a hot cup of coffee. She tucked her phone into her purse and removed the blanket from under the door. All was quiet.

Maybe he'd left.

She bit back a snort. Not a chance in hell. She closed her fingers over the cool, smooth metal handle and inched the door open. Her gaze fell to the rumpled, vacant pullout bed. She pinched her eyebrows together. Where had he gone? Maybe he'd needed something from his vehicle. If so, she had seconds to escape.

She cracked open the door the rest of the way and stepped into the living room. Next to the room's only exit was the bathroom. The door was slightly ajar but the light was off.

She gently bit the tip of her thumb. Indecision warred in her mind. She didn't have enough time to grab all her belongings and retrieve the ledger from its hiding spot. And it'd make things worse if he caught her trying to escape. She'd go downstairs and grab a coffee from the café, and if he still wasn't back when she returned, she'd take it as a sign from God that he'd abandoned his pursuit— and she'd run.

"Going somewhere?"

She inhaled and her body tensed. Slowly, she turned around. He stepped out of the dinette nook tucked beside the bedroom. She'd walked right passed him. She hitched her thumb in the purse strap at her shoulder and met the bastard's steely eyes. He still hadn't shaved, and the stubble on his jaw was almost blacker than the hair on his head. The sunlight from the window caught the jagged scar that sliced through his eyebrow, it's lighter tone sharply contrasting his olive skin. The aromatic scent of coffee wafted to her nose from the steaming paper cup in his hand.

She pursed her lips and dipped her gaze down his tall, stacked body before bringing her attention back to his unshakable grimace. "I don't suppose you grabbed one of those for me," she said evenly.

The top of his cupid's bow twitched, and for a second, she expected a smirk. It didn't come. He brought the edge of the cup to his lips and took a long, leisurely sip. "Not a chance."

She turned toward the door. "There's your answer."

Large, rough fingertips circled her bicep and wheeled her around to face him. His toes bumped into hers, and his face was close enough that if she moved, her hair would rub his chin.

His breath tickled her cheek and his eyes simmered like ancient coals. "You're out of your mind if you think I'm going to let you leave this room."

She clamped her teeth into the sides of her tongue and yanked her arm from his grasp. "I wouldn't leave all my belongings here if I were planning to run. I just need some coffee."

He nodded at the small table near the entrance. "There's a coffee maker over there."

She wrinkled her nose. "I'm not drinking that shit. Besides, you didn't." She tapped the café's label on the cup he held. His mouth finally hitched up at the corner.

"I'm not the thief. Have a seat, and after I shower, I'll escort you down to get your fix."

Distaste crawled up the back of her throat. She might have robbed him, but she was a saint in comparison to him. She itched to slam her palms into his chest and gain distance from his warm, musky scent, but she wouldn't give him the satisfaction of getting a rise out of her.

She raised an eyebrow, daring him to challenge her. "I'm going to get coffee and something to eat. Deal with it." She turned on her heel and moved purposefully toward the door, but the hairs on the back of her neck tingled with his pursuit.

His long, hard arm circled her waist, and in one swift movement, he lifted her off her feet. She kicked and squirmed, but he held her tight against the wall of his chest. Her heels connected with his shins, but he moved her effortlessly away from the door and set her on her feet. Fire burned her cheeks, and all attempts at keeping her cool sailed out the window.

"You slimy sonofab—*Hey*," she squeaked, as he tugged her purse off her shoulder. She lunged forward, but he stepped out of her reach. Before she could form an attack, he had the contents dumped on the pullout bed.

He swiped up her various passports and waggled them in the air. "You won't be needing these to get coffee."

She pressed her lips together to stop the verbal assault building on her tongue.

"Or this," he said, lifting her phone. She dove for the device, but he slipped it in his back pocket before she could grab it. "Ah, ah." The smile reached his eyes, softening the dark orbs. "You grab my ass and I get to grab yours." He winked, and her temper went off like a solar flare.

She snatched her wallet from his nosey palm and pressed it to her abdomen, as if that would prevent him from taking it. "If you so much as look at my ass, I'll gouge out your fucking eyes! Understood?"

His eyelids lowered into a menacing glare. "I'd watch the threats, Lexi. I might decide to call your bluff."

"Go fuck yourself." Her fingernails ached to be dragged over his self-satisfied cheeks, but she didn't need to get into a physical fight with an enforcer. Until she had the opportunity to take his gun and turn it on him, she'd have to keep her anger in check.

He didn't follow her, and she didn't spare a glance over her shoulder. She shoved her feet into her shoes, slipped out the door, and strode down the paisley-carpeted hallway. She rounded the corner of the elevator banks and jabbed her thumb into the smooth pewter button. She combed her trembling fingers through the ratty strands of her hair then balled her traitorous hand into a fist and watched the illuminated numbers over the elevator click closer to her floor.

Unbelievable.

One look from Nash Holmes and she was a fiery ball of nerves. He was demeaning, arrogant, and ballsy. She'd enjoy every minute of wiping that smirk off his face. She couldn't wait to stand back and watch his kinship burn to the ground.

The elevator dinged and the doors slid open. She tottered as the cart whisked her down to the main level, and she tightened her grasp on the rail. She'd slept like shit thanks to the enforcer outside her bedroom, and it didn't look like she'd be able to shake him anytime soon.

After exiting the elevator, she followed the Russian signs to the café, where she ordered a latte and a muffin, which she paid for with cash.

She lowered herself into the sofa in the lobby and brought the steaming brew to her lips. The liquid coated her tongue and she closed her eyes, inhaling the rich scent. When she lifted her lids, she saw a man at the front desk wearing a brown leather jacket. A sense of familiarity sharpened her attention, and she ran her gaze over the back of his head and relaxed stance.

Dmitry.

Her lungs expanded like a balloon ready to burst, crushing her chest. Her hands trembled, and the hot coffee sloshed onto her wrist, scalding her. She set it on the table and stood on wobbly knees, the burn already long forgotten. Her legs tingled with the urge to run, but she forced her feet to walk briskly to the elevator. The doors opened and a family poured out. She squeezed past them into the cart and punched the button for the twentieth floor.

Oh god, oh god.

She had to get the ledger and get out before he found her . . .

And killed her.

CHAPTER 5

Nash's Beretta rested comfortably at the small of his back. The gun was as much a part of him as his right hand. He closed the hotel room door behind him. She'd been gone nearly ten minutes, which was seven minutes too long as far as he was concerned. He'd let her go for the coffee so he could tear apart the hotel room and her suitcase in search of the ledger.

And he hadn't found it.

Unless she'd somehow hidden it on her person, which wasn't too much of a stretch, she might very well have been telling the truth about leaving it with a colleague.

A hoard of children raced out of the elevator and down the hall toward him, their shrill laughter like a flock of seagulls to his sleep-deprived brain. He dodged to the side, letting them skirt past him and into one of the rooms. The elevator next to the one they vacated dinged, and the door whooshed open. Alexis barreled out. Her wide cerulean eyes snapped to his and then darted away. She shoved her hands into his chest, pushing him out of the way and charging toward the room.

"What the hell?" He gripped her elbow, but she tore away from his hold. Her hair fanned out around her shoulders like a dark curtain. He jogged to catch up.

"Dammit, Alexis, what are you doing?" He snagged her slight shoulders just as she walked into the room and whirled her around to face him. Her pink tongue swiped her bottom lip and her eyes shifted to the door behind him and then back to his face.

"Someone is here to kill me."

Sonofabitch.

He locked his fingertips on her shoulders. Her chest heaved on an exhale. He worked his jaw and took in the gentle lines of her smooth, porcelain skin. A ring of dark blue outlined the combustible turquoise in the eyes that stared back at him. Dammit, he didn't want to believe her, didn't want to acknowledge that Conrad had sent out the word that fucking soon.

He needed to call Conrad . . .

And tell him what, exactly? That he'd located Alexis but was unable to reclaim the ledger, just as he'd been unable to stop her from taking it?

"Go in the bedroom and lock the door," he ordered. She wrenched out of his hold and turned, leaving him staring at her tense, retreating back.

"They have guns," she called from the bedroom door. The soft click of the lock followed. She'd be safe in the room, and at least he wouldn't have to worry about her escaping. It wasn't likely she'd sneak out a twentieth-story window to avoid her so-called pursuers.

He pulled his gun from the waistband of his pants and pressed his back against the smooth, mauve-colored wall next to the door. Just because he didn't trust her didn't mean she was lying.

Heavy footsteps scuffled outside the door, followed by sharp Russian words.

Nash's spine molded to the drywall at his back, and he raised his gun to the height of his chest. The lock near his hip jostled. A second later, it clicked and the door eased open.

A pale man with close-cropped blond hair wearing a brown leather jacket moved into the room. He turned to Nash, his eyes wide. The the long mouth of a silencer stared Nash in the face. Instinctively, Nash flexed his fingers and jabbed them straight into the gunman's throat. The man grasped his neck and sucked in a gulp of air. Rage filled his eyes and his finger moved on the trigger.

Nash snapped his head to the side, and the bullet whizzed past his cheek.

Crack!

Drywall splintered behind his head, and Nash's stomach twined like the body of a snake.

The sonofabitch would pay for that.

He flipped his Beretta in his palm and slammed

the butt of it against the blond's temple. He staggered against the door, and the gunman barreled in over him. Nash swept his arm around his neck, catching him in a rear chokehold.

"Who the fuck sent you?" he demanded. Nash moved him away from the door, and it swung shut. The gunman's groan rumbled against Nash's forearm. He heaved his elbow closer to his chest, making the man sputter and thrash.

The blond got to his feet and aimed the mouth of his silencer at Nash's forehead. Rusty brown eyes, their pupils nearly as large as their irises, fixated on him. Nash's blood warmed several degrees, and he lifted the corner of his mouth. He pinched his index finger on the trigger of his Beretta, which rested cozily at his hip.

The bastard had no idea who he was fucking with. The blond guy sneered.

Nash fired.

Crack!

"*Blyat!*" The blond's weapon tumbled from his fingers, and he gripped his thigh where the bullet had penetrated. Blood spurted onto the floor and coated the light denim of the man's jeans.

Nash booted the fallen gun, and it skittered across the room. The big brute in his arms heaved forward, trying to throw him. Nash stifled a chuckle and drew his arm back tight until the man tapped frantically against his forearm.

A smooth, slender hand picked up the gun.

Nash straightened, and he brought his gaze to Alexis's face. Dammit, he'd told her to stay in the room. Her gaze lingered on his, then lowered to the thug tossing himself against him. Finally, it fell to the blond cursing a blue streak in Russian. She widened her stance and brought both hands to the gun's handle. It looked so out of place in her hands yet so fucking sexy with her stormy glare behind it.

"What the fuck are you doing, Dmitry?"

She fucking knows him?

Nash grunted and gave the asshole in his grasp one last choke before letting him drop like a stone to the carpet. One long, delicate eyebrow rose, but Alexis didn't bat an eye or move her gaze from Dmitry.

The tidal wave of words continued flowing from Dmitry's lips. Alexis raised her chin. "In English," she hissed.

"You're a fucking dead little *myshka*. Six million rouble on your head. If I don't cash in, someone else will."

Nash took a step forward, cupped the back of Dmitry's neck, and yanked his head back so they were looking at each other. "Who put the hit on her head?"

Dmitry's thin lips spread into a snarl. He pursed his lips and spat on Nash's leg. Nash immediately pulled his fist back and dropped it like a hammer on Dmitry's jaw. The man's eyes rolled back and he crumpled to the ground, his mouth slack.

"Why'd you do that?" Alexis lowered the gun and placed her free hand on her slender, jean-clad hip. "So much for getting any information out of them." She hiked up the strap of her purse and shook her head at Dmitry's motionless form. Nash pressed his lips together and squinted at her. Her suitcase lay waiting less than a foot away. "And you shot him."

"Do you have a problem with that? He was here to kill you—or so you said." He gestured at Dmitry's grimy gun in her hand. "You obviously know him."

Her gaze dropped to the gun that hung loosely in her fingers, and a muscle in her neck twitched. She cleared her throat and tossed her hair back. Her icy eyes darkened a shade.

"He's my cousin."

Well, hell. He moved his tongue across the inside of his teeth, for once short of words. And yeah, maybe he felt a small bud of sympathy for the deceptive vixen.

Nash turned his attention back to the two thugs and caught sight of Dmitry's left hand. A large black onyx set in a thick gold band sported the Lionsgate emblem. He bent to tug the wallet out of Dmitry's back pocket, confirming his identity. Conrad had indeed covered all his bases. A wire tightened around his chest, squeezing the air from his lungs.

Why the hell was she such a big threat?

Alexis dropped the gun into her purse, lifted the handle of her suitcase, rolled it around the limp bodies, and sidled past Nash. "Thanks for detaining them. See you around."

Nash stretched out his hand to stop her, but all he got was a fistful of air. The door clicked shut and he shoved his hand through his hair. She didn't miss a fucking beat.

He jogged across the room to his duffel bag and pulled out a few zip ties—ones that had been intended for an entirely different and dangerously sexy Russian—and knelt to restrain the men. Killing them would only bring more baggage to his door.

He scooped up his bag, stopped in the bathroom to grab what little he'd gotten the chance to use, and charged out the door. If she got in a cab, he'd have a hell of a time tracking her down.

Dare would laugh his ass off if he called him to do facial recognition again because Alexis had escaped. He ground his palm into his forehead and leaned back against the elevator's wall. Since confronting Alexis, his brainpower had plummeted with the speed of the elevator cart. Enough was enough. If Conrad had turned around and put out a hit on her, he clearly didn't have confidence in Nash's ability to retrieve the ledger.

He'd make her cough it up and then decide what to do about the hit—if there was anything he could do.

★ ★ ★

UN-FUCKING-BELIEVABLE. HER OWN family. Granted, her aunt and uncle wouldn't have had anything to do with Dmitry's coming after her. Dmitry had always hated her and her Americanized family. Alina had kept her in the loop regarding Dmitry's dealings, and every story had made her skin crawl. Not only had he joined Lionsgate Kinship at the ripe age of sixteen, but the year after, he'd gotten involved as a drug runner for the Mafia. Now, fifteen years later, it wasn't a stretch of the imagination to believe that he was a very dangerous person.

Family or not.

A frigid blast of air swirled into her coat and over her skin. She shivered and tucked her chin into the mouth of her jacket, keeping her gaze on the slick sidewalk. She trudged to the curb and lifted her free hand to hail a cab. The wind whipped her again, making her eyes water and her breath freeze in her nostrils before it could reach her lungs. She sucked a gulp of air through the pocket of warmth at the neck of her coat and bounced on her toes.

She'd turn to a damn ice sculpture if she stood out here another minute.

"Alexis." Nash's deep, irritated voice rumbled over the wind. She lifted her eyes to the heavily clouded sky, nearly freezing her eyeballs in place, and cast a glance over her shoulder.

He was storming down the sidewalk. His jacket flapped in the wind, revealing his T-shirt. His duffel bag hung loosely in his fingers. It took all her self-control not to snicker at his flushed cheeks and eyebrows so low they nearly shrouded the coals that burned beneath his lashes. She had no doubt that he'd turned the hotel room upside down the second she'd left to grab her coffee. Throughout her career, she'd always been strategic about hiding her source's information. She'd needed time to retrieve the ledger from the cold air return vent near the ceiling of the hotel bedroom. Dmitry had offered the perfect distraction for that, at least.

"Going somewhere?" Nash stopped inches from her, and his long, thick fingers circled the arm of her coat. His heat scorched her skin, even through the cushiony layer. If she weren't freezing, she'd have yanked away, but that tiny bit of contact spread a torrent of heat through her body.

She hooked her lip. "What gave you that idea?"

"That or you have a death wish. Two men tried to kill you five minutes ago and now you're standing on the street corner."

She rolled her eyes. God, he was annoying. "Kind of hard to escape without transportation." She turned her attention back to the street.

Another cab sailed past her, and she let out a puff of hot air.

He released his ironclad grip on her bicep, and her traitorous body ached at its absence. His rough fingertips brushed hers as he grabbed the handle of her suitcase. She snapped her head up at him but he walked away, her luggage in tow.

"Give me that," she growled. The wide expanse of his shoulders blocked the snowflakes that fluttered down like those in a shaken-up snow globe. She drew her hands into fists, digging her nails into her bare palms.

He didn't slow down. Instead, he moved swiftly down the walkway that rounded the hotel, to the parking lot behind it. She jogged to fall into step behind him. The wind swirled her hair in front of her face. She slapped it away and tucked it behind her ear. "What do you think you're doing?"

He didn't stop, nor did he acknowledge that she'd spoken. She reached out and grabbed his thick coat in her fist. "Stop, dammit!"

Beep, *beep*

Her gaze fell to the set of keys that hung from his hand and her mouth tightened. If he thought he was going to make off with her stuff, he had another thing coming. He stopped at a large silver SUV and opened the hatchback.

She grabbed the suitcase handle and tore it from his grip. He swiveled to meet her gaze, his shoulders turned in and his chin tucked, either to shield himself from the chilling gusts or to intimidate her.

It accomplished neither.

"What's your plan, Alexis?" His voice rolled through the air, low and formidable.

She bit her cheek. It was none of his business what her plan was, but as of right now, she didn't have one.

"You going to hop into a cab? And go where, huh? You think they won't fucking find you as easily as they just did? There's a time bomb on your back, and if you don't watch every move you make, you'll be dead in the blink of an eye."

Her breath spiraled in the air in front of her, and frost collected in her nostrils. An anvil settled on her chest, making every breath a struggle. He was right. Dmitry was only the first of many who wanted to collect the reward that had settled on her head like a target. She had to be smart.

He folded his arms and lowered his head closer to hers. "So tell me, what's your plan?"

She dug the heels of her leather boots, unsuitable for this weather, in the dense snow and stiffened her shoulders, weighing her options. "To stay alive long enough to finish what I've started."

A beat passed. Then, a barely audible chortle escaped his smooth lips. Amusement softened his gray eyes. "You're trouble, you know that, Alexis?" He drawled out the words leisurely, and a flurry of movement stirred in her belly at the way her name slid off his tongue.

She lifted her shoulder and let it drop. "Yeah, well, you're sure as hell not any better."

"Touché." And just like that, his expression hardened. "Get in the car." He hefted her suitcase into the air and dropped it in the back of the SUV before loading his duffel bag. He pulled her cellphone from his back pocket and tucked it into the outside pouch of his duffel bag.

She couldn't take it back now, but as soon as he wasn't watching, she'd retrieve it and call Alina. She chewed the swell of her bottom lip. He was an enemy, a cold, ruthless murderer who would hand her over at the first chance he got.

Only he hasn't yet.

Why? He could have let Dmitry kill her or done the job himself the previous night. It had to be the ledger holding him back. That old leather-bound book was the only thing keeping her alive. If she ran from Nash, he'd pursue her. But if she went with him for now, until she could reach Alina, she might just make it out of this unscathed.

She hoisted her chin up a notch and met his stare. "Fine."

His eyebrows lifted, nearly touching his hairline. She turned on her heel and rounded the vehicle.

"Hurry up, it's freezing."

She opened the passenger door, sank into the leather seat, and buckled her seatbelt. A moment later, Nash climbed in the driver's side. His eyes raked over her. Then he clicked his seatbelt in place and jabbed the key in the ignition. Frigid air blasted through the vents. Alexis shivered and folded her arms in front of her, waiting for Nash to speak. She needed to put as much distance between the hotel and her as possible. There was no saying how long it would be before the next Lionsgate member came after her.

As Nash pulled out of the parking lot, she cleared her throat. "Where exactly are we going?" The vehicle bounced over deep, icy ruts, and mist from a snowdrift scattered across the windshield.

"Don't you think you should have asked that before you got in?" His words flowed out of his mouth like smooth, aged whiskey. The sound warmed her chilled skin, just as his touch had earlier. A niggle of distaste stung her mouth, and she inched closer to the door.

Maybe she'd been wrong to use him as an avenue of escape. He'd served a purpose earlier, with Dmitry, but she couldn't forget that he wanted her dead. Besides, just because he'd taken out two intrusive armed men didn't mean he was going to protect her from everyone else. Hell, for all she knew he was driving her to Moscow's House.

A low, tired sigh broke through his lips. He rubbed his coarse fingers over his stubble, creating a crackling sound. "Look, Alexis. I don't want to hurt you—"

She didn't attempt to stifle her snort. "You're joking right?" She narrowed her eyes at him. His gaze flicked to her and then back to the white road. God, everything was frozen here. It was almost as if the entire city had been coated in thick, glossy ice and then dusted over with shimmering sprinkles. If it weren't so god-awful cold, she might appreciate the city's wintery beauty.

He continued. "If you really thought that, you wouldn't have gotten in the car."

Boy was he wrong. She was using him, and she'd ditch his malicious ass the first second she got.

"All I want is my ledger. Regardless of your motives, you stole from me. If you hand it over now, I can offer you immunity."

Her eyebrows stretched so far north that her forehead ached. "Immunity?" she squeaked. "You're shitting me, right?"

His hands tightened on the steering wheel. "I'm a lot of things, honey. But not a liar."

Acid boiled in her stomach, whether as a result of the endearment or his pledge of honor, she wasn't sure. She balled her icicle-like fingers until they threatened to snap. It took every effort not to throat-punch him. "Let's say I was stupid enough to believe you," she said. "Do you honestly think I'd be stupid enough to walk away? That I'd let Lionsgate hurt more people? I'm an investigative journalist—even if I wanted your so-called immunity, I wouldn't take it."

He shook his head and shrugged. The movement of his large shoulders invaded her space. "You're not leaving me many options."

She tucked her hands under the sides of her thighs, searching for any warmth her body might offer. She might have Russian blood running through her veins, but it didn't help her acclimate to the weather.

She was sick of going back and forth with Nash. She had a ton of work to do, her boss was probably losing her mind because she hadn't touched base in days, and more than anything, she needed to get a hold of Alina and find refuge until she could piece her case together. Nash was used to people cowering at his presence and surrendering at his scowl. He wouldn't find that here. Not from her.

She lifted her arms and tucked them tightly beneath her breasts before shifting in her seat to face him. "Make your move, Mr. Enforcer. You're not scaring anyone."

CHAPTER 6

J ESUS HELP ME.

No one called his bluff. Ever. And until now, he'd never really had to bluff. Usually a single demand got him what he was searching for. Alexis's small, arrogant turned-up nose and set mouth dared him to do his worst. If she were a guy, he'd oblige. But there wasn't a whole hell of a lot he was willing to do to a woman besides intimidate her.

Not that it had worked.

He forced the muscles in his hand to relax on the wheel and let his fingers slide slowly to the base. He watched her gaze flick down his arms to his hands and then back up to his face. He dragged his eyes back to the road, taking in the soaring skyscrapers as they exited the heart of downtown Moscow. He needed to get off the main streets and to a quieter area.

"Thing is, Alexis, you're in no position to challenge me. You know who I am and what I'm capable of." He spoke low. "You don't have to trust me, but I haven't tried to kill you yet."

She remained silent and turned her face toward the passenger window.

Ten minutes later, he steered the vehicle into the parking lot of a takeout restaurant. "I need some food. Don't try to run. If you do, you won't be happy when I find you." He shifted into park and released the key from the ignition.

"Hey, I'll freeze." She grabbed at the air where the key had been.

He chortled. "Not a chance, baby."

"Don't call me that." Her eyelids lowered and her pupils torched him. He chuckled before stepping out of the vehicle.

Inside the restaurant, the scent of frying meat and garlic assaulted his senses, making his stomach churn. Russian words were scrawled across the menu. Shit. He moved to the counter and ordered items that appeared appetizing in the picture.

Once he'd paid, Nash stepped toward the large window facing the parking lot, gazing past the vacant room. Lunch hour was approaching and more diners would likely arrive. Alexis's oval face stared back at him, and her scowl reached him even from where she sat.

Christ, she was a pain in the ass. He pulled his phone from his pocket and hit Conrad's number. There was a long pause before the call went through and the line rang in his ear.

"What the hell is going on?" Conrad barked.

Nash winced and jabbed his free hand into his pocket. This shouldn't have been difficult. He'd known Conrad for more than half his life. He'd never feared him, and he sure as hell didn't now. He didn't fear anyone. He wasn't the terrified little kid in the group home anymore.

But he'd disappointed the Grand Chancellor, and dammit, that lessened his ability to move through the ranks. His only route of redemption was to retrieve the ledger, take it back to Conrad, and finish the order Conrad had laid out. He shifted his gaze back to Alexis.

That meant killing her.

He cleared his throat. "Hey, sorry I've been out of touch. It was a long day traveling and things got a little hairy."

"What does that mean?"

He moved his fingers over the change in his pocket. "For starters, two men stormed her hotel room and tried to kill her. Do you know anything about that?"

Conrad grunted. "I hadn't heard from you and wanted the bases covered. You've obviously located her, so I assume you're calling to tell me you have the ledger and are returning?"

Nash stretched his neck from side to side. The knots in his shoulders didn't ease. "Not exactly. She claims she doesn't have it."

Conrad snickered. The sound was low and out of place in the conversation.

Nash's spine stiffened. "Something funny?"

"No, it's not fucking funny at all. You're trying to tell me that a 120-pound woman has your balls in a vice? You saw her take it, goddammit. Stop screwing around. You have until this time tomorrow to straighten this shit out."

Heat spread across Nash's face, and he tightened his hand on the phone. "Or what?"

The phone went dead in his ear. Nash closed his eyes and gripped the plastic in his hand. It took all his control not to smash the fucking thing into the wall.

A voice announced his order and Nash strode to the counter and snagged the bags. He nodded a thank you and turned toward the door, slipping his phone into his pocket. He pushed the door open, and his gaze landed on Alexis. Her lips were moving. He narrowed his eyes to get a better view of her. Her hand was nestled close to her cheek, her chin tucked.

Shit, shit, shit.

Dammit, she'd found her phone.

"I'M GOING TO kill Dmitry," Alina hissed.

"Yeah, well, we shouldn't have expected any less from him." Alexis combed her hair away from her cheek, and her fingers tangled in the strands. God, she needed a shower.

"Where are you? I can leave work early but not

for another couple of hours."

Alexis gave her cousin the name of the restaurant. Her stomach growled, bringing her attention to the window in front of her. Nash's eyes locked on hers, and he stomped across the parking lot, his face crinkled in a deep scowl.

She wet her lips. "Shit, Alina. I have to go. I'll call you—"

"Wait, we need a meeting place in case something happens. Meet me at the church at four—"

The driver's side door flung open and cold air blasted into the vehicle. Without a word, Nash got in his seat, reached across the small gap between them, and snatched the phone from her hand.

"Stop!" She clambered after her only lifeline, but the seatbelt restricted her.

He pried off the back of her phone, took out her battery and placed it in the cupholder. "Are you out of your damn mind? I'd prefer not to have to fight off any more bullets today."

She reached for her phone, but he dropped it into the inside pocket of his coat. "Who do you think is after me, the FBI? Street thugs won't have the resources to trace my phone."

He shook his head. His eyes lit with amusement. "That so? How do you think I found you?"

She gasped. "You tracked my phone?"

A rare smile graced his face. Had it not been full of disdain, it would have been almost attractive.

"No. I used facial recognition and followed your many disguise changes." He opened the takeout bag on his lap.

She clamped her lips together and fought the surge of panic that had sunk its greedy claws into her skin. The heavy garlic scent that erupted from the wrapper made her press her fingers to her lips, and she fought a wave of nausea.

Nash's eyes widened at her over the sandwich clamped between his teeth. He pulled it away, and a muscle in his jaw twitched. "You going to puke?"

She waved him off. "No, I'm fine." She grabbed one of the water bottles from the bag and opened it.

"I'm not sure which wig I liked the most—the platinum blonde one or the red one. Then again, your natural color suits you." He tugged on a strand of her hair, and she jerked out of his reach.

"I don't give a shit what you like." She brought the bottle to her lips and let the cool liquid coat her throat and stomach.

He pulled out a napkin and wiped his mouth. "Is that any way to talk to someone who bought you lunch?" He dropped the bag at her side and she curled her lip. "You should eat. You might not get another chance for a while."

She didn't want to ask what he meant by that. Instead, she reached into the bag and pulled out a salad, avoiding the other heavily packed sandwich he'd gotten for her. She didn't like Nash, not one bit. As a matter of fact, just looking at his hard, arrogant face made her want to deck him. But she wasn't going to turn down food.

"Who were you talking to?"

She jabbed the tongs of a plastic fork into a tomato and a crisp piece of lettuce. "None of your business."

"Someone you called for help?"

She shifted her eyes to him and then rolled them back toward her salad. She took another bite, ignoring his question.

"C'mon, Alexis. I'm not stupid. You have family here and a story you want to work on. You can't do that if you're stuck with me."

She sighed, crumpled a napkin between her fingers, and rested her head back on the seat. He wasn't going to let her free, not while she had the ledger and he didn't have a shred of dignity.

"Fine, you caught me," she said dryly. "As soon as you blink, I'm going to escape."

He polished off his sandwich and wiped his hands on a paper napkin. "You're impossible," he mumbled.

"True. And you haven't killed me yet. Why?"

He folded his arms across his chest again. The pose made his body look as if it were about to explode from his coat. "I need you and you need me."

She laughed, a deep, throaty guffaw that vibrated in her throat.

His eyebrows rose and pinched together. "Laugh all you want, but I saved your ass a half hour ago. If it weren't for me, you'd be dead."

Her shoulders shook on the last wave of her giggle. He was right, of course. But if she let him believe that she needed him, he'd have the upper hand. Besides, all she had to do was survive a few hours until she could ditch Nash and meet Alina.

"So what's *your* plan?"

He lifted a shoulder. "Easy. I give you some options and you make the choice."

She scrunched her face at him. "What's that supposed to mean?"

"It means that you have about thirty seconds to produce the ledger—"

"I told you. I don't have—"

He held up his hand, and she sank her teeth into her tongue.

"Before I search every inch of your bags ... and you." He lowered his hand and her pulse dropped with it. Heat flamed across her chest and up to her cheeks, leaving a tingling path in its wake.

"You won't touch me," she whispered through gritted teeth.

He watched her, his expression unchanged. "Twenty seconds."

While he was inside the restaurant, she'd tucked the ledger in the bottom of her suitcase. As much as she didn't want him searching her person, she couldn't let him get near her bag. She had to think of something. There was no way she'd let him strip her naked.

In college, she'd taken self-defense classes, though for the life of her she couldn't remember a single thing except the acronym SING. What the hell did that stand for? "Scream" and "groin" were all that came to mind, and hell if those were even correct. She lowered her gaze to her purse, cuddled against her thigh. Inside lay Dmitry's gun.

"Ten seconds," he said, his voice smooth and holding more than a hint of delight. He stretched his arms in front of him, as if warming up for a sporting event. In one swift movement, she unzipped her purse and reached for the smooth metal.

Nash lunged across the seat; one large fist covered her hand and another tore her purse away from her lap. The barely eaten salad tumbled into the footwell. She winced as his grip tightened.

"Don't even think about it." The words leaked through his gritted teeth, and a dark stain tinted his cheekbones. She wrestled her wrist out of his hold and as soon as she did, he unbuckled her seatbelt. "Get in the back seat."

Defiance climbed the back of her neck, and she knotted her hands to avoid hitting him. If she tried to escape now, he'd catch her before she even got out of the vehicle. Without a weapon, she was powerless. She flicked her gaze around the empty parking lot and toward the busy street several dozen feet away.

"There's no one around to save you, and by the time anyone gets here, we'll be done. Now take off your coat and get in the back. I don't want to have to drag you."

She brought her fingers to the zipper and nodded at the vent in front of her. "Turn the heat up."

He flicked his fingers over the dials, and warm air hummed through the vehicle. She climbed over the console and dropped into the back seat, scanning the floor and seat pockets for some kind of weapon as she shed her coat. A blast of flurries rushed in through the open door as Nash got out of the driver's seat.

A tire iron would be golden right now.

Nothing. Not a damn thing.

The rear driver's side door opened. Nash climbed in. She shuffled over, and her side dug into the arm of the bench seat.

His hand shifted on his lap, and her gaze dropped to the gun he held loosely.

"Last chance to hand it over." His tone rang with authority, and his eyes never left her face. The fact that he didn't lower his attention to her cleavage, which her V-neck shirt showed off, earned him half a point.

She hoisted her chin up a notch.

"C'mon. You're starting to make me think you

want me to strip-search you."

Her temper threatened to overboil. What were the chances he'd shoot her if she punched him in the face? Probably slim, since he didn't have the ledger . . . yet. In all actuality, it was only a matter of minutes before he found it. If she were smart, she'd avoid the whole process and just give it to him. But she couldn't. She was waiting for a distraction, a spark of inspiration to hold him off just a few more hours.

Not even the glow of an ember sizzled to life in her brain.

He raised the gun and aimed it at her chest. "Shirt off."

She pressed the pads of her fingers into her palms and fought to swallow over the bowling ball that had formed in her throat. Would he shoot her after he got what he wanted?

She sucked in a breath through her nose. He was one of them—of course, he would. She'd learned how to disarm someone. She could do this. Goosebumps raced over her skin at the thought of touching the menacing piece directed at her.

Screw it. She wasn't going to die here.

She shot her hands forward. Her right hand clasped his wrist and her left palm slammed the gun to the side. His arm faltered, but the weapon didn't leave his grasp. His left hand grabbed her throat, propelling her to the seat. Terror bit through her flesh, and she clawed at the hand that pinned her down. Instantly his grip went slack, but he kept his palm at the base of her neck, holding her in place.

"Jesus, I could have fucking shot you," he snarled. "What the hell is the matter with you?"

"You were going to shoot me anyway." She squirmed beneath his hold, but he didn't back off. Instead, he leaned in closer. His breath stirred the hair that fell beside her cheek, making the long strands tickle her jaw. The faint scent of coffee mixed with beef filled the vehicle. It should have made her want to vomit, but it didn't. The tiny hint of yellow in his granite irises glowed, and the straight bridge of his nose hovered inches from hers. Her gaze lingered on the stubble over his lip, and fascination sprouted inside her.

Despite who he was and what he'd done, he was a good-looking man. An asshole, but that didn't change his rugged handsomeness.

"I told you I wouldn't hurt you." He pulled his hand away from her throat and his scowl deepened.

"Oh, right. As you point a gun at my chest." She rolled her eyes and he released a breath through his nose. "I told you I don't have it and I'm telling the truth. The person I was speaking with was my cousin, and she has it. She's going to meet me in a few hours and arrange a place for me to stay until I can get home." The lie rolled off her tongue easily, and thank god it actually sounded believable.

"Is this the same cousin who tried to kill you?"

"No. She's his sister, and she's one of my best friends."

He raised an eyebrow and snorted. "So you landed in Moscow, met her and gave her the ledger, and then went to a hotel? Why wouldn't you stay with her in the first place?"

"Because I didn't want her in any danger." The fabrication slipped easily off her tongue. She wasn't usually one to stretch the truth, but she had no choice. She needed more time and she needed to stay alive to avenge her family.

He deposited the gun in its spot behind his back. "Fine. You've got until 6:00 p.m., Lexi. After that, no more leniencies. I can promise you that."

She'd worry later about how she'd ditch him after she met with Alina. Right now, she just had to get by, one minute at a time.

CHAPTER 7

NASH LEANED AGAINST the tiled pillar less than ten feet from the Victoria's Secret entrance. He crossed his arms, not bothering to hide his annoyance. "Hurry the hell up, alright? And don't try anything funny. I won't hesitate to go in there if I think you're trying to sneak out a back exit."

They had an hour to kill before Alexis needed to meet her cousin, and there was only so much driving they could do around the city before someone else found them. The mall was like the concourse of a football stadium—full of people.

And apparently, she'd forgotten to pack bras and frickin' panties.

Alexis lifted her chin, which held an impish dimple, and smiled so broadly her eyes crinkled. She couldn't have picked a faker expression if he'd paid her.

"I wouldn't dream of it." She patted his bare forearm, and her touch sent a ripple of heat right to his dick. "Hold this, will you?" She tossed her coat over the parka on his arm.

"Ten minutes," he warned. And fuck him, his words teetered on the empty threat. Goddammit, he hated how she did that to him—called his bluff, challenged him on everything, and basically made him look like an idiot for trying to have the upper hand.

Conrad's laugh echoed in his head and Nash's gut clenched. Was he losing his edge? Conrad seemed to think so. The man had threatened him for god's sake.

Alexis's effect on him had nothing to do with the blue balls she'd left him with. Nor did it have to do with the fact that she was a woman. He'd had confrontations with women before, and he'd always held his stance.

What did she do to him? Her cryptic reasons for needing the ledger could have something to do with it. And he'd been involved to some degree with the death of her family. Was that it? Maybe his thirty-third birthday two weeks ago had given him the gift of a conscience.

Yeah, that had to be it.

She'd lost her family. But hell, there had to be more to the story than that. They hadn't been innocent targets. Later, he'd talk to her more about what her family had been involved in, and maybe that would alleviate the crushing weight on his chest.

She wriggled her fingers over her shoulder at him as she entered the store and headed to the table of panty bins. His irritation grew. His conscience had to be acting on a subconscious level. He exhaled heavily and lifted his gaze to the ceiling before lowering it to scan the crowd.

It wasn't likely that they'd be found here. Alexis's phone was long gone. He always used a burner, so his wasn't a liability either. Unless someone had stuck a GPS under his SUV or had been following them around the city for the last two hours, they were safe for the time being.

He kept Alexis's light brunette head in view as she flitted around the store. To her credit, she didn't stray too far from the entrance, so he didn't have to go in after her. Nearly twenty minutes later, she exited the store with a large black-and-pink bag dangling from her fingers.

A tremor of hunger rippled through him at the prospect of what the bag held. The memory of her in the black lace bra and panties flashed through his mind and hit him like a punch to the gut. Her hot, wet tongue had flicked over his skin with promise. His mouth went dry. He'd never get that sensation out of his head. She'd been soft and sensual, assertive yet demure, and he'd wanted nothing more than to drive himself into her musky heat.

"I'm ready." She pulled her coat from his arm and he cleared his throat, which failed to banish the images from his head. He gave a tense nod, and she raised her eyebrows at him. "I need your phone to call Alina. I should probably do that now, so we know where we're going."

Nash pulled his burner phone from his back pocket and handed it to her.

"This one is safer. Make it quick and tell her we need to meet now."

She accepted the device, her slim fingers sliding over his like silk. He stuck his hand in his pocket and pressed his shoulders back against the pillar. Alexis thumbed over the screen and a second later pressed it to her ear. She took a step away and he reached out, turning her on the spot.

"Stay put." His voice came out harder than he'd intended, earning him a glare. Tough shit. He wasn't giving her the opportunity to plan anything. As it stood, he could already be walking into a trap.

"Hey, it's me," she said softly into the phone, not breaking eye contact with him. She listened, and his insides twisted with the need to know what her cousin was saying. "That's fine. Can you be there soon?"

A beat passed, and then she said goodbye and handed the phone back to him. "She'll meet us there in twenty minutes."

He slipped the phone into his pocket and caught her elbow before she could waltz away. "Where are we going?"

Her lips stretched like a rubber band into a mischievous smile. "You'll see."

★ ★ ★

"HERE?" HIS VOICE rang with disbelief. He shifted into park and swiveled to face her. If she could have snapped a picture of his wide-eyed expression, she would have.

Alexis stifled a laugh with her knuckles and scanned the parking lot. Alina's headlights cut through the glitter of flurries. She nodded and slung her purse—a hell of a lot lighter without Dmitry's gun—over her arm.

"Let's hope the walls don't burn down when you go inside." She opened the door and slipped out of the SUV. Alina had pulled up right in front of the entrance to St. Philip's Cathedral. Nash's heavy footsteps crunched swiftly behind her.

Alina's straight blonde hair lay underneath the knit hat pulled tightly over her head. The bottoms of the long strands fluttered around her shoulders. She smiled, her arms wide. A black fabric bag hung around her wrist. Her gaze shifted over Alexis's shoulder, and her eyes darkened.

"Speak in Russian," Alexis whispered next to Alina's ear as they embraced. Nash's formidable presence hovered near her back, making her spine stiffen. If he didn't know Alina spoke English, he wouldn't be able to question her and the safer Alina would be.

Alina pulled away, her smile frozen and her brown eyes as sharp as a tack.

Alexis closed her fingers around her cousin's

gloved hand.

"Who's this?" asked Alina, in Russian. Alexis turned and took in Nash's dark stare. He shoved his hands in his pockets. A small ripple of pleasure at his annoyance spread through her.

"He's, uh . . ." She struggled for the right word in Russian. *A murderer, a thug, and the man who saved my life hours ago.* "He won't be here long."

Alina's perfectly waxed eyebrows rose, and skepticism sparked her chocolatey irises. "He looks scary, Lex. But in a super hot way."

Nash's eyes narrowed, and Alexis covered her laugh with a cough. "Can we go in? I'm freezing."

Alina nodded and gestured them to the door. She pulled Alexis up the snow-covered steps and then dropped her hand to fish a set of keys out of her pocket. "Father Abram happily agreed to let you stay the night. There's a nice space in the basement."

She bumped her hip into the old wooden door and it creaked open. Alexis followed her inside with Nash close behind her. He remained uncharacteristically quiet, but he was likely trying to dissect Alina's words.

Warmth surrounded her in a tight hug, and she shook off the chill. Her shoes scraped over the stone floor as Alina led them down a long corridor off the entrance and away from the sanctuary. Ornate stained glass decorated the door at the end of the hall. Alina inserted a key into its lock and pushed the door open. The hinges groaned. She flicked on the light, illuminating the carpeted staircase.

Alexis wrapped her hand around the slim railing and followed Alina down the stairs. "Thanks for arranging this, Alina. I appreciate—"

Nash's warm hand closed over her shoulder, tightening enough that she slowed her step.

"In English," he whispered against her ear. His breath was hotter than his skin. Its gentle rhythm stirred the hair at her cheek, making her shoulders tense with apprehension.

She turned and met his eyes, which appeared onyx in the dim lighting. "She doesn't speak English, so deal with it."

Nash bared his teeth but looked away. She turned in the direction of his gaze. Alina stood at the bottom of the stairs, her face pale and her eyes wide, watching their exchange. Alexis pulled her lips into a taut, reassuring smile and descended the rest of the stairs.

The open-concept room held a small kitchenette. The black bag Alina had been carrying now sat on the clean laminate counter. A couch that had seen better days faced a small flat-screen TV.

"Father Abram said you're welcome to anything in the fridge. They had a potluck last night, so there's quite a bit of food, but in case you need something more familiar, I brought a frozen pizza and some snacks."

Nash moved toward the counter, his gaze locked on the bag. Alexis stepped in front of him and rested her hand on the rough canvas. Damn him, he was already in search of the ledger, which was still hidden in her suitcase. No need for him to find out she'd been lying yet. Not until Alina was gone. Unless she could come up with something else to tide him over—but judging by his testy attitude, she was fresh out of cards to play.

"There's a bathroom over here," Alina continued, as she fluttered around the room. "And an office in case you need a computer."

Yes. Before she crashed for the night, she'd check in with her boss. It was too bad she didn't have any material to send her. She'd had the ledger in her possession for three days and still hadn't had the chance to read it.

Nash cleared his throat and Alexis fought her reluctant neck to look at him. He stared at her, the muscles in his jaw tense, but less murderous than they had been. Probably because he'd already freaked Alina out.

He wanted the ledger and to have her out of his hair. Which was perfectly fine. No one would think to look for her here, and tomorrow she'd arrange her flights to return home. What a wasted trip this had been. She'd come to get help from her family and had been attacked in return.

Alina tapped her fingers against the side of her thigh as she retraced her steps back to the kitchenette. Her eyes lowered and shifted. A boulder of regret dropped into Alexis's stomach. She shouldn't have gotten Alina involved. She pulled her cousin into another hug. "Thank you. And don't worry, I'm fine."

Alina snorted. "Yeah, this guy looks like he either wants to pile-drive you or kill you. I'm not sure which."

A hiccup of laughter caught in Alexis's throat, but despite her amusement, heat rose to her cheeks. She didn't want to analyze Alina's impression of Nash. But if she had to guess, she'd say he'd be more inclined to kill her than pile-drive her.

Especially when he found out she wasn't going to hand over the ledger.

A laser burned into the back of her head, scalding her scalp. She didn't have to glance over her shoulder to know Nash was scowling about their secret exchange.

"I'm fine," she repeated. "I promise. I'll call you tomorrow, okay?"

Alina nodded and pulled away. Her gaze drifted to Nash, and the muscles beneath her smooth skin turned to steel. She brushed past him and stopped at the stairs to wave.

Alexis forced a confident smile until the muscles in her face ached and watched her cousin disappear up the stairs. Nash shed his coat and rested his baseball-mitt-sized hands on the counter.

The thick cords in his forearms bunched before disappearing along with the thick flesh beneath his short-sleeve shirt. A strand of unkempt ebony hair fell over his forehead.

His lips curved into a slow, lazy smile. Her stomach muscles clenched, and her cheeks tingled. God, he was too seductive when he smiled. Whether it was intentional or not, he had her muscles achy, her temples sore, and her stomach in a tangle of ribbons.

"I don't think your cousin likes me too much."

Her fingers went to her zipper, and she eased it down her abdomen. Nash's gaze lowered to her exposed body, and his Adam's apple moved beneath his whisker-covered throat. She hung her coat over the chair nearest her and folded her hand on top.

The air caressed her neck and turned her nipples into tight buds. Dammit, she needed to find the thermostat, but she couldn't move under Nash's stare. She cleared her throat. "In her defense, you don't really make the best first impression."

His mouth split into a grin, and he tilted his head back as a deep, throaty laugh rattled his shoulders.

"What?" She folded her arms.

He shook his head and pinched the bridge of his nose as if to stop his chuckles. "I find that pretty amusing, considering how we met the other night."

Her knotted stomach seized, sending an explosion of butterflies through her midsection. She pressed her tongue to the top of her mouth, but that did nothing to stifle the fire that burned all the way to the top of her head.

"In case you haven't figured it out, let me spell it for you." She drew up her shoulders and used every ounce of control she had not to lose her cool. "I was using you to get to the ledger, smart-ass."

"And you were very convincing. I've never seen—"

She held up her palm. "I'm not engaging in this conversation." She shook her head and let loose a deep breath through her nose. She reached for the snacks Alina had brought. The cold pizza box cooled her skin, taming the fire he'd started within her. Dammit, how did he get such a rise out of her?

He moved toward her. Keeping her gaze down, she tried to round the island toward the fridge. His hot, firm hand on her hip froze her in place.

Her breath stopped in her throat and swelled against the delicate walls until her lungs ached. His strong, wide arm pressed against her shoulder and side, boxing her in and heating her to her core.

She didn't move.

Couldn't.

All she could do was struggle to suck tiny puffs of air through her nose. And in doing so, she filled her lungs with his warm, heady scent.

"Before we part ways, should we finish what we started?"

Panic shot through her veins, snapping her head up. And god help her, a thrill followed it. Hot and pumping with need. The sensitive nerve endings between her legs tingled, begging her to give in to the damp throb that she hadn't been able to shake since Nash had touched her days ago.

No. No matter how badly she needed sex, no matter how good his body felt against hers, she wouldn't stoop to sleeping with him. Visions of the heinous crimes Lionsgate Kinship had committed flashed through her mind. Crimes that he very well could have committed himself. Crimes that she'd put a stop to if it killed her.

She whirled around in his arms and pressed her palms against his abs. She shoved firmly on the steely muscle until he inched back. "I'm not interested."

His scarred eyebrow arched, and his mouth slid into a sexy smirk. Her rebellious fingers pressed into his pecs, savoring the delicious muscle stacked there.

"You sure? I'm picking up on something else." His hand rose from its happy place at her hip to brush a lock of hair from her cheek. He rested his hand on the crook of her neck, his hold gentle and firm—confident.

Lord help her, she wanted nothing more than

to melt into his strength. To accept every pleasure his touch dangled in front of her. Her lips burned with the desire to part, to bring his tongue into her mouth and revel in its wetness. Delight littered her skin with goosebumps, making her need raw and desperate.

She squeezed her eyes shut to avoid looking at his face, but limiting her vision only enhanced every other sense. His fingertips twitched on the back of her neck, and his other hand was welded to her waist. If he moved either of those extremities, she wouldn't be able to resist. His hot breath swirled over her mouth, warning her that his lips were there for the taking.

"No." She turned away, breaking his hold on her neck. Her body cried at the loss of contact. He took a step back, but not far enough. She risked opening her eyes. He stood with his hands up in front of him as if in surrender.

"Understood." His tone was tight. Strained, even. It seemed he was also fighting the battle of lust that arced between them. She wrapped her arms around her, as if they could shield her from the intensity of his granite eyes.

"Thank you," she said softly. Why the hell was she thanking him? For god's sake that was as bad as apologizing. His mouth tensed and he gave one brisk nod. Like a melting glacier, the mountain of dislike she felt toward him receded an inch.

He could have forced himself. Although she

would have fought him, he wouldn't have broken a sweat overpowering her. And if she was going to be completely honest with herself, it would have ended in her satisfaction.

But he'd respected her, and she appreciated it.

"If that's off the table, how about you cough up the ledger so I can be on my way?" His gaze shifted to the bag.

She turned back to unloading the food. "Of course. A deal's a deal." She glanced over her shoulder as she slid the pizza in the freezer. Hunger stirred in her stomach. The second he left, she was going to fire up the oven. "But would you mind bringing my bag in for me? It's freezing in here and I'd like a sweater."

"Sure. Just give me the ledger first."

She chuckled, the sound brittle. "Why, so you can make off with all my stuff? Sorry, but that bag holds my passports, and I wouldn't be surprised that once you get what you want, you'll tell everyone where I am."

Shit, shit, shit. That possibility hadn't occurred to her until the words left her mouth. Once he left, she was a sitting duck.

He scoffed. "It's really ironic that you're the one with trust issues. I'll get your damn bag, but the ledger better be waiting when I get back." He lifted his jacket from the chair, fit his arms through the sleeves, and stormed upstairs. As soon as his footsteps hit the stone floor above, she darted for the stairs.

She hovered near the top and kept her gaze trained on his tense back as he strode down the long hall. When the front door opened, she sprinted for it. She fumbled the cold deadbolt in her fingers and snapped it into place.

She needed to hurry. She didn't have long.

CHAPTER 8

S HE WAS THE most infuriating woman he'd ever fucking met. He dropped her suitcase in the snow that had collected in the church's parking lot. And the damn blizzard was only adding to his anger. It didn't matter. In a few minutes, he'd get the hell out of here.

His stomach tightened. The thought of ridding himself of Alexis should be giving him sanity. Instead, a war clashed inside him. Goddammit to hell and back, people still wanted to kill her. Conrad would likely lift the bounty on her head once the ledger was produced, but he couldn't be certain of that. Besides, it would take time for that word to spread.

He rubbed his hand over his hair and groaned into the storm swirling around him. Christ, he couldn't leave. He'd call Conrad in the morning and insist he spare Alexis's life. If she didn't have the ledger, she was no longer a threat. He'd stay with her until they could catch a flight out of Moscow and be done with the whole fucking thing.

He snagged the strap of his duffel bag and hefted it over his shoulder, shut the hatchback, and then bent to grab her suitcase. He trudged through the snow, which was getting deeper by the second, and the cold dampness clung to his jeans and spilled into the tops of his boots. He shivered. Now that he didn't have to worry about her taking off, he could have a hot fucking shower. He climbed the steps and stomped his feet on the concrete just outside the church's door. His fingers molded to the icy metal door handle and he shoved. It didn't budge. He frowned, tightened his hold, and pushed again.

She locked me out.

Sonofafuckingbitch!

He thumped his fist against the old wooden door. Once, twice, three times. His breath circled around him in small clouds. No longer frozen, flames roared against his skin.

She'd tricked him.

Again.

He let loose a growl and banged on the door so hard it shook on its hinges. She wasn't going to open the door—and he wasn't leaving. He dropped the bags against the corner of the stoop and pounded down the steps.

Rounding the building, he spotted a basement window well. He dropped to his knees and cleared the snow away from the glass with his bare hands.

The snow melted beneath the heat of his legs, soaking him to the skin. A light shone from inside, illuminating the lounge beneath the church. His gaze immediately went to the kitchen, and then the couch, but she wasn't there.

A warm glow flooded the small hallway where the office and bathroom were. What the hell was she doing? He rapped his knuckles against the glass until his skin threatened to split. If she didn't come out in two minutes, he'd break the glass. At least his hand would be numb enough to blunt the pain of the piercing shards.

"Alexis!" he bellowed into the whirling snow. He banged six more times. Still no sign of her.

Motherfucker, he was going to lose his shit when he got a hold of the little heathen. He bent his arm and aimed his elbow at the window. Then he drew it back and slammed it into the glass. Pain shot through his arm and down to his fingertips. He shook his hand and breathed a curse, and then wound up again.

A flutter of movement from inside stopped him. Alexis gaped at him from the hallway, her eyes round, blue saucers and her lips in a giant O shape.

"Open the fucking door!" he screamed against the pane. She turned on her heel and headed toward the staircase. He pushed to his feet and stormed through the snow. If she made it to the door before he did, he had no doubt she'd collect both bags and leave him to turn into a bloody snowman.

He reached for the handle just as the door tore open. "What the hell are you doing?" he growled.

Her narrow shoulders lifted, and she shook her head. "I was wondering what was taking you so long. I—"

"Save the bullshit. You locked me out." He dropped the bags inside and shouldered his way past her.

"I didn't. I was—"

He wheeled on her. "You're going to lie in a church? Hell, even you should have more integrity than that."

Her lips drew together, and she shifted on the balls of her feet. "The door must have stuck. I wouldn't have let you back in if I'd locked you out." She bent, picked up the handle of her suitcase, and wheeled it down the hall toward the stairs. He dusted the large flakes from his coat and peeled it off along with his boots. He opened and closed his hands at his sides. It was possible she was telling the truth. What reason would she have to lock him out while he had her passports and belongings?

Unless she'd hidden the ledger.

It didn't matter. He was getting the damn thing now.

He lifted the strap of his bag to his shoulder and followed her down the hall. The warm scent of melting cheese met him at the stairs, and his stomach growled. He usually ate frequent small meals throughout the day, but today he hadn't eaten since lunch. As his feet touched the carpet of the basement, his eye caught Alexis's bent-over form reaching into the oven. Her snug jeans hugged her hips and pert ass, and her black shirt showed off her small frame and full breasts when she turned around.

His mouth went dry and his fingers twitched at his sides. He pulled the strap from his shoulder and let the bag fall to the floor. Her head snapped up and her eyes, crisp and blue, landed on him. She'd fastened her hair into a ponytail at the crown of her head, and the style highlighted her high cheekbones and alabaster skin.

She might be a thorn in his side, but she was a gorgeous one.

Her lips rolled in, and she peeled her fine-boned hands out of the oven mitts. "Lots to eat if you're hungry." The blood suddenly drained from her face like sand through an hourglass. Her eyes shifted, and she tucked an invisible strand of hair behind her ear and then turned to take out plates from the cupboard.

Desire spread through his thighs and filled his dick, which was like a loaded gun. She said she wasn't interested. Bullshit. But who the hell was he kidding? He couldn't blame her for not wanting to get involved. A woman like her didn't have sex just for fun, and certainly not with someone of his ilk.

Even if every small tremor of her hands and lowered lids screamed otherwise.

Sex with her would be fucking heaven. Three nights ago, he'd been so close to hearing her scream. She was tight. Her pussy had clenched around his fingers like a vice with the perfect amount of wetness.

And as much as lust was sucking at him like a riptide, there was more to it than that when it came to her. She intrigued him, dammit. She was smart and quick, willful and so fucking stubborn. And yeah, he had to admit he admired her.

He opened and closed his hands to alleviate the tension in his muscles. It didn't work.

"Thanks." He waited until she'd filled her plate with two pieces of pizza, macaroni salad, and some kind of chickpea-vegetable mix. "I saw you come out of the office. What were you doing?"

She set the spoon back into the bowl and a muscle near her eye twitched. "Nothing. I had to check on something for work, but other than that I've been getting food together."

She squeezed behind him, rounded the island, and sat at one of the chairs across from where he stood. He piled up his plate, not skimping on any of the food she'd laid out. Her eyes widened on his fifth slice of pizza, and he froze midair. "Do you want more?"

The corner of her mouth tucked in with amusement, accentuating the cute dimple in her chin. "No. Finish it, please." She held out her hand, signaling she didn't need the temptation, and he dropped the last slice on his plate.

He stood at the counter and lifted a slice to his mouth. After taking a bite, he said, "Dinner is perfect timing and all, but I'd appreciate it if you'd give me the ledger now."

She dabbed her lips with a napkin and rolled her eyes to the ceiling. "Can't wait until we finish eating?"

He swallowed a mouthful of cheese and pepperoni and glowered at her through lowered lids. "What are you trying to pull? Every time you agree to give it to me, you stall." He dropped the slice of pizza on the pile on his plate and pressed his palms to the counter. "You have about three seconds before I lose my patience."

She took a bite of her pasta, completely unfazed. "You're so dramatic." She set her fork beside her plate and stretched across the counter to the canvas bag tucked against the wall. Her hand disappeared inside and a second later, she pulled out the leather-bound book.

His chest tightened. She had it. She wasn't playing any more games, and no matter what, it was his again. The cords in his neck loosened and his shoulders lowered.

He held out his palm. His skin itched for the familiar weight. Her small thumbs tapped an erratic beat against the face of it, her top teeth pierced her bottom lip, and her eyes focused on his beloved book.

One millimeter at a time, her lashes rose. Her aqua eyes met his, the bright blue of her irises pushed out the ocean green. Gone was the defiance she'd shown him from day one, gone was the hard, relentless determination, and gone was the spirit that both angered and attracted him like lightning to a metal rod.

The air whooshed from his lungs, and all the annoyance she'd caused him vanished as if it had never been there in the first place. In those eyes, she was stripped naked of the armor she'd stacked around herself, and fuck him, he barely even recognized her.

This was important to her. Her fuel was avenging her family. He understood. If someone hurt one of his brothers, he'd kill. Yet here he was, robbing her of justice.

She expelled a long, low breath, leaned forward and stretched out her arm, the book clamped between her thumb and fingers, and then dropped it in his palm. His hand closed over the rough, deeply worn material.

"Thank you," he said, his voice damn near hollow. She nodded, her gaze down. Well, fuck. He should be elated. Should be doing a jig right now. Instead, he felt like shit. Guilt burned in his guts. The emotion was so unfamiliar that it pissed him off.

And that made his head throb.

She scooped up a few more bites of food and stood. "I'm going to shower and crash. I have a lot to sort out in the morning."

He nodded and watched her approach her suitcase, which sat at the bottom of the stairs. She froze. "Why did you bring your bag in?" Her voice shook. She turned to face him. Her skin had turned chalky.

He should have known he wouldn't be welcome. He lifted his shoulder. "I decided to stick around for the night. There's about two feet of snow on the ground and no sign of it letting up." It was a pathetic excuse. The weather had nothing to do with why he was staying. His reason why stood stark still, as rigid as a scarecrow at the prospect of being around him another minute.

Her hand toyed at the base of her throat. The sharp outline of her teeth moved beneath the skin of her cheek, indicating that she was abusing the inside of her mouth. "I don't understand. You have what you want, Nash."

"Yeah, well, we've been stuck together this long. What's a few more hours?" He crossed his arms and curled his lips into a smile.

She shifted her weight to one leg. "I suppose that's fine, but I'm leaving first thing in the morning—alone."

He nodded. "Ditto."

She grabbed the handle of her suitcase and

wheeled it to the bathroom. The door shut, and he pressed the small of his back into the counter, letting his chin drop to his chest. He ran the pads of his fingers over his jaw until his skin stung.

He was too soft, too attached and involved with her. He shouldn't give a damn about her reasons or ambition. Since when had anything wavered him from his oath to Lionsgate? Never. But that's what was happening. For the first time, his faith and loyalty were being tested. And he needed to know why.

ALEXIS KNEW LOCKING Nash out had been a risky thing to do, but it had saved her ass. There was no way she'd have been able to get out of giving him the ledger. Her lies were the only thing that had kept him from taking it before she'd been ready. She splayed her fingers under the shower's warm spray, but it didn't heat the chill that had bit into her bones.

It had taken almost fifteen minutes to photocopy the most important pages in the ledger. She'd much prefer to have the original, but there would have been no stopping him. He would have torn apart every stitch of clothing in her suitcase—and on her back—to get it.

She turned in the slick basin and tilted her head back. Rivulets of water ran over her cheeks and fell to her chest to cascade over her puckered nipples.

She combed her fingers through her strands and then reached for her shampoo. After filling her palm with the vanilla-scented liquid, she lathered it into her hair.

She didn't need him around another second, let alone another night. It had taken everything in her not to press herself into his body and accept the sex he'd offered. A tremor spread through her belly, warming the wet lips between her legs. God, if he came onto her again, she wouldn't be able to say no.

She squeezed her eyes tight and washed the suds from her hair. This was crazy, all of it. She shouldn't be horny right now, and sure as hell not for him. Reaching for the conditioner, she pushed Nash from her mind.

After scrubbing her body, she soaked up a few more minutes of heat and then shut off the water. She reached for her towel, quickly dried herself off, and got dressed while her teeth chattered.

She hadn't lied about needing to check something for work. She'd sent her boss a quick email— too quick. Lauren would be livid when she read the two-sentence email promising she'd call as soon as she got the opportunity to do so safely. Lauren had always given her a lot of leeway, but considering her silence over the last few days, Alexis assumed she'd be lucky to have a job to go back to.

She combed her hair, brushed her teeth, and

exited the bathroom. Nash still stood in the kitchenette, a toiletry bag and fresh pair of clothes hanging over his arm. Heat swelled in her face, and she fisted her hair in her hand and swept it over her shoulder. Nash pushed away from the counter and strode toward her slowly, his eyes locked on her. Her insides twisted with the need to take a step back, but she rooted her feet to the spot in the hallway and waited for his approach.

"Mind if I get in there?"

She cleared her throat—no way would she attempt speaking while the tension was lodged there. She nodded. "'Course. I'm going right to sleep, so help yourself to the extra pillows and blanket in the office."

"Thanks." He angled his shoulder back to allow her to pass, but her hip brushed his as she did so. The door closed behind him and her muscles went lax. She rubbed her fingertips over her forehead and shook her head. This was going to be one hell of a night.

A glance at the kitchen showed he'd tidied up and put away the leftover food. A glimmer of appreciation sparked inside her. She'd been prepared to tackle the mess, but he'd done it.

Another tally in his favor.

As the water turned on in the bathroom, she scurried to the living area and tore the large cushions from the couch. She dragged up the hideaway bed and fetched a pillow and blanket from the office. Then she turned off all the lights except one, in the kitchen.

She lay down and settled herself under the blanket, and her chest rose and fell in sharp, jerky movements. Her pulse thundered so hard that it pumped in her fingertips. She took a long, deep breath to steady her nerves, but it didn't work. She let her gaze roam around the room. Her back was to the kitchenette, so she wouldn't see him exit the bathroom. One rigid armchair sat kitty-corner to the couch. Where would he sleep? She scooted over so she lay smack dab in the middle of the bed. He wasn't dumb enough to try to get into bed with her . . . was he?

Please, God, don't let him be that dumb.

Less than five minutes later, the water turned off, and she heard Nash shuffling around the small space. Her ears were so sharply attuned to his every movement that they picked up on his barely audible footsteps over the carpet. He rounded the end of her bed, and she snapped her eyes shut with such force that her head pounded.

He said nothing, but the air crackled as he shook out a blanket. A pillow landed on the floor with a soft thud. She focused on her shallow breath and willed her eyes to fight the temptation to open and look at him. He grunted as he lowered himself to the floor, and a tiny pang of pity struck her. He was so large, nearly gargantuan, and sleeping on the floor would likely kill his back.

Oh well. He'd live. However, if he got into bed with her, she'd surely go into cardiac arrest. The gentle ticking of the clock on the wall echoed through the room. She flopped onto her back and pressed her hand to her diaphragm. A slow, constant throb pulsed through her core, filling her clit with need. Dammit, she should have relieved herself in the shower. There was no way she'd attempt to calm the tide of desire inside her with him only feet away. If she didn't chill out, she'd never get any sleep. She shifted her legs beneath the blanket, but it only increased her yearning.

She rolled over again, so her back was facing Nash. If she could pretend he wasn't there, then maybe—

"Alexis, are you all right?" he said gruffly, with a tinge of annoyance.

She moved her tongue over her lips and her blood warmed further. "I'm fine." Her voice strained over the frog in her throat.

"You've been fidgeting for the last twenty minutes."

She pressed her palm to her forehead and suppressed a groan. "Sorry, just restless. Good night."

Silence greeted her words. She drew her knees in closer to her stomach and began counting down from one thousand. Each number landed in sync with the rhythm of desire now pounding between her legs. With each passing minute, her heart rate slowed and her breath became less ragged. She was tired. Exhausted. But her pesky, neglected sex drive was through the roof.

The mattress dipped behind her, and her hip rocked back to connect with Nash's. She whipped her head around, and a muscle in her neck screamed.

"What are you doing?" she hissed, terror clipping her words.

"It's freezing in here and I'm not sleeping on concrete." His voice rumbled against her spine, weakening her muscles. "We both need sleep and aren't going to get it with all the moving around you're doing."

She nestled her cheek into her palm and pressed her knees together until they ached. She thought about kicking him, or at least moving away, but her body wouldn't be denied the contact. Not now. The gears in her brain worked, trying to form a legible sentence that would get him away from her.

Heat arched between their bodies, blazing a fire beneath the sheet. She pressed her closed fist into the mattress and dragged in one mouthful of breath at a time. He shifted, and his knee probed the backs of her thighs.

"What are you doing?" If she could have applauded the strength she'd managed to force into her voice, she would have.

He snaked his arm over her hip, enveloping her in a cocoon of warmth. Her body melted with the speed of butter in a hot skillet. *Oh god. Oh god.*

Oh god.

"You're fidgeting because you're cold. Now hush." He nestled his face close to her hair, and goosebumps prickled beneath her hair follicles. His shins brushed her bare feet. The hair on his legs prickled her skin. She curled her toes but couldn't move away. He shifted, and his chest snuggled against her back.

Every muscle in her body turned to stone. God he was warm. The bulge of muscle in his forearm weighed down on her side. Heat and pressure surrounded her, and despite the need pulsing inside her, she didn't fidget. Maybe this contact would be enough to settle the raging lust that wanted to arch her back against him and welcome his girth inside her. She closed her eyes and breathed in through her nose.

She needed this.

"Is this okay, Lexi?"

On his tongue, the nickname sounded like velvet. She wet her lips and inhaled. His sandalwood scent made her muscles sag. It was like aromatherapy.

His thumb tapped against her hip. "I need to hear you say it," he said softly.

She should say no. Hell, she should draw her knee up and kick him in the shin. But she didn't. The sweet temptation won. In the small bed, it would be almost impossible for him not to touch her. And he was right, the air was damn near frigid. If she didn't let him sleep in the bed, she would freeze. He held her close, but not so close that it was a come-on. His hand had dropped from her hip to rest on the mattress next to her midsection, and her side fit into the crook of his elbow. If it weren't for the delicious pulse of need between her legs, she'd have slipped into a coma.

She sucked in her bottom lip, moistening it, and then nodded. "Yes." A shiver jerked her muscles as the word left her mouth. Whether from the chill or his proximity, she wasn't sure.

"Sleep." The single word was gruff, as if he were halfway asleep himself. She lifted her lashes and pushed a breath through her nose. Here she was, horny as hell only an hour after he had offered himself to her, and now he was completely unaffected by her.

She shifted her palm beneath her cheek and stared into the darkness until the desperate need for release slowed to a dull hum. Little by little, Nash's warmth made her lids close. A soft rumble of a snore rattled against her back, and she slipped into sleep.

CHAPTER 9

NASH RUBBED THE base of his palm over his eye sockets, but the sandpaper texture still clung to his lids. Switching off the bathroom light, he slipped out the door. He balanced his weight on the balls of his feet and inched his way toward the pullout couch.

Two times in the last few hours, he'd snuck out of bed to relieve himself of the raging lust that coursed through him. He'd respected her for not wanting to have sex with him, and he couldn't go back on that word. Even if it killed him. He'd woken up to the gentle cadence of her breathing and her ass snuggled into his groin.

His thigh brushed against the thin mattress and he paused. Alexis laid on her stomach, her knee drawn up to rest beside her, the blanket pulled back to expose the creamy skin of her leg. Her hair tumbled in dark waves over the white pillowcase, and her cheek was cushioned in her palm.

She'd passed out within minutes of him getting into bed with her and hadn't so much as flinched since. He'd fully expected her to kick him out. He dragged his gaze away from her cozy form and rounded the end of the bed. His still-hard cock strained against his boxers as he slid beneath the blanket, pausing to tug the material over her leg.

He molded his body around hers and fit his arm around the indent of her waist as if he were the last piece in a puzzle. Her back rose and lowered on a deep sigh, and her ass wiggled back into the cavern of his hips.

Jesus Christ. He wasn't going to get a second of sleep. And he'd be damned if he got up to beat off again. Her warm vanilla aroma wafted from the tendrils of hair draped over her shoulder. He took a deep breath and forced his eyelids shut, embracing her feminine assault on his senses as fatigue pulled down his eyelids and his mind turned off.

Slam!

His eyes snapped open, and he jolted into a sitting position. He lowered his gaze to Alexis, but she hadn't moved. Shit, was he hearing things? The noise had been distant, so it was possible he'd dreamed it. He lifted his wrist and pressed the tiny button on his watch. 4:01 a.m. He'd gotten a few hours of sleep, at least.

But what the hell had woken him? He didn't startle easily, but his brain was beyond sleep deprived, so he couldn't rule that out. He tossed back the covers and tugged on his sweatpants. No way he'd be able to get back to sleep until he checked it out.

He pulled on his T-shirt, grabbed his Beretta, and strode quickly for the stairs. Each step creaked beneath his weight as he bounded up. It was probably nothing, but after what had happened in the hotel, he couldn't be too careful.

The main level was several degrees warmer than the basement. He kept his gun aimed toward the floor, his index finger on the trigger. Taking wide, soundless steps, he approached the front door. A flash of light burst through the window and a vehicle pulled to a stop in the parking lot.

Shit.

Keeping his back pressed to the wall next to the tall, narrow window beside the door, he peered outside. A large white SUV sat under the street-lamp. Beside it stood two men dressed in black. The lights on the second vehicle cut out, and he pressed his teeth together. There were a lot of them this time.

He double-checked the dead bolt and raced back to the basement. "Alexis!" he called, the second his feet touched the basement carpet. The mound in the bed didn't move, and he didn't dare turn on a light. He crossed the room and tore the covers away from her chin. Keeping his Beretta pointed at the floor, he jostled her shoulder. "Lexi, wake up, dammit!"

Her head jerked up, and wide, sleepy eyes landed on him. "What's wrong?" She pushed herself into a sitting position and rubbed her eyes.

The dead bolt wouldn't hold them long. He needed to get her out of sight and take out the fuckers who would be inside any second. He set down his gun on the mattress and closed his hands around her shoulders, lifting her from the bed.

"Hey, what—"

"They're here. You need to get in the office and hide." He picked up his gun again and hustled her to the small hallway and into the office. Her bicep turned to stone in his palm, her warm skin icy in a matter of milliseconds. She whirled to face him.

"Who's here? How'd they—"

"Doesn't matter. We don't have much time. I need you to listen to me, all right?"

Her hands clenched in front of her abdomen. She nodded briskly.

"Push the chair up against the door," he said, gesturing to the wooden-backed chair against the wall. "And don't open it until I come for you. Got it?"

Her chest lifted and the fine muscles in her jaw tensed. "Okay."

"I mean it. Don't open that fucking door."

Her lashes flickered and she swallowed.

He backed up to where his duffel bag sat, next to the office door, and kneeled. He unzipped the bag, dug inside it, pulled out Dmitry's gun, and stood. "Do you know how to use this?" he asked.

"Yes," she said, her voice strong as she reached

forward without hesitation. Skepticism brought his eyebrows together. She pursed her lips and lifted a shoulder. "My brother taught me how to handle one years ago. I'm not a pro, but I know what I'm doing."

And hell if that didn't make admiration prickle his skin.

Ping!

He snapped his head up and held his hand in the air. "Shhh." He cocked his head.

Alexis wet her lips and wrapped both hands around the butt of the gun. "What was that?"

The floor above their heads groaned softly. "They're in." Nash moved across the office to the electrical panel on the wall and turned the breakers off.

"How many are there?"

"Not sure, but at least four or five."

"Nash, you can't . . ." She stood in his way as he turned from the box.

He fit his fingers around her shoulder and brought his nose close to hers. Her lips parted and her chest swelled in the space between them. "I've been up against worse odds. Don't leave this room." He gave her shoulder a tight squeeze and sidled around her. He shut the door softly behind him, and his fingers hovered on the knob, as if it were a line of connection to Lexi. The soft clank of wood against wood assured him she'd barricaded the door.

The creaking above grew louder. His muscles bunched beneath his clothes. He hadn't been lying—this wasn't the first time he'd been outnumbered. But it was the first time he had someone else to worry about. The good thing was, they didn't know where he was. His feet grew roots in the carpet outside the office door. As much as he wanted to, he couldn't stand guard. His best bet at taking them out was to remain out of sight and shoot them as they came down.

As slow footsteps scuffed down the stairs, he tore himself from the door and moved to the sofa. He crouched and aimed over the arm. Sweat collected at the back of his neck, tickling his skin. He narrowed his eyes, closing off the shadows around him. His vision had adjusted to the darkness, and he focused his gaze on the bottom of the staircase.

A tall, lanky form came into view. Right on his heels was another man. Nash's blood pressure rose several notches. He moved his finger over the trigger, exhaled slowly, and fired.

Crack!

The gun jerked back in his hand, but he didn't break focus. The first man grabbed at his chest and staggered to the floor. Man number two froze in place, swiveling his gun around the room. Nash pulled the trigger again.

Crack!

His target's head snapped back, and he

dropped to the ground like a stone.

"Shit. They're down. Move!" Four thick bodies charged down the mouth of the stairwell and spread out around the room. He aimed at the man he had the clearest shot of and fired.

"Ah, fuck!" the guy bellowed. When the other three men spun to face their wounded partner, Nash bolted from his shelter. He fired at one of the men, then slammed his body into one of the others, tackling him to the ground.

Crack! Crack! Crack!

Bullets rained down around him. His body jolted with every shot.

★　★　★

LEXI COVERED HER mouth. Her fingernails bit into her cheek, and a veil covered her vision. Terror bubbled up from the pit of her stomach, burning the back of her throat. The muscles in her hand trembled around the handle of the gun.

All those shots . . .

He could be dead.

And if he was, it would be a matter of seconds before she was, too. She bit the knuckle on her thumb. He'd tried to save her. That didn't make him a hero, but it also meant he couldn't be a complete monster. His life sure as hell would be easier right now if he'd turned her over to Dmitry or the thugs outside the door.

She scanned the room. There was no window

in the office, and even if there were, she wouldn't run. Not when Nash could still be alive. He'd told her to stay put, but if she didn't act now, they'd find her anyway. At least she was armed.

She sucked in a deep breath, but the air entered her lungs as if she'd inhaled through a straw. Gingerly, she lifted the chair and moved it from the door. Her chest constricted as she closed her hand around the cool doorknob. Easing the door open, she peered through the small crack. Russian slang spewed out of the men's mouths. Three of them stood around a motionless body on the floor.

Nash . . .

One man pulled back his foot and then swung it forward into Nash's side. A low grunt erupted from his motionless body.

"Where the fuck is she?" he demanded in broken English. A beat passed, but Nash didn't make another sound. The man cursed and motioned to the other two. "Search the basement," he said, in his native tongue.

Now was her only chance.

She pulled open the door, stepped into the hall's concealing shadows, then settled both hands on the gun to steady it. She aimed it at the group. Her elbow trembled and her pulse roared in her eardrums like water over Niagara Falls. She moved her index finger and pulled the trigger.

Crack!

Her upper body jerked violently backward, but

she regained her balance. One of the men grabbed his abdomen and crumpled to the floor like a wet towel. A flurry of movement on the ground brought her attention to Nash. One of the other men tripped over Nash's outstretched leg and fell into a grapple with him. The third man turned toward her, the whites of his eyes and the gleam of his teeth visible in the dim room. Her stomach coiled into a spring and her breath came out in rough pants. She had to finish this.

She fired again but he charged, and the bullet cracked into the wall behind him. He came at her full speed, his arm lifted, aiming. He'd be on her any second.

She fought the wave of tremors that threatened to steal the strength from her limbs and focused the barrel of the gun on his heart.

Crack!

Her body slammed against the doorjamb, and her arm dropped to her side as if a bucket of sand had been tied to her wrist. She staggered into the office. Heat spread through her midsection, and she lowered her chin to look down. Blood . . . *so much blood* . . . hot and sticky, seeped into the material of her shirt. More shots were fired, but the sound echoed in the distance. A shrill ringing screeched in her ears.

Oh god, oh god, oh god . . . I've been shot.

A thick, inky fog permeated her consciousness. She sank to the ground. Her back connected with the floor, forcing the air from her lungs. Any second, the man would come through the door and put the gun to her head.

Pain seared her abdominal muscles, and she sucked breaths through her gritted teeth. She pressed her shaky fingers to the wound, and her flesh throbbed against her palm. She had to stop the bleeding. She couldn't die like this.

She wouldn't.

Tears stung her eyes and she fought down the tsunami of panic that thundered through her skull. She couldn't pass out. If she did, she wouldn't wake up.

"Alexis?" A distant voice broke through the gray vapor clogging her mind. "Fuck." Nash was next to her. She opened her eyes and searched the shadows for the steely granite of his eyes to anchor her, but she couldn't make them out. His hand, warm and firm, grasped her shoulder.

He shifted and pulled his phone from his pocket. A bright glow blasted the darkness, bathing her. She winced and turned her head away from the beam.

"Sorry," he mumbled. "You need to move your hand so I can look, okay?" His strong, resolute voice should have calmed her, but instead it made her want to curl into his warmth and cry.

She'd refrain if it killed her. Her palm molded itself to her abdomen, as if her blood were made of glue. His fingertips gripped her wrist and tugged.

"Lexi, please. You have to let me help." His solid voice turned tender, almost fearful. Her heart palpitated, and a sinking weight crushed her ribs into her lungs.

"Hey," he said. His fingertips brushed her cheek, but she didn't dare look at him. Not until she could combat the paralyzing fear taking over her. His thumb trailed her jaw, and goosebumps rose over the back of her neck. "You're going to be okay, I promise. I won't let anything happen to you."

She swallowed and pressed her lips together. How the hell could he say that? She'd been shot, for god's sake. He wasn't a doctor. But he was all she had and for the moment, her life was in his hands. She let him lift her hand and set it on the floor at her side.

Inch by inch, as if he were handling a piece of fine china, he lifted her shirt. His palm rested on the skin at her side, and he leaned in so close his nose nearly touched her navel. His fingers probed near the wound. She flinched and turned to look at him despite the bright light.

"You're losing a decent amount of blood, but I think it grazed you."

The crushing weight on her chest lifted a fraction. "You *think*?"

He straightened away from her, and this time she was able to focus on his iron eyes. There was blood near his temple, but aside from that, he showed no other sign of injury.

"I'll have to clean it to be sure, but we need to be quick. They can't be the only ones who've found us." He fit his phone into her hand and stood. "I'll be back in a second. Hang tight."

He disappeared into the main area and her muscles clenched. Where was everyone? Surely they wouldn't have run. But they couldn't be dead. There was no way he'd taken on six men and come out on top.

Quick footsteps scraped over the carpet, and he dropped next to her again. In his hand was a tall glass bottle. She pinched her brows together and moved the light over him and the familiar vodka logo.

"This is going to hurt like a bitch, but I don't want to bandage you without cleaning it. Think you can handle it?" He unscrewed the cap and waited for her acknowledgment.

She snorted. "Give me that." She snaked her free hand around the neck of the bottle. He chuckled but hung on tightly to the booze. He shifted his hand under the back of her neck and lifted her head from the floor.

"Atta girl."

She guided the bottle to her lips as he bore the weight of the full bottle of alcohol. The room-temperature liquid touched her tongue and slid smoothly down her throat. A tight burn followed all the way to her stomach. She didn't let him pull the bottle away when he tried. The soft vibrations of his laugh warmed her to the bones almost as quick as the alcohol.

"Okay, that's enough." He pried the bottle from her lips and let her neck go. She coughed and her shoulders shook. Heat spread through her body like wildfire, and she dropped her head to the carpet. The room spun, and she welcomed the buzz that would dull the pain soon to tear through her flesh. Nash tucked something soft underneath her, and she noticed a fresh towel resting over the waistband of her pants. "Ready?"

She sunk her teeth into her bottom lip and shook her head. "Just do it. Hurry."

The liquid was as cold as ice against her heated skin. He cleaned around the wound first, making the anticipation of the burn that much more drawn out. She kept her gaze on his long, dark lashes as he worked with the precision of a surgeon. His eyes lifted to land on her face and softened.

He poured again, and the sharp sting through her sensitive muscle made her jolt. She tensed the muscles in her legs and clamped her lips tight, but the scream bubbled through. Nash tensed but continued pouring the liquid over the wound.

She sucked in a breath and he pulled the bottle away. "Done." He moved the towel from her waist and patted around the wound.

He angled the light at her midsection, and the muscles in his face relaxed. "It's a graze. Hurts like a bitch, I'm sure, but you're not going to die from this."

She let out a low breath, and her heart slowed to a near normal rate. Paper crinkled next to her, and Nash pressed something to her side. He wiggled his hand beneath her shoulder and lifted her into a sitting position.

"Easy. I just need to secure this around you."

She held her shirt up and took the phone from him and held it so he could see and use both hands. He pressed the gauze to her again and wrapped a bandage several times around her waist.

"Is that too tight?" He rested his palms on either side of her waist, pressing harder on the wounded side. She covered his hand with hers and inspected his handiwork.

"No, that's perfect."

"You'll need stitches, but we'll save that for later. Right now, we need to get the hell out of here. Can you stand?" He wrapped his fingers around her palm, steadying her.

She straightened and nodded. Now that she knew she wasn't on her deathbed, she could get through anything. His free hand circled her waist and together they stood, her weight heavily supported. Her head swam and her legs trembled.

"You all right?"

She forced her head to nod. "Just the vodka."

He laughed, and his shoulder jostled hers. "I'll get our stuff together, take it out to the vehicle, and then come back for you."

She froze midstep and lifted her chin to gaze through the shadows at his face. "I'm not staying here with them."

His lips twitched. "Good point, but I can't carry you and our bags."

"You don't need to carry me. I was shot in the side, not the legs."

"It's not a short walk, and I don't want the bleeding to pick up." Concern laced his voice, and a tremor of delight wormed through her belly. His fingers flexed on the small of her back, and she cleared the gravel from her throat.

"I'll move slowly." Her attention shifted to the darkness beyond the hall. "Are they . . . ?"

He brushed his thumb over her knuckles. Her hand was still snug in his. "Four are dead and two are restrained."

She snapped her gaze back to him and her mouth turned to cotton. "How did you do that?" she rasped.

He stiffened. "If you hadn't taken that shot when you did, we'd both be dead. So thanks for not listening to me."

She grinned at the backhanded compliment and let him lead her from the room. He could give her the credit all he wanted, but the fact was he'd taken on six men. He'd been on the floor when she emerged from the room, but there was no way in hell he would have died there.

Her initial impression had been spot-on. Nash was a savage.

CHAPTER 10

"WE NEED TO do something about the bodies," Lexi said.

Nash held firmly to her elbow as he led her through the snow, matching her slow pace, his duffel bag slung over his shoulder and her suitcase in his free hand. Her statement made him curse internally. In Seattle, there were people he could call after this type of event. But not here. Not when people of his very brotherhood had just tried to kill them.

Lexi kept her arm pressed firmly to her waist, and her breath was labored. Small clouds puffed out of her mouth. She should have stayed in the damn room, but he'd been in a dire situation, laid out on the ground with his gun knocked out of his hand. He'd been distracted taking out the man on the floor when he saw another man charge for her and heard the shot.

Walking into the room and seeing her sprawled on the floor had been like taking a cannonball to the stomach. He'd been scared shitless. And that sharp, piercing rod of pain had ricocheted through him with familiarity. It'd been decades since he relived the kind of terror he felt the night Summer disappeared.

That time, he'd been helpless.

"I'll call Alina," Lexi said. "She'll have someone dispose of them."

He stiffened his jaw and glanced down at her through the flurries. "What do you mean 'dispose of them'?"

The tip of her tongue slipped over her bottom lip, and she lowered her eyes to her feet. "We're in Russia. Dead bodies aren't exactly a rare occurrence. She'll know who to call without getting the authorities involved."

He snorted. He knew all too well about disposing of bodies. But the words were just plain wrong on her lips. "Who would do that for her?"

She lifted her shoulder. Distaste touched the back of his throat. He didn't want to think about the types of people who would do that sort of job—people who were in the Russian Mafia. They needed to get the hell out of here and somewhere safe.

He dropped her bag next to the side of the SUV and pulled the key fob from his coat pocket. He hit the unlock button and pulled open the door. Lexi shuffled closer and gripped the handlebar above her head.

"You're going to hurt yourself." He bent down

and tucked one arm under her legs and the other around her back. She fit snugly against his chest, her body stiff in his hold. "Am I hurting you?"

She shook her head.

He lowered her into the passenger seat and clipped the seatbelt beside her hip. She shifted and winced. His fingers ached to touch her, to take away the lines of pain etched on her smooth forehead.

"I'm fine," she insisted.

He worked his jaw and drew his hands into fists to avoid the urge to lift her coat and check her wound. He stretched across her, inserted the key into the ignition, and turned the heat on. Then he shut the door, loaded their luggage into the hatchback, and rounded the vehicle. Sliding into the driver's seat, he buckled his seatbelt.

"Where are we going?" Her words rattled over a shiver and her teeth chattered. Shit, he should have grabbed one of the blankets from the church.

"I'd like to know how they found us, for one thing. But for now, we'll go to a motel. I'll book us on the soonest flight out of here." He shifted into gear and pulled out of the parking lot. The sooner they got moving, the quicker the vehicle would warm up.

She nodded vigorously and stretched her hands toward the barely lukewarm air coming from the vents.

How the fuck had they been found? Alina was

the only person who'd known they were at the church. Aside from the minister . . .

"My email," Lexi said. The word came out on a breath. "Could they have tracked my email and found us through the IP address?"

Fuck. He tightened his fingers on the steering wheel and exhaled through his nose. "Yeah, that's more than likely." He'd underestimated the people they were up against. Clearly, he wasn't the only one within the organization who had connections to hackers.

Light from the streetlamps flashed over the windshield as the SUV bumped over the icy terrain. The engine still hadn't warmed enough to take the shiver from Lexi's body. With her loss of blood, she'd feel the godforsaken temperatures even more.

She blew a breath through her lips. "God, I feel so stupid. Both times they found us because of me."

He let go of the steering wheel with one hand and brushed his fingers over her knee. The lithe muscle beneath her thin pajama pants flexed against his fingers. An image of her soft, supple skin pressed against his flashed through his mind. He jerked his hand away as if she'd burned him. He sure as hell wouldn't be getting the kind of relief his dick so desperately craved. It'd do him good not to set the fire that already burned inside him into a fucking wild blaze. He flicked his gaze down the side of the street.

They'd passed a few motels, but he hadn't wanted to go to the nearest ones. He was the stupid one for not calling Conrad the second they got to the church. First things first—he'd stitch up her wound and get her comfortable, then he'd take the bull by the horns and make Conrad back the fuck off.

"Can we stop at the next one?"

He glanced at Lexi. Her lips were pinched, the smooth contours of her cheeks set into a tense grimace, her brow creased. Her head rested back on the seat, and her usually pale skin was downright pasty.

Fuck.

"You should go to the hospital." He leaned forward, looking for a place to pull over. He'd have to map out a route.

"No," she said, shaking her head. "No hospital. I just need to be horizontal, that's all."

He scrubbed his knuckles over his jaw. The bullet had grazed her, of that he was certain. Lexi had likely never been shot before, so her body would experience more shock and trauma than his would. Add in two shots of vodka and she was done in.

A neon-blue sign caught his eye. He changed lanes and slowed down to pull into the parking lot. He unbuckled his seatbelt and turned to face her. "Will you be okay for a few minutes while I check in?"

Without opening her eyes, she nodded. "I'm fine."

He pressed his tongue to the backs of his teeth. She was far from fine. But he'd get her inside and assess her before deciding what to do. He left the SUV running and hopped out.

In the lobby, a tattered red carpet welcomed his wet boots. From the ceiling hung a single dim bulb, which offered the only lighting other than a small lamp on the receptionist's desk. Soft-soled black shoes sat on the counter, and Nash's gaze followed their owner's legs and landed on an old, weathered face. The woman's mouth hung open, and soft snores broke through her lips.

The rooms had better be nicer than this shithole of a lobby.

He cleared his throat and the woman bolted forward, her feet dropping to the floor. They had a short battle of words, she speaking Russian and he English. Then she handed him a key and pointed to the east side of the parking lot. He thanked her and left.

Cold wind blasted him in the face as he stepped outside. He tucked his chin into his coat and jogged across the parking lot to the vehicle. Snow collected on his lashes and turned to ice. He climbed in the SUV. Lexi hadn't moved. Her hands lay stiffly against her abdomen. A trickle of dread rolled down his spine. He pulled out of the parking spot and drove the short distance down the length of the motel. Overhead lights between each suite illuminated the room numbers.

He parked directly in front of their room and jumped back into the cold. Snow caked around his pant legs, adding to the previous dampness. He opened the passenger door. Lexi's lashes lifted but she kept her gaze down. She reached for her seatbelt, but he unbuckled it before her fingers found the button.

She stretched her fingers out for him to help her from the seat, but he scooped her up in his arms again. Her head dropped to his chest and her fingers caught the material of his jacket. He took wide steps through the snow and stopped at the door marked 110.

Without putting her down, he shifted her weight and pulled the single key from his coat pocket. He jammed it into the lock and kicked the door open. As he entered the room, Lexi lifted her head. She squirmed in his arms until he lowered her to the floor. She shucked off her coat and stepped out of her boots, her movements slow and concentrated.

"I'm going to grab our bags. Why don't you get comfortable?"

She nodded and turned to the only bed, in the center of the room.

After retrieving the bags, he dropped them beside the door and tugged off his coat and boots. His gaze landed on Lexi sprawled on her back on the rumpled comforter. He arched his lip as he took in the rest of the room. Christ, he should have asked to see it first before checking in. The worn carpet was rough against his socks, and the wallpaper near the bed was peeling. He poked his head into the bathroom, and the disgust in his stomach settled. It needed some touch-ups, but at least it was clean. He washed his hands, grabbed a towel from the rack, and headed back into the main room. He pulled his small survival kit out of his duffel bag.

When he turned around, he found Lexi staring at him, her blue eyes tired and lacking the fire that usually dwelled in them. His stomach muscles clenched, and he switched on the lamp beside her.

"Let's get you fixed up, shall we?"

ALEXIS EYED NASH through narrow slits as he pulled a chair close to the bed and laid out the contents of the safety kit. Sleep lugged at her eyelids. Her sockets were dry and grainy. But she'd be wide awake in a few minutes, when he started sewing her up. If it weren't for the exhaustion weighing her down, she would have tried to run away.

"Do you know what you're doing?" She aimed for casual but fell short. His mouth twitched and his eyes sparked. Geez, had she really never found him attractive? Then again, she was seeing a side to the enforcer that few had. His dark features and the hard, straight lines of his face made him intimidating. But fear wasn't what stirred the nerves in her belly and made her skin warm in the chilly room.

He picked up a small white tube. "I've done this on more than one occasion."

She lifted her eyebrows. "To who?"

"Mostly myself. But I've stitched up a couple buddies before." He lifted the object in his hand. "Lucky for you I have some numbing cream. It won't be nearly as good as freezing, but it should take the edge off. Are you still feeling the vodka or do you want another sip?"

The blurry vignette around her vision, and the liquor sitting heavily in her stomach made it an easy decision. "No, I'm fine. Just get it over with."

His eyes darkened. He reached forward and folded her shirt to just beneath her breasts. She lifted her head to gage the wound. Dark red, almost black, blood oozed at the fine mesh pressed against her. Nash pulled out a tiny pair of scissors, cut through the material, and peeled it away from her skin. It tugged on her freshly abused flesh, and she winced.

Nash squinted, and the skin of his face etched with sympathy. "Sorry."

She craned her neck to get a better view, and the metallic scent of blood rushed in through her nose. The graze was no bigger than a golf ball, not apple-sized, as she'd imagined. Nash's fingertips floated over her skin, making ripples of pleasure skitter down her thighs. She lowered her head back to the pillow and kept her focus on his face and not on his ministrations.

His gaze skated over her belly, and he froze.

Blood pounded through her skull. *Shit. Shit. Shit.*

"What the hell is that?" He nodded at her abdomen.

"What?" God, she didn't want to get into the story. Didn't want to rehash the night that had stolen everything from her . . . including a piece of her soul.

He lowered his free hand to her stomach and ran the tip of his thumb over the two-inch scar below her ribs. The lighting in the church would have been dim enough to obscure it.

She cleared her throat and kept her eyes on her rising and falling chest. "It's a scar."

"From?"

God, he was pushy. She slid her gaze up to meet his. "From a knife, okay?"

His hand turned to stone on her belly. A vein bulged next to the dark hairline at his temple. And just like that, the enforcer was back. Every crinkle of kindness that had creased his skin for the last few hours turned to concrete. Even his soft lips hardened, and the slight bow on his upper one tensed.

"Who did it?" he said, his voice as rough as sandpaper.

She swallowed and shook her head. "I'm too exhausted to talk about it, Nash. Can you please just finish this so I can rest?"

His expression didn't change, but he rolled his shoulders back and smoothed some cream around her gash. She kept her gaze on the ceiling and counted the little white popcorn-like balls on the surface. Nash leaned closer. "Do you feel that?" he asked. The sharp, stinging pain had eased but the dull ache remained.

"I can feel the pressure, but it's numb."

He straightened and screwed the lid back on the tube. "That's probably as good as it's going to get." Plastic crinkled as he pulled a sterile needle out of its package. After threading it, he lowered it to her skin.

She sucked in her breath and molded her hands at her sides in anticipation. Out of the corner of her eye, she watched the needle pass to his waiting hand.

Pain shot through the wound and across her stomach. She let out a curse.

"Hang on, you won't need many."

She squeezed her eyes shut and started counting down from thirty.

Twenty-nine, twenty-eight, twenty-seven—

He moved the needle through her skin again, and her nerve endings screamed. Stupid cream hadn't done a thing. Her chest ached, needing a deep breath of air, but she didn't dare move her abdomen. He threaded two more times.

Twenty-four, twenty-three, twenty—

"Try to relax."

She nodded sharply and inhaled through her nose.

"That's it, you're doing great. One more, okay?" His hand was poised over her skin, waiting for her permission.

"Just do it," she hissed. He lowered his face and sunk the needle into her skin for the fifth time.

Nineteen, eighteen, seventeen, six—

"Done." He lifted the scissors next to him. Only his fingertips fit into the small openings, but he managed to snip the thread. He gave her arm a light shake. "You'll live." The tension around his mouth receded, but his eyes were distant. He stood and packed the kit in his duffel bag. "It's almost 6:00 a.m. I have some calls to make, so I'm not sure how much rest you'll get."

Fatigue tugged at her eyelids and pushed her body into the lumpy mattress. "I don't think I'll have a problem sleeping."

She shifted and tucked her legs under the blanket. Part of her craved another hot shower, or at least a soak in the tub, but there was no way she could do that before sleeping. Besides, she'd have to cover up the stitches, and that would be too much work.

Nash appeared next to the bed and gripped the edge of the blanket. He lifted it up, and she snuggled onto her good side and let him spread the material over her.

"If I'm too loud, just tell me and I'll take my calls in the vehicle."

Her eyes lowered with the weight of sandbags and the muscles in her face went slack. His large, firm hand pressed down on her shoulder. His warmth invaded her body through the covers, enclosing her in a cocoon of security.

"Mmm . . ." The hum of acknowledgment turned into a soft moan as sleep pulled her into its waiting arms.

CHAPTER 11

S HIT.
Nash dropped into the tattered green chair in the corner of the room and lowered his face to his hands. His insides tossed and the cords in his neck tightened like guitar strings. He should be exhausted. He should be ready to pass out. What he shouldn't be doing was raging over the goddamn scar on her midsection.

A knife wound.

The implications of that small slash of damaged ivory beat through his skull. He'd been stabbed before, so he was certain that it was relatively fresh. It couldn't be more than a year old, if that. He barely knew Lexi, but he knew she was ballsy, intrusive, and downright strongheaded. He could only imagine the dangerous situations her fucking investigating got her into. Jesus, if she'd pulled what she had with him on any other enforcer, she likely would have faced the fate Conrad had laid out for her.

A ragged inhale sounded from the bed, and he

lifted his head. Her body faced the opposite direction, so he didn't have the pleasure of seeing the softness of sleep melt the frown she usually wore for him. He pushed up the cuff of his long-sleeved shirt and checked his watch.

Almost 6:30 a.m.

He had to get a flight booked and call Conrad. He hated to risk waking her, but with the help of vodka and exhaustion, she'd likely sleep through his conversation. He took out his phone and pulled up Conrad's contact.

The line rang in his ear. He was eleven hours ahead of Seattle, so that made it 5:30 p.m. Conrad's time. No reason for him not to pick up.

"Hello." Conrad sounded as if he'd just run a marathon.

"It's me," Nash said, pushing his spine into the back of the chair.

"I was hoping you'd call."

Is that because you're preparing to put a hit out on me too? He bit back the words. Pissing off Conrad wouldn't make their situation any easier.

"Just leaving the gym," Conrad said. "Give me a sec while my Bluetooth connects." A car door slammed and a soft click pierced the line. "All right, shoot."

"I have the ledger and am coming home. Hopefully leaving today if I can get a flight."

A beat passed. "And Alexis?"

"She's dead. Six men ambushed us a couple

hours ago. One shot her in the midsection. I took her to the hospital but she didn't make it." He'd hoped to persuade Conrad to call off the hit on Lexi, but there's no way Conrad would have believed she'd cooperate. And for some godforsaken reason, Conrad wanted her dead. He wouldn't stop just because Nash told him she'd given up. Telling him she was dead was the best option he'd come up with.

He pinched his temples together with his thumb and forefinger until his skull threatened to buckle. The men who survived would report back to Conrad that Lexi had left the church alive. The fact that she'd been shot was the only thing that made his lie believable.

The momentary silence that washed through the line pulsated with satisfaction.

"It's unfortunate things had to turn out this way, but it's for the best. You see that, don't you, son?"

Anger reverberated through Nash's nerve endings. He gripped his knee to prevent himself from chucking his phone against the wall. His tongue burned. No, he didn't fucking see how Lexi's death would be a good thing. His gaze floated from the peeling wallpaper to Lexi's still form. His mind churned. He needed to find out what Lexi's family had done to deserve the spotlight of hate from Conrad. Under any other circumstance, he'd flat out ask Conrad for full disclosure. But if he didn't play his cards right, this shit could blow up in their face. Lexi wouldn't be safe in Seattle. Hell, she wouldn't be safe anywhere. Not if Lionsgate—and Conrad—suspected she was breathing.

He had to buy them some time. Get to the root of why Lionsgate was so damn threatened by her and pacify Conrad in the meantime.

"I'm not sure I agree."

Conrad knew him well. The Grand Chancellor would have picked up on Nash's soft spot for Lexi when he didn't kill her as requested, so if he didn't show some remorse over her death, Conrad would be suspicious. Nash listened to the dull roar of the highway driving on the other end, his senses on high alert.

"Understood. This isn't the way I like things handled either." Conrad's tone rang with defeat. "Safe travels, Nash. Call me when you get in and we'll meet for coffee."

The line went dead in his ear and Nash lowered the phone to his thigh. He brought his attention back to Lexi's sleeping form and his chest tightened.

He'd done all he could to keep her alive so far. And damn him, he couldn't wrap his head around the reason why. She'd been a royal pain in the ass. Detouring Conrad should have lifted the weight from his chest. Instead, the call had crushed his lungs. A sickening thought gnawed at him.

I can't trust Conrad.

★　★　★

LEXI OPENED HER eyes, and pain exploded through her skull. She squeezed them shut again, but it didn't help. The events of the last twenty-four hours hit her with the force of a hurricane, and she groaned. She rolled onto her back, and her headache immediately evaporated as an excruciating pull on her side tore through her. She let out a hiss and grabbed her abdomen.

"Yeah, it will probably be pretty tender for a while." Nash's lazy drawl lifted her eyelashes, and her gaze fell to the form sitting in a chair across the room.

She made a face but couldn't muster a response through the cotton that had collected on her tongue. She dared to stretch her arm to the nightstand and opened the bottle of water there. She didn't bother to lift her head as she sipped the liquid.

"How long have I been out?"

Nash brought the screen of his phone to life. Its soft glow illuminated his face in the dim room. The shades were drawn. "A good four hours."

She lifted her eyebrows. "Holy shit. You shouldn't have let me sleep so long." She tossed the covers back, rolled to her side, and pushed into a sitting position. "We have to—"

"You needed the rest."

Her skin tugged on the fresh stitches again and she winced. Her fingers itched to lift her shirt and survey the wound, but she'd wait until she was alone.

"How's it feel?" Nash nodded at her belly, and she lowered her hand to the bed.

"Not bad. It's tight and sore, but that's to be expected."

His mouth twisted and he rose to his feet. "Let me take a quick look." His slow, relaxed stride made tiny butterfly wings beat against the lining of her stomach.

"It's fine," she squeaked.

Ignoring her protest, he dropped to one knee and peeled up the edge of her shirt. His lips softened into an easy smile. She didn't fight him, mostly because part of her needed to know that the gash wasn't turning black or oozing pus.

She looked down, but the awkward angle made it impossible to properly assess the wound. She shifted her focus to Nash. With his lashes lowered, she could take in the contours of his face— contours she'd originally thought were hard as metal, just like the man beneath. Which maybe wasn't the case.

His thumb smoothed the skin beneath the stitches, and a ripple of pleasure tightened her abdominal muscles. "Looks good. No sign of infection, but I'm sure it hurts like a bitch."

She worked her tongue through her mouth and fought the urge to reach for the water again. She shrugged and rolled her shirt down. "Thanks."

His gaze lifted to hers, and he didn't budge from his position at her feet. Her palms dampened, and she swallowed while his attention drifted over her face. His hand rested on the bed next to her hip, and his knuckles twitched against the material of her pajama pants, making goosebumps skitter across her body.

"I booked our flights." He pushed to his feet, breaking their eye contact. "We depart this afternoon and arrive in Portland tomorrow night."

She snapped to her feet and she winced at the searing pain in her side. "Portland? Why?"

He tugged the string that dangled beside the blinds and they swung open, washing the room in sunshine. "Because I just told Conrad you died." The string bounced off the wall as his stony irises flicked over her face. "He knows I'm returning in a couple of days, and if he doesn't believe me, he could have someone stake out the airport looking for you."

He'd lied . . . for her. He'd endangered himself . . . for her. He was risking everything to keep her alive. A rock formed against her diaphragm, making each breath shallow. She sank back to her seat.

"Why did you tell him that?"

He broke his steadfast focus on her and shoved his hands in his pockets. "Because he won't stop until you're dead. Whatever you have on him is enough to make him go to great lengths to see this through." His voice dropped to a whisper, and grief rattled the words. "For my own sanity, I need to find out what's going on. From here on out, we stick together."

Her stomach dropped to her feet, and she brought her fingers up to tangle in the strands at her shoulder. Stick with Nash? She could think of worse fates. He waited for her response, eyebrows bobbing.

"Ah, okay." God that was weak. "Sure, whatever you think is best." She forced her lips to curve into a smile, even though her skin burned with the need to cross the room and mold her body to his. "The traveling might be the death of me, but I'll try."

He winked. "I'll see to it you make it back in one piece."

She wasn't exaggerating. She still hadn't caught up from her last overseas journey. Another twenty-something hours of traveling, this time with a bullet graze, sounded as feasible as climbing Mount Everest.

"Couldn't find anything direct to Portland, I take it?" she said jokingly. God, direct would have been heavenly.

He snorted and moved to the door. "Not a chance. I'll grab us some food and coffee. Do you want to rest a bit more before we head out?"

She scrunched her nose. If she so much as put her feet up, she'd be a goner. "No, I'm fine. I'm going to freshen up."

He stuck his feet in his boots and gave a brisk nod before exiting the room. Yesterday, she would have made a run for it. But he'd saved her life more than once, and now he wasn't the threat. But what exactly was he to her? She couldn't call him a friend, but maybe, just maybe, he was an ally.

She dug her teeth into her lip and stood. Her legs wobbled beneath her weight, and she steadied herself on the wall. Filling her lungs with air, she moved toward the bathroom.

What would happen when they got back to Seattle? After the events of the last twenty-four hours it was hard to imagine Nash wouldn't keep her safe. The question was, would he be able to handle the allegations against Lionsgate and his fellow brothers?

★　★　★

FOUR DAYS. ALMOST four frickin' days since she'd stolen the ledger from Nash and still she hadn't gotten the chance to read it. The photocopies were tucked neatly into the lining of her suitcase—in cargo, beneath the plane.

Nash slid into the seat beside her and his shoulder pressed against hers, forcing her closer to the window. She was too tired to care. They'd just had an eight-hour layover in Amsterdam and were on their last flight to Portland. As much as she hated to admit it, traveling without him would have been hell. He'd carried her bags, led them through the airport, and reminded her constantly to eat and drink.

Which told her she must look as shitty as she felt.

"How are you holding up?"

She fought the urge to make a face. Complaining would only make her more miserable. "Not too terrible. I'll probably pass out for a week once I get home." Realization stabbed through her as the words left her mouth. Who was she kidding? She wouldn't be able to go back to her cushy condo. In Seattle, she'd be right in the lion's den, waiting for someone to put a bullet in her head.

Nash had assured her that she was safe, that he'd done everything in his power to detour Conrad away from her trail. She anchored her fingers around the edges of the armrests. She hated that she still had to hide. Since that fateful night six months ago, she'd been under the radar, carefully forming her investigation and, finally, her plan to move in on Lionsgate.

And now, she was working with one of them. Amusement tickled over her and her lips twitched. Had she known the night she'd drugged him that he would help her, things would have ended very differently—and very pleasurably.

But he was still one of them.

Was he *really*, though? Had he committed or allowed other members to commit the heinous acts her brother had discovered? It didn't ring true.

A flight attendant made an announcement over the intercom and a few minutes later, the plane taxied down the runaway and lifted into the air. The propellers roared beneath her window and her seat vibrated with the force. She closed her eyes and pressed the back of her head into the seat. Maybe she'd be able to sleep on this flight. It would be a long ten and a half hours, so she sure as hell hoped so.

Nash shifted closer to her. "I have something for you."

She cracked an eye open and turned her face toward him. He was staring at her, his deep-coal gaze sharp. His focus flickered, but not before she caught the streak of hesitation that crinkled the skin at the corners of his eyes.

"What is it?"

He pulled his hand from the inside of his jacket, and she looked down at the object.

The ledger.

She snapped her gaze back to his and wet her lips with her tongue. A surge of energy brought her sleepy limbs to life. As quickly as he'd revealed the leather, he slid it back in place.

"It's yours. I'll hand it over to you for your investigation, but I want something in return."

Her excitement deflated, and she twisted her mouth into a sneer. "Of course you do." Little did he know that she possessed the same contents he dangled before her. If he wanted to play some sort of head game, he was shit out of luck because she'd already won. The drawback was that it would be another day before she could be alone with the copied pages. A tingle of worry ran through her brain. She'd been in a rush when she photocopied them. Had she put them in order? Had she gotten every page that seemed important? The ledger would be far more reliable, but if he was going to be an ass, she'd make do.

Nash wagged a finger at her. "Don't jump to conclusions. I'm giving it to you no matter what. But I'd really like it if you'd share something with me."

She pressed her lips together. "I can't tell you what the case entails. I'm sorry. I appreciate you sharing it with me, but it's just too risky." Sighing, she turned toward the window. For months, she'd kept the details of the case to herself. She'd even managed not to tell Lauren. She'd told her boss about her suspicions regarding the brotherhood but kept back the gruesome details. The temptation to let it all out, to release even just a fraction of the burden, hummed through her.

Nash might not be involved with the scum she was after, but Lionsgate was his brotherhood. Her own relatives hadn't turned their back on the organization—so why would he?

"I figured you'd say that," he said. "But what I really want to know is how you got the scar."

CHAPTER 12

NASH TENSED HIS fingers on the book resting against his side. He hadn't asked her to share her life story, nor had he asked about the case against Lionsgate. Yet, her eyes darkened and her pupils dilated with dread.

She toyed with the neckline of her shirt, as if it had shrunk two sizes. "I don't want to talk about it."

"Please," he said, and fuck if his voice didn't turn gruff. Why the hell did the scar bother him so damn much? Had he seen it on any other person, he wouldn't have given it a second thought. But on Lexi it wasn't fucking right.

Her shoulders went lax and her breath sailed through her lips. "Fine." She cleared her throat, shifted in her seat, and glanced around at the other sardine-crammed passengers, who were paying them no mind.

"It happened the night my parents' house was set on fire. I woke up to the suffocating scent of smoke." Her gaze drifted to her knees and then swung to his face. "I rarely ever spent the night there. But I was up late helping my mom put together donations for the women's shelter and crashed in my old bedroom." Her skin had taken on an ashy tone. "For some reason the smoke detectors didn't work. Which makes no sense because my dad was anal about things like that."

She smoothed her fingers over an invisible wrinkle in her pant leg before continuing. "My parents met me in the hallway, but a wall of fire separated us. They had access to the staircase, so I shouted at them to get out and assured them I'd go through the window." She tucked her hair behind her ear, and her fingers trembled with the movement.

Distaste hit Nash's palate. He shouldn't have pressed her, especially in her weakened state, but there was no way he could stop her now. He had to know.

"My room was above the garage, so all I had to do was jump out my window to the roof and then drop to the ground. When I got onto the roof, I saw a man dressed in black run from the back door. Without stopping to check if my parents had made it, I jumped down and chased him."

Nash closed his eyes and pressed his fingertips so hard into the book he was sure he'd leave an indent. Nothing he could say would take back her actions from that night, but he wanted to shake her.

"He must have heard my footsteps. When we reached the treeline of the woods behind the backyard, he turned around. I tackled him, but he jammed a knife into my stomach." She snorted, glanced out of the window, then glanced back. "You don't have to look at me like that. I know what I did was dumb, but I just couldn't let him get away. All I was hoping for was something to identify him by. Anyway, he pulled the knife out and ran. I heard the sirens pull up and then saw firefighters running around the house. I dragged myself across the ground, screaming for help, but no one heard me. I passed out and woke up in the hospital." She lifted her shoulders.

Nash knotted his fingers in his hair and fought the urge to tug on it. Jesus Christ. Out of everything she'd told him, the thing that had shaken him the most was the image of her lying on the ground, bleeding—alone. She could have died cold, terrified, in excruciating pain, and only yards away from help.

His airways tightened. His gaze vacillated on the seat inches from his nose and his muscles bunched with the need to pace the aisle.

"Nash?" Lexi's fingers brushed over his wrist then hovered. It didn't matter that she wasn't touching him—electricity exploded through his veins. He gripped her fingers. Her sharp inhale brought his attention to her face. Her normally pink lips were almost as white as the skin around them. Her eyes were wide turquoise dishes, and the beauty of her irises struck him. She didn't pull away. Didn't move. Didn't breathe.

He forced a swallow, releasing the boulder that had formed in his throat. "I'm sorry that happened to you." He grazed the pad of his thumb over her knuckle. His senses tingled with the tantalizing softness of her skin, and his lips ached to bring the back of her hand to his mouth. As if the gesture would wipe away the terrors of her past.

But it wouldn't.

Crossing the line would only drive the wedge they'd set aside right back between them. She blinked and he watched, transfixed, as her heavy lashes kissed her cheeks.

"Thank you," she said. "I had internal bleeding, but fortunately they were able to treat it with surgery." Her face softened enough to produce a genuine smile. "I'm fine now." She shrugged, and her fingers inched away from his. His palm burned with the need to pull her hand back into his.

Instead, he passed her the ledger. "Keep it concealed. You never know who could be a member, and it's very recognizable to other brothers."

"Thank you," she said, her voice raspy. He didn't have to give it to her. As a matter of fact, it was the last thing he should have done. But he wanted to know more. And the only way to do that was to not stand in her way.

He winked at her. "Try to keep it down. I'm

going to get some shut-eye." He tilted his ball cap down and folded his arms over his chest. She'd already opened the book. Not a single line of fatigue etched her face.

★ ★ ★

NASH WEAVED THROUGH the airport. Lexi lagged behind him. After all she'd been through, it was a miracle she was still standing. He'd slept most of the flight, but almost every time he'd stirred, he'd found Lexi with her nose buried in the ledger. Once, he'd woken up to a slight weight on his shoulder. Warmth had spread through him at the sight of her asleep on his bicep, his discarded sweater tucked over her and the ledger pressed to her belly.

She was silent as they collected their luggage, her movements slow and awkward as she accepted her bag from him. In minutes, they were in the cold Portland air heading to the car-rental terminal.

"I don't understand how this is going to work," Lexi said. Her breath expelled out into the night. February wasn't as cold in Portland as it was in Moscow, but still damn chillier than he would have liked. Snow fell but didn't stick to the ground.

He stopped at the truck he'd rented, unlocked the door, and hefted their bags into the cab. "What's there to understand?"

She dug her hands into her coat and her teeth chattered.

"We'll talk in the vehicle," he said jerking his head to the passenger door. She nodded and positioned herself to climb inside. He snagged her hips before she tore open her stitches and lifted her to the seat. Pink flared her cheekbones. He clicked her seatbelt into place and rounded to the driver's side.

"If Conrad is suspicious, won't he have someone staking out your place?"

He turned the key in the ignition and blasted the heat, but only cold air came through the vents. He glanced at the clock—just after 9:00 p.m.

"I never gave him a definite arrival time, just said I'd call when I got in. He could have someone watching my place, but I know how to spot a tail. It'd be more likely he'd place someone at the airport, where I wouldn't be as likely to catch on."

He pulled out of the lot and flicked his gaze to the rearview mirror. Seattle was three hours away and he wanted nothing more than to crash somewhere. But as much as they both needed a bed, getting home would be a hell of a lot better than dragging out their travels another day.

Lexi kept her face turned toward the window, and her fingernail scratched against her coat on her opposite arm. Tension radiated from her, and he noticed the clench in her satiny smooth jaw. God she was beautiful. Exhausted, moody, and unpredictable, but beautiful. He ached to drag his thumb over the tight muscle in her face.

"My life is here. My condo, my job . . ." The unspoken words hung in the air. She brought her gaze to his, then ducked her chin to focus on her knotted hands on her lap.

Her family.

A wire tightened against his chest, and with his peripherals, he took her in again. Her face had been scrubbed clean of makeup at some point during their flight, and her hair was tied in a bun at the top of her head. Loose strands fell around her cheekbones, once pale with fatigue but now flaming with temper.

"I hate that I can't go home." Her voice broke, and a dam inside him rattled.

He cleared his throat. "It's only temporary. We just need a few days—"

She chortled. "Right, and then they'll shoot me in the back of the head if they see me alive. I know how these guys work."

The jab at Lionsgate wasn't directed at him, but it was a cold reminder of her opinion of him. "I get that. But we don't have many options."

She pressed her fingertips to the sides of her head. "Unbelievable. You're still protecting them."

He slowed to a stop at a red light, and the hairs on the back of his neck prickled to attention. Either his senses had picked up on something around them, or her words had cut through his conscience.

He turned to her and gripped her elbow between his fingers. "In case you haven't figured it out by now, I'm on your side. Or at least I'm trying to be, but you won't let me in."

Her hand fell away from her face and wild, stormy blues seared into him. "Let you in? I'm trusting you with my life, dammit. They'd kill me without batting an eye."

"They would, but I haven't let that happen, have I?" He shot back. Her lips clamped shut and the hard line quivered. Christ. Her stamina was running thin. The last thing she needed was grief from him.

"No, you haven't." She crossed her arms and a cloud of breath spiraled from her lips in the still-cold interior of the truck. "But you're still one of them. It's hard for me to see past that when they've torn my entire life apart."

The light changed, and he let go of her arm to accelerate. Guilt expanded through him, and he dragged his dry palm over the scruff around his mouth.

"I don't know what more you want me to do here, Lex. Do you suggest I tell him that I want answers as to why you and your family have been targeted? What the hell do you think that will accomplish besides raining bullets on our heads?" He shook his head and turned onto the interstate. "Jesus. With your profession, you should understand. And for the record, I want to know the truth. I want that truth to be Lionsgate's innocence, and if helping you further your investigation achieves that, then I'm slap-fucking-happy."

"Well that's good to know," she hissed.

He sighed. "I want to help, and I won't let them hurt you. Please believe that."

She shifted the seat into a reclined position and closed her eyes. "I'm going to rest. Let me know when we get there."

He jabbed the button for the radio and music flooded through the speakers. The next time he glanced at her, her cheeks were slack and her breath was coming out in a steady rhythm. She was ferocious and damn near paranoid, but she was right. He hated that she'd lost everything because of them, that by association he had robbed her of her life. He fought the urge to pull over and apologize. She needed sleep.

Two and a half hours later, he pulled into the underground garage beneath his condominium. He'd rounded the block a few times and hadn't caught sight of anything suspicious. With the rental vehicle, he was at an advantage. Tomorrow he'd return it to the airport and pick up his truck from long-term parking.

He pulled into his designated parking spot and rested his palm on Lexi's shoulder. "Hey, we're here." Her lashes flickered as if they wanted to resist opening, and her forehead creased. "If you can make it upstairs, there's a big comfy bed waiting for you." The image of her falling naked into his sheets invaded his brain, and his dick constricted in his briefs.

She pushed herself into a sitting position. "Wow, I can't believe I slept the whole way." She unbuckled her seatbelt and stretched her arms in front of her like a lazy cat.

"You needed it," he said, getting out of the vehicle. He grabbed their bags, and Lexi followed him to the elevator. When they reached his floor, she fell into step beside him. Lexi's heat crowded his back as he stopped, inserted the key, and kicked open the door. She followed him inside, and her gaze raked the entryway. For a second, he'd almost forgotten that she'd been here before. In fact, the last time he'd been home had been the day after she left him drugged on his bedroom floor.

"I'd offer to show you around, but I think you scoped out the place last time."

Amusement lifted the heavy corners of her lips. She tugged off her boots and dropped them on the mat. He pulled off his coat and took hers from her hand. "I did. It's a nice place," she said teasingly. Then her tone turned sharp. "They must pay you well." She brushed past him and into the living room.

"That's not all I do, you know."

Her eyebrows crept up her forehead and she gave him a chilly look. "That so? I'm afraid to ask."

He narrowed his eyes. "All right, I deserve the skepticism, but cut me a little slack." When her brows stayed at their extended height, he continued. "I'm a day trader."

She snorted. "That's hardly a job."

Annoyance nipped at his insides. He folded his arms across his chest in an effort not to take the bait. "It's a source of income and takes time out of my day, so I beg to differ."

She waved her hand in the air and yawned. "You obviously do well for yourself. By the way, I'm going to need a cellphone. I have a job I have to report back to."

"I have a burner you can have. One sec." He disappeared upstairs and returned a few minutes later. "I hope you remember your important contacts phone numbers, it's not worth it to put the battery back in your old phone. Even for a minute." He peeled open the package and passed it to her.

She accepted the basic device. "I memorize phone numbers. It's my superpower," she said as she fired off a text to Lauren and Alina, the only two people who she cared to reach her.

He grunted.

"Do you have an extra pillow or something? I don't think I can keep my eyes open a minute longer." She sauntered farther into the living room and dropped onto the white leather couch like a melting popsicle.

"You can take my bed." He stretched out his hand to her. She glanced at it, and he almost curled his fingers away, but then she fit her hand into his. He hauled her to her feet, picked up their bags, and followed her upstairs.

"I don't mind taking the couch."

His gaze lingered on her heart-shaped ass, and need pulsed through him. He swallowed over the constriction in his throat. "Don't sweat it. There's a spare bed down the hall. I'll sleep there," he said, gesturing in the opposite direction of the bedroom she'd entered. "You'll have your own bathroom in here."

He lowered her bag to the floor as she turned to him. "Thanks, I appreciate it."

The annoyance that had crept over him evaporated. Appreciation had softened the hard, skeptical look in her eyes. She lifted her hand and yanked on the elastic binding around her hair. As her rich brown locks tumbled in a mass of waves over her shoulders, his pulse slowed. Her white T-shirt fit snug around her full, pert breasts. Her nipples poked at the material.

Jesus. If he didn't stop staring, he'd never be able to leave. He nodded briskly, and the motion took more effort than it should have. "Let me know if you need anything."

"Night," she said softly. He closed the door behind him, and it took all his willpower to tear his hand from the knob.

★ ★ ★

LEXI GROANED AND pulled the thick down duvet over her head. Her phone buzzed, and her eyelids protested at the prospect of checking it. The buzzing stopped momentarily then started again. She dropped the blanket and stared at the blast of sunlight that covered the ceiling. All she wanted was another eight hours or so of sleep. Was that too much to ask?

She lifted her phone from the bedside table and sat up. Lord, she'd slept more than ten hours. Lauren's number flashed on a missed-call ribbon across the screen. There was also a text from her.

Where are you? I'm worried. Please call.

She rubbed the pads of her fingers over her forehead. No wonder Lauren was worried. Last night she'd sent her a random text telling her she had a new phone and her old one was toast. Lauren would have a slew of questions. Make that a damn inquisition that she was ill prepared for even wide awake. She needed a shower and coffee before she could face the music. She swung her feet over the bed, and the stitches in her side pulled on the tender skin. She grimaced, gripped the sore muscles, and stood. A piece of paper on the nightstand caught her eye.

Had to run out for an hour. Make yourself

at home.

Oh god, Nash had come in while she'd been asleep. She closed her eyes and let out a breath. Her face had probably been nestled in a puddle of drool. She pushed Nash from her mind, and found some plastic wrap to cover her stitches. With her wound covered, she got in the shower, dressed, and made her way to the kitchen. Her thoughts were on Lauren as she filled the coffee pot with water. Her boss was going to give her the third degree.

Click, click

She looked at the front door just as the handle stopped turning. Panic catapulted into her throat.

Nash would have unlocked the door, not tried the handle first. The clank of metal on metal reached her ears, and the dead bolt rattled. She lowered the pot to the island's granite surface. Terror beat through her chest and a tremor overtook her. She fisted her hand in her hair and turned in a circle, taking in the open-concept living area.

There was no place to hide. She had nothing. Her gaze flicked over the knife block. A knife would do nothing against guns. She didn't even know Nash's damn phone number. There was no other route of escape except the front door.

If she hid, she'd be a sitting duck.

The dead bolt rattled again. Adrenaline fired

through her veins. She tore her feet from the floor and charged for the balcony door off the living room. Moving aside the heavy gray drape, she fumbled her fingers over the lock. The front door jumped with more urgency.

Any second and they'd be inside.

The lock released and she eased the sliding door open. Brisk air washed over her, and she stepped her bare feet onto the balcony's frigid concrete. She shut the door behind her and moved to the far end of the terrace. A break in the curtains allowed her to peer inside.

Two men dressed in jeans and hoodies entered the condo. Her heart raced against her breastbone and her mouth turned to sandpaper. Each held a black automatic. Their footsteps were long and ginger as they scoped out the living room. Terror turned her spine into an icy rod.

She didn't have much time.

She moved away from the glass and gripped the metal rail. A blast of wind caught her hair as she stared down the twenty-story drop to the frosted grass below. Her limbs shook and she squeezed tighter, as if her hold would anchor her. Nash's balcony overlooked the small patch of concrete that was guest parking. A maroon pickup truck idled at the curb, thankfully facing away from the building. The outline of a baseball-hat-covered head was visible through the back window. Was he waiting for the men who were now inside Nash's condo?

More than likely. Even if she could get down, she wouldn't be able to run for it. And if the driver saw her on the balcony, he'd alert the others. She wet her lips and took a deep breath, focusing on steadying her heartrate. She couldn't stay here.

She hefted her leg over the rail and boosted herself over the side. Her stitches pulled with every movement, and she clamped her lips together to keep from yelping. Her toes balanced on the sliver of concrete that stuck out beyond the railing. A sub-zero gust of air danced around the hem of her shirt, snaking its way around her torso.

She hooked her arm through the rail and peered over her shoulder. Dropping to the balcony below would likely tear her stitches open.

The sliding glass door rattled open and she snapped her head up. A long, denim-covered leg stretched through the opening.

Go, go, go!

She crouched, gripped the bars, and swung her feet to the metal beam below. Her toes didn't touch. The muscles in her arms screamed as she dangled in the air.

"No one's out here," said a deep male voice. "He must have fucking took her somewhere else." The glass door slammed shut, cutting off the rest of the conversation.

Shit. They'd be on their way down now. If they glanced back at the building on their way to the truck, they'd see her hanging like a set of human wind chimes. She swung her feet to the stucco-covered wall next to her and scaled them up the surface. Her shoulders screamed, but she managed to hook her toe on the concrete ledge. She shimmied her hands up the thin bars, pressed her weight into the ball of her foot, and stood.

She dropped over the other side, landing on the hard concrete. Pain radiated through her side and her breath came out in fast pants. She crouched, and a heartbeat later, the two men exited the building, focused on the maroon truck. She inched behind the barbeque just in case they decided to glance up.

As the truck peeled away from the curb, she dropped her chin to her chest and dug her fingertips into the unrelenting cement.

Nash, where are you?

CHAPTER 13

*S*ONOFABITCH.

Nash turned down his street and forced the muscles in his hands to loosen their death grip on the steering wheel. Smoothing things over with Conrad had taken more effort than he'd anticipated, and it had also cost him the ledger. He couldn't shake the dread in his stomach. Lexi needed the ledger for her investigation, but he'd had no choice. By handing over the ledger, he'd bought Lexi some time and proven himself to Conrad. He needed to stay on common ground with him so Conrad didn't sense they were enemies.

Are we enemies?

Memories of his youth flashed through his mind. Conrad hadn't been the most happy, easygoing father figure, but he'd been solid and reliable, and he'd given Nash a better start to life than he would've had otherwise. But goddammit to hell and back, something wasn't right.

He flipped his hat off and tossed it to the seat next to him. A maroon truck sped past him.

Nash's skin prickled. He did a double take in the rearview mirror.

He knew that truck.

He'd seen it numerous times in the House's parking lot, but he didn't know the owner of it. He pressed the ball of his foot to the gas pedal. The truck shot forward, and he pulled into the parking lot in front of his condo. The tall stucco building sat unbothered in the brisk morning. The fact that the building was still standing did little to calm the jitter that jerked his hands. He steered into the underground parking garage, slammed into his spot, and jogged up to the elevator. The doors dinged, and he skirted around an old woman walking her dog and jabbed the plastic 20.

The familiar scent of lemon cleaner hit his face as the doors opened on his floor. The fragrance stirred the acid in his stomach. He sprinted down the hall, and his neighbors' doors rattled as his feet pounded down the carpet. He pulled out his key, jabbed it into the lock, and shoved the door open with his shoulder.

Lexi stood at the island, her hands braced on the counter, her dark hair hanging to her breasts. She jumped a foot and slammed her palm to her chest. "You scared the life out of me," she hissed. He let the door fall from his hand, not taking his gaze off her. Her glassy eyes were rimmed with red. Moisture clung to her lashes, bringing out the blue in her eyes. His senses told him to scan the condo, but tearing his gaze from Lexi was akin to ripping his eyes out.

"What happened?" He moved across the hand-scraped engineered hardwood floor, not bothering to remove his shoes. She met him at the edge of the island, her body moving like a thumbtack to a magnet. She burrowed her face in his chest and her hands knotted the front of his shirt exposed under his open jacket.

He wrapped his arms around her waist and lowered his face to her hair. Tension gripped the muscles in his back. The urge to shake her to find out what had happened rattled his bones. But the tremor of her spine kept him in check.

"They came while you were gone."

He snapped his head up, pulled away, and gripped her biceps. "Who?"

The moisture left her eyes, but the dark shadow of fear remained. She shrugged and her bottom lip moved—not quite a tremble, but it was clear she was badly shaken.

"I heard them trying to pick the locks, so I went onto the balcony."

He breathed a curse and ran his hand through his hair. "I'll fucking kill them."

His promise didn't throw her. Instead, she gave a tiny nod. "They got into a maroon truck. I saw it idling outside."

"They didn't see you?"

Her gaze dropped to the floor. Dammit, he

needed to hold her and chase the terror from her body, but more than that, he had to know what she'd endured. If they'd hurt her . . .

No. She wouldn't be alive—or here, for that matter. They fucking played him. There was no chance it was a coincidence they'd came while he was meeting with Conrad. At least he could pretend that he didn't know about the break-in and keep up the fucking charade.

"I tried to swing down to the balcony below, but I couldn't reach. They came out when I was hanging onto the rail. Thankfully they didn't see my hands. I managed to pull myself back up after they left."

"Jesus Christ." Rage vibrated through his core. "You could have fallen, for god's sake."

Hot breath erupted from her nostrils and her lips puckered. "I had greater chances of being shot."

He let his gaze fall over her body. Her bare feet peeked out from her gray leggings, and her toes were painted a delicious pink. No sign of injury, but the biggest concern was her stitches.

"I need to have a look at your wound." He tightened his grasp to lead her from the kitchen, but she cemented her feet to the spot.

"I checked. They're fine."

He growled with impatience, gripped her hips, and lifted her to the counter. He shed his jacket and tossed it to one of the chairs at the island.

"Nash, please. I—"

"Just let me look, dammit." He kept his hands on her hips. Heat glowered from her eyes. The fire that easily turned on within her brought a tug to his mouth. "Please," he said softly.

Her jaw worked, but she pressed her hands to the counter behind her and thrust her breasts forward, offering him access to her shirt. His fingers tingled as he lifted the hem. The urge to tug it right over her head amped in his muscles. The image of her in the black lace bra flashed through his mind. He'd never forget the fullness of her breasts, the taut nipples straining the lace. His tongue burned, begging to taste her again. She watched him carefully, one brow lifted as if challenging him.

With the satin of her belly exposed, he leaned close and inspected the wound. Dried blood that hadn't been there the last time he checked dotted the suture, but there was no sign that the stitches had been pulled out.

He pressed his lips together and lifted his eyes to meet hers. "It definitely looks like they tugged, but I don't see any damage. You'll have to be careful. No more acrobatics, all right?"

She folded her arms over her chest and her foot swung in the air beside his thigh. "Maybe you should leave me a gun next time."

He grinned. "Touché. But I won't be leaving you alone again."

At his words, all the humor left her eyes, and her gaze burned through his soul. Regret lodged in his throat. Lexi was tougher than fucking nails, but it didn't change the fact that he'd endangered her by leaving.

Next time, he wouldn't let her sleepy, pouty lips sway his decision to wake her. He lowered her shirt then dropped his hands to the granite on either side of her thighs.

She sat up straight, bringing her face inches from his. "You don't have to protect me, you know." Her tongue peeked out of the corner of her mouth, and the blood drained from his head and into his dick. He rubbed his thumbs against her thighs—the only contact he permitted himself. If he touched her any more than that, he'd lose himself . . . if he didn't, he'd fucking combust.

Her teeth followed the line of her tongue, and he pressed his knuckles into the impenetrable stone. She was right. He didn't have to protect her. Hell, she wasn't going to make the effort easy. But he couldn't walk away.

"I know that," he said. It took all his power to keep his voice strong and not melt into her warm vanilla scent. "But we're in this together, and I'll be damned if you end up in that position again."

She inhaled, and her pulse pummeled against her throat. His blood pressure ratcheted up a notch. Her hand lifted, and she curved her fingers around the back of his neck. Her ass inched forward on the counter. Her eyelids lowered and she sealed her lips over his.

Her lips were soft and her fingers cool as she held his head in place. Her tongue pressed between his teeth, and flames scorched every inch of his body. He pressed one hand to the small of her back, holding her in place. His other hand moved to tangle in her loose, silky strands. As her tongue swept over the inside of his mouth, his dick throbbed with need. Her warm, feminine taste with a hint of toothpaste turned his muscles lax.

Holy Christ.

He moved his hand under the hem of her shirt and reveled in the baby-soft skin at the small of her back. Her knees closed against his hips in response, and her shoulders trembled. Curving her lips into a smile, she broke away. Pink stained her cheeks and her lips were swollen and red. Her hair dangled over his wrist, and he moved his thumb over the column of her throat. His tongue ached with the need to have her mouth on his again.

"I'm relieved to hear you say we're on the same side." Her voice, barely above a whisper, carried the strain of someone whose shoulders had harbored the weight of a great burden for far too long.

That was about to end.

"You need to tell me everything, Lex. Now."

ALEXIS'S BACK STIFFENED, and she lowered her hand from the breadth of his neck. His gaze flicked over her eyes, gaging her reaction. She swallowed.

He wants to know everything.

His warm palm was settled on the sensitive flesh at her back. His other hand still cupped her neck. God, the thought of letting everything leak out was so tempting. The only other person who knew about Lionsgate's endeavors was Brooks. A stab of pain split her heart. Six months and she still didn't even know if he was alive. All because of them.

"Lexi, please." His fingers twitched at the waistband of her pants, the only indication that he was on edge. Gentle creases formed around his beseeching eyes.

Slowly she shook her head, and a laugh bubbled from her lips. Tell him everything? The suggestion was almost crazy. Where would she start? It'd be like pulling a thread. There'd be no end.

"It's not that simple." She flicked back the strands of hair next to her cheek. "You don't understand—"

"So help me understand. I won't take no for an answer. Start wherever you want, take as long as you want, but you're telling me everything." His voice was hard. With the force of a bucket of ice water being dumped on her, she was reminded of exactly who he was. "I can't be in the dark anymore, and I can't help when you keep shutting me out. If you want me on your side, then I need you to be on mine, too."

She blew a breath through her lips. "You're not going to like it."

"I'll manage."

She straightened her shoulders. "Fine. Will you put on a pot of coffee?"

He stepped away from her. "Good call."

As Nash prepared the brew, Alexis worked out where to start while letting her eyes wander over the hard, muscular lines of his back. Goodness, he was so thick and strong. She curled her toes at the musky taste of him, still lingering in her mouth. She'd half-expected to take the kiss to another level, to "finish what they'd started," as he'd suggested at the church.

She'd been more than ready. Pulsing and hot, she'd burned with the need to feel his long, solid fingers run over every inch of her body. But more than that, she needed his warmth. She needed to have him erase the terror of the last hour, and to completely lose herself in pleasure. But he hadn't made a move and dammit, she wanted more.

"Feel free to start any time," he said over his shoulder, as he slapped down the lid of the coffee maker.

Did he have to be so damn unaffected? She tucked her fingers around the edge of the counter and pushed all images of Nash's naked body on top of hers from her mind.

Thank god he wasn't a mind reader.

She cleared her throat. "My father and brother were Lionsgate members. Yuri and Brooks Ivanov. Did you know them?"

He turned to face her, pressing his back into the counter opposite her. "Yeah, I knew Yuri. He was good friends with Conrad. I'm sure I crossed paths with Brooks at some point, but nothing jumps out at me."

"I'll show you his picture later." She lowered her gaze to her knees. Talking about the investigation was brand-new territory. Her lips didn't want to cooperate. "My brother had picked up something about the organization . . . something pretty damning. He went to my father, but at first, he didn't believe him. He was in denial. My father was treasurer at the time, and Brooks had started snooping around some of Lionsgate's files and found things that didn't add up. That's when he took it a step further and broke into Conrad's house and—"

"Whoa, whoa. You're losing me." He folded his arms across his chest. "Go back to the beginning. What did he pick up that made him suspicious in the first place?"

She let her shoulders droop, and a deep exhale sputtered through her lips. Of course Nash wouldn't make this easy. He bounced his eyebrows at her, prompting her to continue.

"He was filling in for my dad on his treasury duties. My dad had had a minor heart attack and was taking some time off. Brooks was going over the books, and a sum of money didn't add up. He asked my dad about it and apparently, he'd come across the same thing and brought it to Conrad's attention—but it was dismissed."

"What was it?"

Her throat constricted and anger simmered her blood. "It was a record of ten thousand dollars . . ." She cleared her throat. "For a sale."

Steam whirred from the machine behind Nash, and liquid began to fill the pot. He twisted his face into a grimace. "A sale of what?"

"It didn't say. Brooks did more digging and found some other things that didn't add up. That's when he broke into Conrad's house and found more information. It indicated the sale had been for a . . ." She swallowed. The muscles in her abdomen flexed. "A teenage girl."

Nash jerked forward, away from the counter. His eyes flashed. The look in them as truculent as a raging storm over an inky black ocean. "What the fuck are you talking about?" He moved closer to her. A gorge opened up in her stomach. If he insinuated she was lying, or that her brother was, she'd lose her shit.

"I don't remember the exact wording of what he saw, but he wrote it down for me. It said, 'Female, age fourteen, ten thousand dollars.'" Her voice came out haggard with the effort to keep her tone even. Just uttering the words filled her mouth with acid.

Nash gripped the edge of the counter on either side of her hands. After their kiss, the lines of his face had been soft and unguarded, but now the hard tension was back. He met her gaze dead-on.

"If you're wrong about this—"

"I'm not."

His lips compressed into a solid line. "How can you be sure?"

His skepticism grated her nerves to chalk dust. She'd gone from wanting him inside her to wanting to hit him. "Because my brother would never make false accusations. Aside from that, he did more digging and found other evidence. But he needed the ledger to decode the transactions."

Nash turned from her and paced the stretch of hardwood between the island and the stove. He cupped his jaw in his hand, his fingertips brushing over the bristles. "There aren't any encryption codes in the ledger."

"You're right, there aren't. Brooks was so certain the ledger would hold the answers to what he'd already found, but instead, it's more information we need to decode."

Nash shook his head. "No. It can't be. It doesn't add up. They wouldn't have been that sloppy."

She let his words fall between them. Time to go

in for the kill. "Don't you find it strange that it's not inconceivable that they would do it, but it's inconceivable that they'd be stupid enough to get caught?"

He stopped pacing and turned. His knee brushed hers as he lowered his hand from his jaw. His gaze fixated on her with the sharpness of a dart. "I've been with Lionsgate for half my life. They're like my damn family. If this has been going on and I had no idea . . ." He shook his head. The corners of his eyes tightened, and he pressed his hands to the counter beside her and lowered his head. Her fingers tingled with the need to reach out and touch him.

"If that's true," he continued, "I'd be at fault." His voice was gruff. The skin on his knuckles turned white.

Pain curdled in her belly. She gave in and let her fingers coast down his forearm before placing her hand on top of his. "Not if you didn't know."

He lifted his chin. His dark, ebony eyes melted. It wasn't heat or lust that had softened him, but raw guilt. "Conrad is like my father. I'm there day in and day out. To have no inclination, to be completely fucking unaware . . . Jesus, Lexi." He dropped his head again. "I know you want to nail them with this, and I promise you if there's even a shred of truth to it I will make sure that happens. But I hope to hell you're wrong."

Her tongue grew thick in her mouth. She

couldn't lie and say the possibility of her being wrong was there. It just wasn't.

"What's our next step?"

She chewed the inside of her lip. The fact that it was Nash looking to her for direction made warmth spread through her. "I need to bring up the files Brooks left for me and compare his findings with the ledger, to see if there's anything I can link together. I'm not sure if this will give us all the answers, but the records are coded for a reason."

Nash squinted at her, and the corner of his lip lifted in a grimace. "I gave the ledger to Conrad." He lifted his free hand to circle the wrist that touched his knuckles.

Her body tightened.

"I had no choice. If I would have hung on to it, he never would've believed I was still on his side." He scoffed and shook his head, sweeping his thumb back and forth over her wrist. "Not that it did any good. They used me to get to you."

She lifted her shoulder. "Well, it's a good thing I'm always one step ahead of you. I photocopied the ledger when I locked you out of the church."

His lips hooked into a grin. "Wait a minute"—he wagged his index finger in front of her nose—"you said you didn't lock me out."

A giggle bubbled up her throat. "Oops." She covered her mouth with her hand, but he snagged her wrist.

"You're lucky," he breathed.

She pursed her lips. "Why's that?"

"Because I like kissing you." He brought his mouth down on hers, and an electric current shot through her body. Heat blazed through her and settled between her legs. His hands came to rest at the back of her head and on her hip. His tongue moved between her lips, caressing hers.

A moan gurgled in her throat and she arched her back, needing more. His mouth left hers to trail kisses down her neck. He moved her shirt aside and his tongue flicked over her collarbone. Her fingernails dug into his biceps, and her nipples turned to rocks.

"Ah, god," she wheezed, through her narrowing windpipe.

Ring, ring, ring

Her heart dropped into her stomach at the interruption. Ever so slowly, Nash pulled away. He pressed his forehead to hers and let out a chuckle. He pulled his phone from his pocket and glanced at the screen.

"I'd better get this. Why don't you get your stuff ready? I'll fix our coffees and we'll take them to go. We need to get you somewhere safe."

She slid off the counter, but he stopped her with a hand on her waist. He lowered his face and brushed his mouth over hers. "We're going to finish that later."

Delight spread through her. "If you're lucky,"

she shot back.

He laughed and pinched her chin between his thumb and forefinger. "We'll see who's lucky."

She turned and made her way to the stairs. Nash answered the phone, and his greeting carried to her ears but fell away as gravity sucked her back down to earth.

She had an important call to make, too.

CHAPTER 14

NASH'S BLOOD HUMMED through his body. It took every ounce of restraint to keep his feet rooted to the floor and not chase Lexi's perfectly shaped retreating ass.

She'd kissed him. That move had propelled them into the sex zone. He wanted her. More than he'd ever wanted anyone. Just breathing her scent, watching her move, and the odd touch of her hand sent his desire into a blazing fire. She'd told him at the church that she wasn't interested, and although her kiss belied that, there could be truth to those words. She might be interested but not want to get involved with him. He couldn't blame her. The question was, what the fuck could he do? All he had to go by were her signals, and he'd follow them to a T if it killed him.

He brought his attention back to the phone in his hand and swiped to accept the call.

"What the hell, dude?" Cole barked into his ear.

Nash winced at his brother's pissed-off tone.

He'd promised to call him when he got to Moscow. "Sorry, man. It's been a shitshow."

He dragged his hand over the counter, wiping a small pile of crumbs into the sink. Lexi had dropped a fucking bomb on him, and his brain was still trying to pick up the pieces. If Lionsgate was involved with what she claimed, he couldn't turn his back. If he was guilty by association, he needed to make amends. He'd be damned if he let any child suffer under the name of his brotherhood.

Cole grunted. "You should have called me."

"I know. Look, I need your help with something else. But I can't tell you over the phone."

"All right, I can come to you. Are you home?"

"We're about to leave. I can be at your place in an hour."

"Who's 'we'?"

Shit. Nash pressed his fist to his forehead. He planned on telling Cole about Lexi, but he needed to ease him into it. When he'd called Cole after Lexi stole the ledger, he'd been on a rampage. Now he was hiding and protecting her.

A beat passed. "Never mind," Cole said. "Dare showed me the picture of the woman who drugged your stupid ass. I get it." Cole's voice pitched in amusement.

"Yeah, yeah. Go ahead and laugh. But hold your breath until we chat. I need your help and this is dangerous territory."

Cole's laugh subsided. "You know I'm down

for whatever."

"Good." He pulled the phone from his ear, ready to disconnect, and then quickly brought it back. "And Cole."

"Yeah?"

"Don't breathe a word about this to anyone. Don't even mention you talked to me."

"All right." It was the first time he'd ever heard Cole's voice flounder.

Nash disconnected and turned his attention to the coffee. A few minutes later, Lexi came downstairs. Her cheeks were flushed and her eyes somber.

He passed her a travel mug. "Everything okay?"

She wrapped her hands around the steel and inhaled the aroma before taking a long sip. "Mmm. Thank you." She kept the mug at her lips, and her eyes drifted to his. "I just talked to my boss."

Nash raised his eyebrows. It hadn't occurred to him that Lexi would need to answer to someone about her investigation. Probably because she was so personally driven. He sucked back a mouthful of coffee, and the much-needed caffeine hit his bloodstream. "And?"

"She's not happy that I have to keep her in the dark. She wants something handed in by the end of the week." Lexi brought the mug down to rest on the edge of the counter. "But I can't do it. I trust her completely, but leaking information to anyone right now could be detrimental to our investigation."

Pleasure spread over him and his lips quirked at her use of "our." "Did you tell her that?"

She sighed and shook the loose strands of her hair back from her shoulders. The motion sent a surge of desire through him, and he folded his hand tighter around the mug to keep from touching her.

"Yes. But she's not taking no for an answer. If I don't have something concrete to her by Friday, she's pulling me off the story."

Nash cursed. "Can she do that?"

Lexi's mouth pulled into a pucker and her forehead creased. "Professionally, yes. But I'll lose my job before I give up." She sighed and drove both of her hands into the roots of her hair. "It's fine. I'll cross that bridge when I get to it." She lowered her hands to her hips. "So where are we going?"

"I have a place we can stay. But we need to make a stop first."

She squinted at him. "Oh? Where's that?"

"My brother's. I'm going to see if he can do a bit of digging for us."

The corner of her mouth dipped, and her eyes glowed with interest. "Is he the one who helped you find me with facial recognition?"

"Nah, that was my other brother, Dare. Cole,

well, he's more . . . rogue than Dare or Dallas."

Her eyebrow cocked into a perfect arch, and she folded her arms across her chest. "I know he's your brother, but we need to be careful. The more people who know about this—"

Nash held out his hand. "I agree, and there's no one I trust more in the world. Truth is, we need all the help we can get. And if anything happens, it's best that at least someone knows what's going on."

Her pupils receded and her irises expanded; sharp blue pushed out the ocean green. It was a reaction he was beginning to link to her suppressing emotion. He reached out and smoothed his fingers down her arm. "What'd I say?"

She shook her head, but when his hand reached hers, she snagged it. "It's just . . . that's what my brother did. If he hadn't left me his findings, I wouldn't have a shred of anything to go on."

"He didn't tell you about his investigating before the fire?" Questions churned through his mind, but the last thing he wanted to do was press her. Her gaze kept flicking from him to their surroundings. Talking about her brother was a soft spot, but Nash needed to know if he was alive or if it was another body chalked up for Lionsgate.

"I knew something was going on with the organization, but he wouldn't tell me. He said it would only put me in danger." She sucked in a shaky breath and her shoulders trembled. "The night he disappeared, he called and told me that if anything happened to him, I needed to go to our secret place—the woods behind our parents' house—and retrieve the information he'd left me." Her focus dropped to the counter.

"That was the last time you spoke with him?"

She nodded, and her eyes lifted to meet his gaze. "He's not dead. I can't believe that." She shook her head firmly. "But they did something to him." Her lip trembled and her eyes turned glassy.

"Christ." He dropped her hand, pulling her against his chest. Disgust released bile into his stomach, and the sharp burn of it climbed his esophagus.

No wonder she'd been so fucking hell-bent on taking down Lionsgate. He couldn't blame her one bit. He'd have done the same if they'd hurt one of his brothers. She'd been through more than anyone should have to go through, and all this time she'd been swimming against the current on her own. Her hands pressed to his back, and she turned her cheek to rest on his sternum. Every atom in his body pulsed with the need to pick her up, lay her on his bed, and take away the pain that had her body wound tight.

She was so much smaller than him. Her shoulders easily fit between the expanse of his chest, her head lay well below his chin, and her slim belly snuggled up against his groin. He let his hand run down her back in long strokes and inch by inch, her tension dissipated until she melted against him and her breath evened out.

"I'm going to find him," he said into her hair. "I promise you that."

She tilted her head back to stare at him. Her irises had returned to their warm aqua shade, and her forehead was now smooth.

"Thank you for saying that, but I don't expect you to." Her tongue ran over her teeth, pressing her pink top lip forward.

He ran his hands around the small of her back and let them land on her hips. His thumbs moved as if they had a mind of their own, stroking the denim at her waist. He inched her away to shield her from the growing member straining against the zipper of his jeans.

Jesus. He was worse than a pubescent teenager.

"Leave it to me," he said, over the sand that had collected on the inside of his throat. "Let's get going." He turned her away and ushered her from the kitchen. If he didn't get her out of the house and as far away from a bed as possible, they'd be holed up for days.

LEXI BURROWED HER chin in the neck of her coat and took the steps to Nash's brother's apartment two at a time, not waiting for him to catch up. Nash grabbed the door handle before her fingers could close around the steel. "Slow down, will you? I need to scope things out before you go charging from the car."

She slipped inside and waited until Nash's body crowded her back. "I thought you said you could trust him?"

Nash nodded to the concierge, a heavyset man with sandy hair cut close to his scalp. He bore the stern look of a bouncer at a club. They sailed past him, their boots scuffing against the slick marble floor. Nash loosened his coat, and her gaze dropped to the Beretta nestled in his palm, the mouth of it hidden under his jacket. Her windpipe contracted.

"I do. It's everyone else I don't trust." His hand circled her hip, and he led her down the marble hallway to the bank of elevators.

She dropped her voice to a whisper. "Is your brother with the organization too?"

Nash scoffed and jabbed his thumb into a button, calling the elevator. "Hell no."

The doors whooshed open, and Lexi stepped in with Nash on her heels. He pressed the button for the ninth floor and the doors glided shut.

"What does he do?"

Over the last several days, Nash hadn't shied away from any topic. But now, he kept his gaze on their reflection in the shiny elevator door. His hand remained buried in his jacket, the butt of the gun just visible from where she stood.

She swallowed over the boulder that had settled

in her throat. The urge to question him again burned on her lips, but his eyes landed on her face before she could form the words.

"I guess you could say he's self-employed." His tone held a hint of humor, but his eyes were dark with hesitation. The doors opened, and before she could ask more, his hand fell to her shoulders and he led her down the hall.

The building was as prestigious as Nash's—maybe even more so. They passed a tall vase filled with fresh flowers on a glass table tucked into the elevator vestibule. A wide brown-and-gold-vined runner lined the hall, showing just enough of the marble on either side to leave a lasting impression.

Nash stopped at an oversized wooden door and rapped his knuckles once on the surface. A lock clicked, followed by two more, and then a chain rattled against metal.

What the hell?

A ball of unease collected in her chest, and she snapped her head to Nash. His jaw tightened beneath his stubble, but he didn't look at her. The door opened and a man about an inch shorter than Nash stood in the doorway. Being that Nash was of gargantuan height, his brother was still stagger-ing. He wore a black T-shirt and dark jeans, and his slick, ebony hair was pulled back into a low bun. Nash's hand pressed at the center of her back, and he urged her inside.

"Lexi, this is Cole," Nash said, as Cole shut the

door and fastened the locks and the chain. She worked her tongue over the backs of her teeth and clasped her hands in front of her, hoping neither of them would notice how they trembled.

Cole turned to her and nodded. His eyes were almost as dark and hard as the sedimentary rock of the same name. They swept over her and then landed on Nash.

"Glad you made it out of Moscow. Have a seat," he said, gesturing to the black leather couch in the living room. Light hardwood floors caught the glow of the sunlight from the window. Lexi slipped off her boots and dragged the zipper of her coat down, taking in the space. The kitchen wasn't as warm and inviting as Nash's, but it had smooth, modern lines and glossy white cabinets. She sank down on the edge of the sofa, and pressed the soles of her feet into the checkered area rug.

Nash snorted. "Almost didn't. Conrad made that damn difficult." He sat next to her. His thigh brushed her leg and his hand grazed over her knee and gave it a gentle squeeze.

Cole sat in a matching leather chair across from them and rested his elbows on his knees. "Is that what this is about? Conrad?" His gaze pierced into Nash, and Lexi took in his long, sinewy forearms. Tattoos and scars littered his olive skin, but it was the jagged scar that peeked out from the collar of his shirt that turned her skin to stone.

"He hired out the hit on Lexi's family and has

been after her since." He glanced at her. "Her brother left her information, and Conrad is going to great lengths to kill her."

Cole's expression didn't change, but his temple twitched slightly. He laced his fingers together. They were covered in tattoos of Roman numerals. "I never cared for that guy." He turned his hard stare to Lexi. Though he and Nash looked faintly similar, looking at Cole was like staring death in the face. His alert, observant eyes bore the experience of someone who had weathered a long, rough life.

"Sorry about your family," he said. Although his face didn't crack, his voice carried a hint of sympathy. "What did your brother leave you that's so damning?"

Lexi cleared her throat and fought the urge to lean toward Nash's heat. She pinched her fingers together and wet her lips. "He, uh . . ." She shifted her gaze to Nash, who nodded, urging her on. "He found evidence that the organization is trafficking children."

Cole's thick black eyebrows hiked up. It was the biggest facial expression he'd made since they entered. His steely gaze shot to Nash. "What the fuck?"

Nash leaned forward, mimicking his brother's pose, and took the baton from her. He explained what Brooks had uncovered, turning to her occasionally to clarify or prod for further details.

Cole settled back. The hard glint in his eyes was downright fatal now. His hand hung over the edge of his knee and opened and closed spasmodically. It looked as if he was fighting to suppress his furor. "Dare and I can hack into his computers and the ones at the House, but my guess is if he's hiding something like this, he'll keep it on a separate hard drive."

Nash grunted. "I was afraid of that. So we'll need to get into his office or his house to look for it."

Cole nodded. They chatted for a few more minutes and Cole promised to update Nash in a few days, once he'd swept through Conrad's devices.

Nash's hand covered her elbow as he led her from the building. He left his jacket open, and his hand hovered on his hip, ready to attack. He opened the passenger door and waited until she got in before rounding the vehicle.

"Do you think someone's following us?"

Nash scanned the mirrors as he clicked his seatbelt in place. "Cole has helped Lionsgate with tasks in the past, so he's not a stranger to some of the members. But I doubt anyone would dare piss him off. Just being cautious."

She fastened her seatbelt and cranked the heat. The shadow that hung over Cole had been chilling—an ominous warning of who and what he was. She pressed her back into the seat and kept her focus on Nash. His calm, easy energy flowed through the vehicle. Her heart rate slowed as she inhaled his musky cologne.

Nash navigated through the streets and then merged onto highway 99. He set the cruise control, and Lexi took in his long jean-clad legs as he stretched them out. His wrist hung limply at the bottom of the wheel. Looking at his thick, bronzed fingers, she was reminded of what they could do to her body. A thrill shot through her.

"I'm sorry I didn't warn you about Cole." Nash didn't take his attention from the road. His voice held a hint of strain. "He's kind of hard to explain."

Lexi looked at his face. She needed to ask the question hanging in the air. She forced down the tremor that threatened to steal her voice. "What does he do, Nash?"

Nash shifted and rolled his shoulders. They sailed over the West Seattle Bridge, and for a minute, Lexi's attention was diverted to the stunning harbor and skyline. With the cold chill in the air, the sky was clear enough to get a good view of the snow-capped mountains.

"He works independently. Freelance, I guess. That's really all I can say."

She pressed her arms against her abdomen. Nausea sloshed in her stomach with the force of a violent sea, and the constriction of her muscles made her stiches ache. "Is he an assassin?" That one word ricocheted through her mind. Everything added up. The hard exterior, the deadly eyes . . . God, why had she asked?

Because she was a goddamn journalist and needed to confirm her suspicions.

"I really can't say anything, Lex." His words came out pained.

Tension pulsated in the air around them.

"He was involved in my family's death, wasn't he?"

"No. He connected Conrad with someone else, who completed the job."

Tears burned her eyes, obstructing her vision. Her shoulders shook on a laugh, the brittle sound derisive.

"He didn't do it."

"But he knew about it?"

"So did I," Nash countered.

Pain throbbed through her midsection and her lungs ached for a deep breath. She sucked shallow ones through her nose. If she gave into the suffocating need for oxygen, it would come out on a sob.

"I didn't ask enough questions. I had my fucking head so burrowed into the brotherhood that it never crossed my mind—"

She pressed her hand against his forearm. "Nash, it's fine. I don't blame you. You didn't know." And it was true. As much as it stung and gnawed at her to know that maybe, just maybe, he could have prevented her parents' death, she couldn't hate him for something he'd been in the dark about.

And in that light, she couldn't blame Cole. But he wasn't cut from the same cloth as Nash. He was a cold-blooded criminal. People with careers like that enjoyed and thrived off the work.

Nash gripped her fingers and lifted her knuckles to his mouth. "I'm so sorry, babe. I'd cut off my hand to go back to that day."

The tears that had built like a wall in front of her pupils spilled onto her cheeks. The endearment had rolled off her shoulder but then circled back and settled over her like a warm blanket.

"If you hadn't connected Conrad to Cole, he would have found someone else to do the job. Let's not talk about it right now." She cleared her throat and dashed the wetness from her cheeks. "How far are we?"

Nash let go of her hand and hit his turn signal. "Almost there." He took the next exit and slowed as they approached a set of lights. A few minutes later, they turned down a tree-lined street. The sun shone through the bare branches, giving the impression of spring. Nash slowed in front of a brick townhouse. She studied the colonial style pillars and large front porch as they pulled into the attached single-car garage.

"Do you own this place?"

Nash hit the button to close the garage door

and got out of the vehicle. Lexi waited at the door inside the garage while he gathered the bags.

"Yeah. I found this place last year," he said, approaching her. "It's a rental, but that's what I wanted." He lowered the bags and then inserted a key in the door and kicked it open, stopping only to flash her a smile. He stepped inside. "That way I could use an alias. No one knows about this place besides Cole."

She pulled off her boots and left them on the mat in front of the door. A laundry room and two-piece bath sat beyond the garage-access door. Her socked feet slid over the smooth mahogany floors as she followed Nash into the main area.

"Do you come here often? It's awfully clean." She ran her hand over the green-and-taupe granite countertop and took in the tall maple cabinets. A big-screen TV hung above the gas fireplace in the living room, and a gray sectional ate up the rest of the living room's space.

"I haven't been here since before Christmas, but I have a cleaner come in once a month to keep it up."

"It's lovely."

"I'll grab the bags in a sec. Why don't you have a look upstairs? The master is yours. I think you'll be happy with the shower."

Her interest piqued, she made her way to the staircase. "Now you've got my attention," she called, as she ascended the carpeted steps. The master wasn't as large as the one in Nash's condo, but it held a wide king bed and a TV. She dragged her fingers along the cream-colored wall and entered the all-white bathroom. A large soaker tub and walk-in shower that made the one in her Moscow hotel appear tiny was the focal point. Her muscles yearned for the heat and comfort the room promised. Nash's footsteps sounded on the stairs and she turned back into the bedroom.

Her gaze swept over the dresser opposite the bed and a slim black card caught her eye. Her pulse slowed and her breath wheezed out of her lungs. She inched her fingers toward the object as if it'd jump up and sever her fingers.

She lifted the thick paper and brought it close to her face.

No.

Nash dropped the bags in the corner of the room. "Not a whole lot of food here other than frozen crap. We can order . . ."

Nash's voice faltered but she couldn't tear her focus from the neatly printed words on the card. *The White Room.*

"Lex?"

Her hand shook. "The White Room?" she rasped. "You . . . you go there?"

CHAPTER 15

NASH'S BREATH SAT trapped in his lungs. Lexi's skin had faded to the shade of white powder. Her eyes seared him to the spot, round and, dammit, filled with disgust. Her fingers pinched the paper as if she were afraid it carried a flesh-eating disease.

Fuck, fuck, fuck.

He rubbed his palm over his face as his brain grasped at excuses as if they were on an assembly line. He could have told a million lies, but none of them would form on his tongue. The worst part was he'd gone to the White Room only once—the last time he'd used the townhouse. That was why he'd left the exclusive card here.

But the big question was, how the fuck did she know about the White Room?

"I promise it's not what you think." He lowered his hand and held it out in front of him as if making a peace offering. Shit, couldn't he have come up with something better?

Her pinky finger flicked the card, and she

dropped it back on the dresser. "Really? I'd say it's exactly what I think." Color returned to her cheeks, and she folded her arms across her chest and drew her lips into a rigid line. He stepped forward and gripped her elbows in his palms. She didn't yank away, but her eyes blazed in warning.

"Listen to me, Lex. Out of all the years I've been with Lionsgate, I went there once. Only once. It was mostly out of curiosity and boredom."

She placed the tips of her fingers on his sternum briefly. "You don't owe me an explanation. I was just surprised." Her shoulders drew up and a cold mask of indifference settled over her features, over the emotions he'd worked so hard to expose.

He dug his thumbs into her forearms harder than he intended. "I do owe you an explanation. I don't want you to think that's the kind of guy I am, all right?" He slid his tongue over his lips. Desperation raked him. He reached over and swiped up the card that he should have burned months ago. He flipped it over and showed her the back.

"See that?" He pointed to the letters in the bottom corner. "Those are my initials. This is my card, and I need it to enter. Downstairs, I told you I haven't been to this condo since before Christmas."

He shouldn't give a damn what she thought. And if she were any other woman, he'd probably laugh it off. But for some fucked up reason it cut him to the core that she'd assume he was a sleaze. The harsh lines of her face softened, but only by a fraction. Her gaze drifted over his face.

"Okay, I believe you." Her shoulders jerked on an almost invisible shrug, and the tension in his spine unwound a bit. He dropped the card back to the dresser and returned his hands to her arms.

"Now you need to tell me how the hell you know about that place." There was no way she'd gone there—unless she'd been a guest, which wasn't a stretch of the imagination considering the lengths she'd go to nail Lionsgate.

But Jesus, if she'd been to the brotherhood's private sex club, he'd lose his fucking mind.

Lexi's top teeth pulled in her bottom lip and her eyes roamed around, straying far away from his attempt at eye contact. No one outside of Lionsgate was supposed to know about the club unless they'd been a guest. But guests were rare and limited. Not all members frequented, but some visited faithfully. To Nash's knowledge, Conrad attended only once a year. But it was a nice touch for the young guys and kept some of their more daring preferences in a contained environment.

Finally, she dragged her eyes to his. "I questioned someone and they slipped the name. They tried to cover it up and wouldn't elaborate, so I dug until I found someone who would."

"Who did you talk to?"

She snorted. "A good journalist never reveals

her sources." She tilted her head back and her chin jutted forward defiantly.

"Fine. What did they tell you?"

She twisted her lips sideways.

"If you tell me I can set the record straight."

"You said you'd been there only once." Her words came out with the force of a bullet.

He closed his eyes on a sigh. "I have. But a lot of brothers go, so I have a pretty damn good idea of what would be accurate or not."

"Fine." She cleared her throat. "He said members who frequent pay twenty-five thousand dollars a year as an annual fee. Is that true?"

"Yes. But your first visit is free."

Her eyes widened. "Aren't there prostitutes?"

Nash winced. A deep throb pulsed through his skull. "I wouldn't say that." He scratched his head, the right words evading him. "The House employs women to ensure the members have a good time."

One of her eyes narrowed into a slit. "You're splitting hairs."

"Not everyone uses those services. Some women frequent the White Room too, and they go for a good time, just like the members."

"So which did you use? The women Lionsgate employs or the women who frequent for a good time?"

A beat passed. "The latter."

Her expression didn't change, and her broiling gaze didn't flinch. He picked up the card again and held it in the air between them.

"I don't care if I ever set foot in there again." He twisted his fingers and the top of the card ripped.

Lexi shot out her hand and grabbed his wrist. "Wait. When do they hold the events?"

He frowned. "First Tuesday of every month."

"That's tonight!" She snatched the card from his hand and slipped it into her back pocket. "We're going," she said over her shoulder as she brushed past him.

"You're not serious," he said with a chuckle.

She knelt in front of her suitcase and unzipped it. "'Course I am. We need to get on the inside, and this is the best way. If children are being trafficked, wouldn't the White Room be the best place to find a buyer?"

He scoffed. "Hell no. It's way too risky. Yeah, there's some scuzzy dudes, but there's also a lot of legitimate men—doctors, lawyers, businessmen: people who wouldn't stand for the extortion of children."

She dug into her suitcase, flinging articles of clothing over the side as she searched for something. "We won't know how things are really going down until we get inside."

Nash rubbed the back of his neck. "Are you forgetting that these are the same guys who just ransacked my condo? Considering the fact you've been wanted dead for the last five days, it's probably best not to walk right into the hornet's nest."

She scoffed. "Shows how much you know. It's called hiding in plain sight. The last thing they'd expect is that I'd be stupid enough to go there. Besides, I wasn't suggesting I waltz in there looking like this."

"Look, Lexi. I really don't feel like fighting off any bullets today—"

She got to her feet and faced him. On each hand balanced a wig: one bleached blonde and the other flaming red. The one she'd worn the night she'd followed Nash to the hotel and picked him up. She bobbed her eyebrows at him and flashed a mischievous grin.

He exhaled through his lips and rested his hands on his hips. "You're not listening to a word I'm saying, are you?"

"Yeah, I heard you. But I think the lives of children are a hell of a lot more important than hiding with our tails between our legs. I'm leaning toward blonde—what do you think?"

ALEXIS'S SHOE CAUGHT one of the cobblestones in the drive, and she pitched forward. Nash's hold on her hand tightened, and she caught her balance before she went down. The old stone mansion loomed before her. Wrought-iron lanterns hung outside the front double doors and along the sides of the building. The House. For six months, she'd wanted to get inside these walls.

"I don't know how women walk in those things," Nash said.

She tilted her face up to look at his. Damn, he looked good in a tux. The black suit jacket over the crisp, white shirt brought out the olive tone to his skin. The hard set to his jaw hadn't dissipated since he agreed to go. Okay, so he was going under duress, but there was no help for it. She smoothed her hand over the bottom of her black dress. The material barely reached the tops of her thighs. The blonde wig's glossy strands hung over her shoulders.

If her disguise didn't serve its purpose, they were in deep shit. It was a risk she was willing to take.

They approached a set of stone stairs, and Nash's hand moved to the small of her back. One of the doors opened, and a tall man in a black tuxedo and gelled hair exited the building with his hand held out.

"Evening, Ronnie," Nash said, as he placed his member card in the man's palm.

The doorman's eyes fell on her, and his thick black eyebrows pulled into a scowl. Her chest tightened.

"Who's your guest?"

Alexis wet her lips and fought the urge to look at Nash. It wouldn't do her any good to show she didn't belong. She hiked up her chin, meeting his gaze dead-on.

"Amber Wallace," Nash said. "Do you want to see her ID?"

Ronnie gave a curt nod. Alexis peeled the zipper of her clutch open and pulled out the fake ID she'd used at the airport. He accepted the card and began to copy the information on a clipboard. Heat scorched up her back, but she didn't dare turn to look at the line forming behind them. Nash had given her strict instructions to keep her face down as much as possible, at least in well-lit areas. The lens of the surveillance camera hung beside the exterior of the double doors. It would likely only catch her profile, which was partially hidden by the wig.

The guard handed back her ID and lifted the fingers of her free hand. After clipping a slim white wristband around her wrist, he let her go. "Guests are restricted to the White Room. Enjoy your night."

Nash moved her through the door, and his fingers circled her wrist. Dim lights cast shadows down the long maroon-colored hallway. Her gaze drifted over the paintings that lined the walls. The thin gold paisley carpet muffled the click of her heels on the hardwood that lay beneath.

"Head down." Nash tapped his thumb against the back of her hand, and she lowered her chin. Two men stepped out of one of the rooms along the hall, and Nash tensed. He moved her behind him as he squeezed to the right side of the hall, allowing the men to pass.

"Nash! Dude, where've you been all week?" Nash slowed and Lexi's nose bumped into his back. The vibration of the man's voice skimmed over her skin, and her scalp prickled.

That voice.

"Hey, Leith. I was out of town. Hope you kept up with kickboxing since I've been away." Nash drove his fist into the guy's shoulder.

Lexi's pulse drummed against her throat. Every urge inside her screamed to peek around Nash's bicep, but she forced her feet to stay still.

"I've slacked a bit. It's hard to stay motivated without competition." The man shifted and peered behind Nash. His clear, almost translucent, blue eyes swept over her, chilling the air, and then flicked to the man next to him. "Drew's not exactly a tough sparrer."

The lean guy next to him ribbed him with his elbow. "Oh, fuck off. You tapped out this morning."

Leith grinned and mumbled something that didn't reach her ears. Then he looked at her again. "Who's this?"

Lexi cleared her throat. "Amber." She stepped forward and pulled her shoulders back.

Nash placed an arm around her waist and grinned. "Amber's an old friend."

Leith nodded and lifted the glass in his hand. "You gotta try the signature drink tonight. It's delicious." He tilted the glass as if toasting and clicked his tongue at her. Lexi's lip twitched with disgust.

"See you guys later," Nash said. He nudged her in front of him and fist-bumped both men. The scuff of their shoes faded away, and she yanked on Nash's elbow until his ear came down to her mouth.

"That was him."

He straightened. "Who?"

"The man you were talking to was the guy who came onto the balcony when I was hiding." Had he recognized her? A chill ran down her spine.

Nash gripped her shoulder and spun her so her back pressed against the wall. Music vibrated through the drywall against her shoulder blades. To her left, a large white double door waited.

The White Room.

"Leith? Are you sure?" His hold didn't loosen.

She nodded. "Positive."

His eyes raked over her face. Heat radiated off his body and into her belly. His gaze drifted to her breasts, which were pressed against his midsection, and then back up. His thumb twitched on her skin, and the pinched corner of his mouth dipped.

"You're sure? You saw him?"

An image of the men moving on the other side of the sliding glass door of Nash's balcony flashed through her mind. She hadn't let her attention linger too long, but she recognized the man's build and the crook in his long, thin nose.

"I peeked in through the glass while I was outside. I didn't get a good enough look to identify them both, but I'm sure that was one of them." She tucked a faux blonde lock behind her ear and resisted the urge to bite her lip as Nash's cologne invaded her. God, why did he always smell so good? The heady scent made her think of a lumberjack in the forest chopping wood in the rain.

She cleared her throat and forced the picture of him shirtless and swinging an ax from her head. "I heard his voice too. Do you think he recognized me from the picture Conrad shared?"

His face crinkled and doubt shrouded his eyes. "He's had quite a few drinks. I could smell it on him. And with this disguise"—his gaze dropped down to her exposed thighs and climbed all the way back up, an inch at a time—"I don't think so. But he might already be on alert."

"Do you think Conrad is convinced I'm dead?"

His fingers left her shoulder and trailed down her arm to catch her fingers. A path of fire tore through her skin in their wake. "He asked a lot of questions. To be honest, it's hard to be certain what he believes. I think him sending Leith and Drew to my condo means he wanted to find out for sure. Since they didn't see you, Conrad might believe me now."

Nash's other hand left her shoulder and pressed into the wall beside her face as the White Room's door opened and someone stepped out. Heat closed in around her body, wrapping her in a welcoming cocoon. His lips came down hard on hers, and her back arched off the wall. She parted her lips, and his tongue sank into her mouth, scalding her taste buds. He gently bit her bottom lip, assaulting her senses and making her body scream for more. Her pelvis jerked forward in a silent plea for his attention, wetness swarmed between her legs, and a moan vibrated through her solar plexus.

As the footsteps faded, he pulled away. She clutched his suit jacket in her fist to anchor her.

"Sorry," he breathed. His mouth hooked into a grin and his eyes sparked at her. "Just being careful." He winked and tangled his fingers with hers. "Shall we?" The amusement still hadn't left his eyes.

He jerked his head toward the double doors, and she rolled her fingers tighter into his palm. His wide hand splayed against the wood and the door swung open. Techno music pulsed into the hallway and a strobe light danced to the rhythm.

If he'd been expecting the sights beyond the threshold to jar her, well, he'd be disappointed. She hiked up her eyebrow and grinned, though her palms were growing wetter by the second.

"It's about time." She shimmied in front of him and entered the room. Her gaze swept the space and her hand dropped to the hem of her short black dress. It was the same one she'd worn the night she picked up Nash, and the only one she had with her. Men and women were scattered across the main level. Some were pressed against the bar and others strode through the room while a few made out on the many couches. A long railing split the room and allowed a bird's-eye view to the lower level. The strobe lights' purple and white rays bounced off the men's white shirts and the women's sequined dresses.

Nash's front molded to the length of her back and his hand came around her waist to settle on her abdomen, inches from where she still throbbed for him. His stubble scraped against her jaw and his lips brushed over her earlobe, sending an erogenous ripple through her breasts.

"Not so scary, is it?"

She tilted her head back. "I wasn't the one who didn't want to come," she said into his ear.

His husky laugh rumbled against her spine. "Let's grab a drink." He rested her hand on the crook of his elbow and led her toward the bar. As she sauntered alongside him, her eyes zeroed in on a tall, leggy blonde. The woman's lips parted, and her wide eyes trailed over Nash.

She knew him.

A stab of jealousy shot through her. Then the

woman's eyes fell to Lexi and she clamped her mouth shut and turned to the gentleman at her side.

Nash pulled out a stool at the bar and Lexi slid into it as he ordered two signature drinks. As much as she wanted to relax, her spine refused to soften. She sat ramrod straight. Her mind wandered back to the blonde woman. She wasn't the jealous type—far from it. But having someone in this environment recognize Nash sent all kinds of dirty images flashing through her mind. She tapped her clutch against the bar's mahogany top.

Nash's brows rose. "You okay?"

She pressed her lips together. Despite her desire not to show her unease, her gaze slipped to the woman in the red dress. Nash followed her line of vision and then looked back at her.

"Ah, she spotted me."

The bartender placed two glasses in front of them, and Lexi greedily sucked the pink liquid through a straw. Hpnotiq and grapefruit juice tickled her tongue, and some of her tension melted. "Friend of yours, I take it?"

He sipped the drink, made a face, and pushed it a few inches away. "Hardly. She came onto me the last time I was here."

"And you brought her home." She bit the black straw and sucked.

Nash shook his head. "No, she's not the one I brought home. She tried hard, though." He rested his elbows on the edge of the bar. "Tell me, now that we're here, what the hell is your plan?" He took another sip of the cocktail.

She dipped her head closer to him. "We need to find the codes for the encrypted sheet in the ledger. We're breaking into Conrad's office."

CHAPTER 16

THE ALCOHOL SLAMMED against his palate and he coughed to clear it. Lexi sipped her drink. Her smirk touched the corners of her eyes. He noted a dimple at the corner of her mouth he hadn't caught before.

"You can't be serious."

She set down her glass. "Seeing as how we won't be partaking in any of that"—she flicked her hand over her shoulder toward the hot-and-heavy couples on the couches—"I figured we should be productive."

He swung his attention from her face to the brown leather couches and noted one couple in particular. A woman with ass-length black hair pulled into a ponytail straddled a man. His face was tucked into the crook of her neck, and her hips thrust in a smooth rocking motion. If they were in any other place, Nash would be game to have Lexi in that exact position.

"We could partake in that if you'd like. Though I'd opt for privacy, given the option."

A dark pink tint crept from her cleavage to her face, and she glanced over her shoulder. She cleared her throat and turned back to him.

"Maybe another time," she said, her voice deep and husky.

"How about we leave the snooping to Cole? There's not much point in breaking into Conrad's office to get to his computer if Cole can accomplish the same thing from a distance." He lowered his elbows to the bar, bringing him closer to the gentle rise and fall of her chest. "We can scope out people here, see if we spot anyone underage." The smooth, creamy exposed flesh of her breasts made his fingers and tongue tingle with the need to touch her, to taste every inch, every crevice, every—

Lexi lowered her feet to the carpet. "I have a better idea." She leaned in close and trailed her fingers along the waistband of his suit pants. His guts clenched and his muscles jumped. "I'm going to the restroom. When I get out, you can either come with me and show me where his office is or stay here. I'm sure there's enough to keep you busy." Her voice hardened on the last words.

He gripped her hand, stopping her before she could turn away. "There's no one I'd rather be with right now than you." His throat grated out the words. Her lips parted as quickly as they had when he'd kissed her. Dammit, he was overstepping. Kissing and groping was one thing, but verbally showing her how bad she affected him was inching out of the comfort zone they'd set up.

Her lips moved into the faintest of smiles, and she tossed her hair over her shoulder. "Good. I'll be back in two minutes." She squeezed his hand and turned toward the wall nearest the entrance, where the restrooms were located. Her hips swung, and her backless dress revealed the soft curve of her spine. The air left his lungs.

There was no way he'd let her wander around the House in search of Conrad's office alone. She had him by the balls and she knew it. Conrad wouldn't be around. He attended only one White Room event a year, and that was on New Year's Eve. Still, there were a lot of eyes and ears in the place, and it wasn't a stretch of the imagination to think that he was being watched.

If Lexi was right and Leith was the one who'd broken into his house, he'd kill the sonofabitch. He brought his fingers to the sweating glass, still full of pink, too-sweet liquid, and forced his temper down to a reasonable degree. He'd known Leith for two years. A fellow enforcer, the man was trained and skilled. Who the hell could he trust now? Though Nash was respected, the guys wouldn't dare cross Conrad. Hell, no one would be stupid enough to do that except him.

He pushed away from the bar and stood. Lexi would be out of the restroom any second. One good thing about his long-standing membership in Lionsgate was that he didn't need to pay for drinks at any events. Or sex, if he wanted it. He hadn't yet paid for sex, and he wasn't about to start. Especially not now. Not when there was only one woman who drove his blood pressure through the roof and made him want to lose himself inside her for days.

He turned from the bar, and his shoulder collided with a solid form.

"Hey man, how's your night?" Drew stood in front of him, blocking his sight line to the restrooms. Nash met his stare and his muscles rippled. Drew was a decent guy—he'd never had an issue with him—but he followed Leith around closer than a shadow. If Leith had been in his house, Drew would have been too.

He pulled himself up to his full height. The top of Drew's head barely reached Nash's chin. With his hands hanging at his sides, he slowly cracked each knuckle of his right hand. A muscle in Drew's jaw jumped, but his smile didn't fade.

"Going good . . . so far." Nash let the last two words hang in challenge. His blood roared through him. Passive aggressive was not his fucking deal. Just plain aggressive—that's how he preferred to handle shit. Pussyfooting around this douchebag would only piss him off more. But he had to be careful. It would serve Lexi and him a hell of a lot better if their enemies didn't know they were on to them. He forced his temper down and smiled. "Been a long-ass time since I've been here." He let his gaze sweep around the room and then back to Drew. "Isn't really my scene, but I needed to get out after a hellish week."

Drew visibly relaxed and nodded. "Yeah, it seems to be getting dirtier and dirtier here. But I hear you. It's difficult going out with outsiders. Nothing like the loyalty of the brotherhood, right?" Drew clapped him on the back, and Nash's hackles rose.

"You can say that again," he said, through his teeth. "'Scuse me. My guest is waiting."

Where the hell is she?

HAD NASH REALLY thought they'd come here just to have a drink and keep an eye out for suspicious people? Geez. She was finally beyond the stone walls of Lionsgate's fortress, and she'd utilize every minute to her advantage. She smoothed her wig and adjusted her dress in the mirror. The stick up Nash's ass had grown exponentially the second she stepped out of the bedroom dressed and ready to go. His eyes had penetrated through her, hot enough to burn the material of her dress to ashes. And he'd looked good enough to eat in his black tuxedo and smoothed-back hair. It had taken all her resolve not to beg him to get inside her when he kissed her in the hallway.

She sighed and forced all sexual images from her mind. She had work to do. Turning from the marble vanity, she opened the restroom door and stepped out, expecting to find Nash waiting. Her gaze absorbed the room. She spotted Nash at the bar and stepped in his direction. Heat scorched her face as if someone was watching her.

Her skin prickled, and she turned her head toward a small table less than ten feet away. Leith was slouched against it, his hand closed around a glass. His bloodshot eyes drooped but didn't blink.

Her shoes planted to the floor as if someone had poured concrete over her feet. Every instinct screamed at her to get to Nash, but she couldn't tear her eyes from Leith. He either had the hots for her or he was on to them. Neither scenario was good.

His gaze tracked leisurely down her body and back up to settle on her chest. Disgust curdled the alcohol swimming in her stomach. She dragged her feet away from the floor and slammed against a solid chest. Her ankles wobbled in her spiky heels, but warm hands closed around her shoulders and steadied her.

"You okay?"

Nash's voice coated her, and immediately her tension oozed away. She tilted her head back and took in Nash's deep scowl.

"I'm fine." She'd tell him about the disgusting encounter with Leith as soon as they were out of range. She glanced over at the table—he was gone. She hooked her arm through Nash's and led him toward the exit. "Let's go."

Nash didn't move. Instead, he turned her in the direction of the heart of the club. "We can't leave that way. It will draw too much attention. There's some eyes on us that I want to lose, so let's go down to where the party is."

He guided her to the stairs and inched her in front of him, linking his fingers firmly in hers. A man moved past them on the stairs. He had a woman on each arm, and both wore outfits covering only the necessities. Nash's fingers squeezed hers, and a chuckle tickled her lips. He kept expecting her to be shocked, but the last thing she wanted was for him to think she was uptight in the bedroom.

At the bottom of the stairs, Nash pressed his hand into the small of her back. Couples gyrated on the dance floor to the beat of the strobe lights' flickering. She moved into a small break in the crowd and her eyes landed on a woman with her dress hiked up to her hips and her legs wrapped around a man's waist. She skidded to a stop and Nash bumped into her back. The woman's head dropped back on an earth-shattering moan, and Nash turned her away. His arm dropped over her shoulder and his chest shook against her.

She snapped her head up to him. "They were having sex," she hissed. "You think that's funny?"

He swiped his fingers over his mouth and continued to chuckle. "Nah, that's not funny. But seeing you glued in awe was." He stopped in the middle of the dance floor and turned her in his arms.

She rested her hands on either side of his waist and moved to the music. His hands coasted down her bare spine and landed just above her ass cheeks. Her skin burned with the need for him to roam further.

Stay focused, Lexi. He's trying to blend in.

She crooked her finger at him, and he lowered his ear to her mouth. "Whose eyes are you trying to escape?"

His chin moved so his mouth brushed the sensitive skin beneath her ear. "Drew. He cornered me while you were in the bathroom. I think you're right—he and Leith are spying on me for Conrad."

"Leith was staring at me when I came out of the bathroom. He gave me the creeps."

Nash jerked his head back, and his eyes locked with hers. "Did he say anything to you?"

She shook her head and trailed her hand up the side of his neck to bring his ear back down to her mouth. God, she just wanted him close to her. His heat, his scent, the constant caress of his fingers on her bare skin. Her nipples puckered beneath the material of her dress. His knee bumped between her thighs, sending a shockwave of desire through her.

She needed him.

But not here. Hell no, not here. She wanted him

naked and stretched out over top of her, his mouth on every inch of her body.

"Lexi?" He breathed against her. "What happened?"

Lord, she couldn't think. She sucked in a breath, hoping to clear her head, but all it did was intoxicate her with the scent of his lumberjack aftershave. If they didn't get done what they were here to do soon, she'd be in a puddle at his feet.

"Nothing. He was drunk and leering at me and then I bumped into you. He disappeared once you came."

Nash's fingers tensed on her back and his ab muscles flexed against her belly.

"Where can we get out that we won't be spotted?"

He pulled back just enough for her to see his face. Hard lines contoured the angles of his cheekbones. Her fingers tingled to drag her hand over the smooth skin, but she pressed her hand to his chest instead, savoring the heat pumping through his shirt.

"There's a set of doors on the east wall," he said, gesturing with his head. "That will take us to the basement. Conrad's office is two floors up."

"Are there any security cameras?"

He shook his head. "Not inside. They're all on the exterior of the building."

She scanned the dance floor. Thankfully, there was an abundance of bodies. People were crammed into every square foot of the space. She lifted her eyes to the second floor and searched the perimeter of the railing. Couples lingered, groping and making out, and the odd single person stared down. Her gaze stopped on the back of the leggy blonde's head. Facing her, Leith gripped the railing. The woman moved her mouth over the column of his throat, but Leith's eyes combed the dance floor.

Lexi pulled away and gripped Nash's sleeve. "Let's go." She tugged him through the sweaty clamor of bodies that pulsed in unison to the music.

God, how many people are having sex right here in front of us? She didn't want to find out. They reached the opposite side of the floor and Nash's palm draped around her hip. He led her to the door marked Exit and eased it open. Fluorescent light greeted them.

Nash stuck his head into the hall. "Clear," he said, and hustled her in front of him. She tucked her hand into his, and he strode toward a staircase at the end of the hall. "We need to move fast. If Ronnie sees that you're outside the White Room he'll throw us out—and it will raise a lot of attention."

The air in the basement was cool. The walls were long lines of concrete rather than drywall. She clenched Nash's hand. "Maybe we should investigate down here first."

Nash shook his head. "If you want to get into the office, we need to go now. People will be leaving soon to, uh, finish what they've started."

As they ascended the stairs, Lexi scoffed. "I didn't see anyone holding back."

"From what I've heard, the club is PG compared to what happens after." They reached the main level and rounded the banister to the second flight of stairs. "We're at the back of the House. There's no need for anyone to come back here except for rear parking. We'll look suspicious if we're found here. Go." He urged her up the stairs toward the dark hallway above. Nash's stride fell into step with hers when they reached the top, and he moved easily through the unlit corridor. He stopped at a large mahogany door and his hand closed around the handle. It didn't budge.

"He'd never leave it unlocked but worth checking." He let out a breath. "Shit, I don't have anything to pick the lock."

Lexi reached beneath her wig and pulled out a long bobby pin. She dropped to her knee, ignoring how her dress hiked further up her thighs, and inserted the pin into the lock. Nash rustled beside her, and the light on his phone flicked on, illuminating her handy work.

"I don't even want to ask how you know how to do that."

The handle clicked in her palm as the lock released. Satisfaction rippled through her. She looked up at him as she secured the pin back in her hair. "You're better off not knowing."

He grunted and pulled her to her feet. She circled her fingers around the smooth metal handle and swung the door open. Nash moved in behind her and shut the door. Darkness swallowed her up. Only a small beam of light escaped through the heavy drapes over the window. She stretched her hand along the wall, trying to find a switch, but Nash's fingers caught her wrist.

He switched on his phone's flashlight again. "We need to keep the light low so no one sees it under the door."

Ugh. She should have thought of that. She nodded and made her way to the oversized desk in the corner of the room. The chair was pulled out as if Conrad had just stood to leave for the day. Bookcases lined the wall behind it and a leather chair sat pushed away from the desk. She sank into the cool brown material and flicked on the computer.

Nash shone the light around the room and then swung it back to her. Shadows concealed most of his face. The computer screen came to life and the cursor flashed on the password ribbon.

"Any chance you know his password?"

Nash snorted. "Nope. And I wouldn't even know the first thing to guess."

She harrumphed and dropped her elbows onto the desk in front of the keyboard. What the hell was she doing? Nash was right, they weren't hackers. She could break into a locked room no problem, but getting through passwords was another story.

She lowered her head into her hands and massaged her temples with her thumbs. Brooks had been so damn certain the answers were close.

All you have to do is get the ledger—it's basically a decoding book.

She rolled her thumbs around and around. It didn't add up. Brooks was thorough as hell. If there had been even a possibility he was off about the ledger, he wouldn't have steered her in its direction. She'd read through the entire ledger on the flight to Portland, and it was far from a decoding book. It contained names, positions, ranks, rituals . . . and a coded sheet.

There was no way Brooks had been that far off target.

"What are you thinking?" Nash kneaded her shoulder with one hand. She sighed and pushed to her feet.

"It just doesn't make sense. The ledger was supposed to hold the answers and it doesn't. It's like a generic information sheet." She flicked her wrist and turned to the bookcase.

Nash chuckled. "To you, maybe. You saw what was going on down there. People don't outright associate themselves with Lionsgate. The members' privacy is a high priority for us." The light shone over her shoulder as she paced down the wall toward the window.

"Hell, people would kill if their corporations or businesses found out they were one of us."

"Given the allegations my brother has against Lionsgate, that's not surprising." The words came out harder than she'd intended. She stopped at the end of the bookcase, where two shelves held some large group pictures and a few awards.

She lifted one of the frames and held it under her nose. Conrad stood in front of a two-story building that looked like a school, a crowd of teenagers around him. His right hand hung protectively around a boy's shoulders, his left around a girl's. She stretched out her palm for Nash's phone and he dropped it into her hand. She directed its glow onto the boy's familiar face. Dark gray eyes stared back at her. His ebony hair reached his earlobes. Even at that age, his chest filled out his T-shirt and his deep, menacing scowl told a story of pain.

"That was my second year with Lionsgate Youth Center." His tone was hard.

An icy hand gripped her heart. *Youth Center* . . .

"Is it a foster home?"

Nash settled on the edge of the desk and shook his head. He held his phone between them. "More like a large group home."

She kept her gaze on the picture, afraid that if

she looked up she'd see a wall of despair. She'd pegged Nash as some troubled individual who'd gotten caught up with Lionsgate and had stayed for the money he made as an enforcer. She hadn't given any further thought to his background. That morning, he'd said Conrad was like his father, and she'd taken that to mean he was a close male figure. But maybe he was more than that.

"When you said Conrad was like your father—"

"He adopted me."

She snapped her head up and sucked in a breath through her lips. "But your last name is Holmes."

He nodded. "Yeah, I didn't want to give up the tie to my brothers."

"But why did he—"

Nash's hand covered the top of the frame. "We don't have enough hours to dig through my past. Let's finish up here and get home. Then we can talk about whatever you want." He set the picture back on the shelf. "I don't think there's much else we can look at in here, Lex. The safe is locked, his computer requires a password . . . I told you we should have left this to Cole."

"Let me at least look through his desk first." She pulled out the drawers and rummaged through thick binders full of accounting sheets and newsletters. Nash set the phone down on the edge of the desk so the light shone inside the drawer.

Her fingers grazed something leather. She pulled it out and tore the zipper open—a shaving kit.

Lord almighty, she was losing her edge. She dropped her head and Nash shifted next to her. "Satisfied?"

She ran her hand over the case, which was made of the same leather as the ledger's cover. Exact same shade of brown, cracked and worn, the Lionsgate emblem embossed on the front.

The air squeezed out of her lungs. "There's more than one," she wheezed.

"What?" Nash asked, leaning forward. She shot to her feet and tossed the case in the drawer. She gripped his elbow and bounced on her toes.

"There's more than one!"

Nash's lips thinned into a slow smile. "Shaving kit? I'm sure there is—"

"No! Ledger. There's more than one. There has to be." She turned around behind the chair and paced the length of the bookcase. "Think about it. Why would they keep everything in one book and one book only? First of all, they'd never be able to fit it all. Second, they wouldn't want every member to have access to all of the information."

She spun around to face him and spread her palms in the air. Nash squinted with skepticism. "I don't know, babe. I've been with Lionsgate half my life and I've never heard of there being more than one ledger."

"But you've never heard of them trafficking children either."

"Which we don't know for certain is true," he shot back.

She growled. "Maybe there aren't a dozen more, but maybe there's one. Conrad's."

Nash shrugged. "You could be right. But why would he care if you had mine? If its contents are so irrelevant that he keeps the real shit in a separate one, why go to such great lengths to get it?"

She dug her teeth into her bottom lip. "Okay, maybe that doesn't add up, but maybe it was never about the ledger. Maybe he just used that to get everyone after what he really wanted."

Nash folded his arms over his chest. "And that is?"

"Me. Dead."

Nash leaned his hip against the desk and tucked the corner of his mouth in. Several beats passed. She was right about this. There was no doubt in her mind.

Slowly, his head moved. "You could be right."

She closed in on him. "I *am* right. Let's go. We need to formulate a plan to get a hold of the other book." She strode to the door with Nash at her heels. He reached his arm past her, pulled the door open, twisted the lock on the inside so the door would lock when they closed it, and ushered her into the hall.

She slapped her palm against his chest before he crossed the threshold. "The chair," she whispered. Nash grunted, turned back into the room, and pulled out the chair to where it had been when they came in.

A strong, hard arm came down across her chest and propelled her backward into the dark mouth of the hall. She tried to scream, but all that came out of her restricted airways was a squeak. Hot breath hissed at her ear and a sharp blade pressed against her throat. Her stomach punched against her ribs. She clawed at the suit-covered wrists, and the man's hold tightened with the force of a boa constrictor.

"Don't fucking move."

CHAPTER 17

L EXI'S HIGH-PITCHED SQUEAK froze Nash in place. He snapped his gaze to the doorway just as an arm yanked her out of view. His heart plummeted.

No!

He bolted for the door and raised his phone. The beam caught her stark white face. Her lush pink lips were the color of her ashen skin and her ocean blue eyes were wide, the dark liner around them making the whites that much bolder. Her chest rose and fell sharply.

He tore his gaze from her face and locked it on Leith's. Rancor shot through his veins, hot and wild. The only thing keeping him from closing the five feet of distance between them and ripping the bastard's throat out was the fact that Leith had a long switchblade pressed against the soft skin over Lexi's jugular.

Nash's Beretta sat cozily at the small of his back, but there was no way he'd be able to grab it and get a shot off before Leith swiped his blade across her throat.

Sweat collected between his shoulder blades. *Think, Nash. Think.*

"What are you doing, Leith?" He let the words leak through his teeth. His face burned under Lexi's terrified gaze, but he couldn't for the life of him look at her. If he did, he'd lose it. "Put the fucking knife down and I won't gut the shit out of you."

Sweat poured down Leith's red cheeks. His lips parted on a drunken snarl, revealing the ridges of his yellow teeth. His brown hair stuck out in all directions.

"You think I don't know this is *her*? You're a traitor. Conrad's going to slaughter you."

Flashes of white exploded in front of Nash's vision, and he bunched his hand into a fist. He couldn't snap. Not while Lexi's life hung in Leith's clutches. He finally lowered his eyes to Lexi, and his fury melted into panic. Tears glistened in the corners of her eyes and she batted them away.

He was fucking helpless. If he moved an inch, Leith would kill her.

Leith took a step back toward the rear of the hall. "This ends here." As Leith's elbow twitched, Nash lunged forward. The phone fell from his fingers and bounced at his feet. A cloak of darkness dropped around them.

He wrapped his hand around Leith's forearm and jerked the knife away from Lexi's throat. She bucked, and Leith's hold broke.

Lexi catapulted against the wall, and Nash twisted Leith's wrist until something popped beneath his hold. Leith cried out and the knife landed on the floor with a soft thud. Lexi's soft pants filled his ears and a second later the light returned. The beam shook more than the strobe lights downstairs.

Nash slipped his hand underneath Leith's chin and twisted it sharply. Bone cracked. The man's body went limp.

Lexi's soft cry penetrated the dark fog that had closed around him. Shame burned his hand, and he released Leith. His body crumpled to the floor like a discarded gym towel.

Nash turned, his chest jerking with every breath he dragged into his lungs. Lexi sat on the floor, her legs bent beneath her, both hands holding his phone as if it took the greatest effort in the world.

But it was her eyes that ripped his chest apart—dark makeup circled them. Barely tampered terror lit her irises, but at the same time laced with concern for his safety. Tears streaked down her cheeks. Her chin quivered and her shoulders shook. He dropped to his knees and extended his hands, but his muscles twitched with hesitancy. He'd just killed a man in cold blood while she watched.

She didn't pull away. The phone slipped from

her fingers, and she threw her arms around his neck and buried her face in his shoulder. A tidal wave of relief washed over him. He dropped his nose to her hair and locked her in his hold.

"Baby, are you hurt?"

She sucked in a deep, shuddering breath against his neck and shook her head. "N–no."

He smoothed his hands down her spine, but her tremors didn't stop. If Leith hadn't been so drunk, his reflexes would have been quicker. If Nash had been a millisecond slower . . . If—

"Can we get out of here?" she said, her voice rising to a near hysterical octave.

He held her to his chest as he stood. "You're damn right we can." He bent to pick up his phone and shined the light over her. He lifted his thumb and smoothed it over the tracks of mascara on her cheeks.

She sniffed. "I'm probably a mess."

His lips tugged into a smile. "Definitely not your best, but still beautiful. Keep your head down and hang tight to me. If you can sway like you're drunk, even better."

She chortled. "I don't think that will be a problem." He pocketed his phone, tucked her beneath his arm, and led her toward the stairs. Her head swiveled to look behind them. "What about—"

"Don't worry about it."

"Do you think they'll know . . . ?"

"Doesn't matter." One thing was for sure: he

wasn't about to waste time moving Leith's body. The last thing he needed was to bump into someone while a dead brother hung in his arms. He'd be burned at the fucking stake.

He turned down the wide hall toward the main entrance and Lexi wobbled dutifully next to him. She kept her chin tucked low, and her temple rested against his side. To onlookers, she'd appear wasted.

Robbie stood at the door. It appeared as if he hadn't moved since they entered. "Have a nice evening," Robbie said, his eyes sliding appreciatively over Lexi.

"I plan to." Nash grinned and nodded in acknowledgment. "I'll be hitting the gym tomorrow. See you there."

Robbie pulled open the door, and Nash guided Lexi slowly down the stone steps. The hair on the back of his neck prickled. He waited for a scream, a bullet, an attack. But it didn't come. They rounded the vine-covered wrought-iron gate and Nash fished his keys from his pocket.

Lexi's body stirred against his. "I didn't think we'd make it out," she said softly. He punched the unlock button and his truck beeped in response. Then he pulled open the passenger door and gripped Lexi's hips to lift her into her seat.

Her hand closed over his wrist. "Nash, I'm fine." Her shoulders straightened and her shaky lips firmed. Respect pounded into his chest. She'd nearly had her throat slit only minutes before and had witnessed him murder someone, yet she claimed to be fine.

"If you're all right, then you have bigger balls than I do." He hoisted her into the seat, clicked the belt into place across her hips, and then rounded the vehicle.

"That's very possible, you know," she said, as he slammed his door shut and settled into the seat. A laugh rumbled in his throat. He fit the key into the ignition and fastened his belt into place.

"I won't argue with you there." He pulled away from the curb. A light rain fell—typical February weather for Seattle. A chill had settled in the air, and the cool leather made the bite that much chillier. Lexi's teeth chattered. He turned the seat warmer and heat on. "Seriously, though, are you all right? Because I'm still shaken."

She tucked her arms across her chest and her body trembled. She put on a tough front, but there was no way shock wasn't settling in.

"I'm okay. Just cold, I think."

He reached out and covered her thigh with his palm. His skin reveled in the silkiness of hers as he stroked his thumb over the top of her leg. "We'll get you warm as soon as we get home."

She dropped her head back against the seat and pressed her legs together, locking his fingers between her flesh. God, he wanted to get her warm in the best way he knew how.

"That sounds nice." Her voice trailed off, heavy with sleep.

His chest constricted. He moved his tongue over the backs of his teeth. He couldn't leave unsaid what needed to be said. He couldn't assume she was completely unaffected by seeing that side of him. Dammit, it cut him to the core that she might think of him as a monster.

"About what happened, Lex—"

Her hand covered his. "You don't need to explain."

"Yeah, I do." The words came out gruff and more pained than he'd wanted. "He knew about you. I couldn't chance letting him go. He'd only come after you again."

Her fingers dragged over the backs of his knuckles. "I know." A beat passed. "It startled me. I've never seen anyone do what you did, but you didn't have much choice. I'm a little less critical than I might usually be, considering he was seconds away from cutting my throat."

Nash's pulse beat into his temples. The memory of that moment, of being so fucking close to losing her, was one he'd never be able to unlatch from his brain. Given the chance, he'd do what he'd done to Leith again to spare her life.

They rode the rest of the way in silence. Her body sunk deeper and deeper into the leather seat. Once they were back in his garage, Lexi's tanned, lean legs slipped out of his truck as he rounded the hood. He hit the garage door button and the steel rattled as it slid to a close. She fell into step behind him as he dug the key into the lock and swung the door open.

He kicked off his shoes but kept his gaze on her back as she moved down the hall toward the kitchen. She tangled her hands in the base of the wig and pulled it off, shaking her dark locks free. Her warm, natural brown hair swarmed her back.

Desire burned through him.

He opened and closed his hands at his sides and mimicked her route. She stood at the kitchen island and gripped the granite counter. After propping her ankle up on her thigh, she tugged off her high heel then repeated the motion on the other foot. Nash's footsteps slowed as he closed the distance between them. His pulse dropped to a low, gentle hum. His breath was trapped in his lungs, and tension hardened every muscle in his body.

His dick had it the worst. It pulsed in the confinement of his pants and his fingers tingled with the need to peel her scant dress away from her body. She tucked her hair behind her ear and turned her face to his. He locked his hands on her hips and lifted her to the kitchen counter. She gasped, and the sharp parting of her lips drove his lust wild. She gripped his forearms, and her wide eyes searched his face. Her warm breath swirled in the air between them as he settled himself between her parted knees. Her hands coasted up his arms, her hold tightening as she skimmed over his biceps. His body vibrated beneath her touch. Her eyes never strayed from his. Big, blue, and round, they bore through him, tearing apart whatever guard he'd had around his heart and sinking their teeth into his soul.

"I never want you to be in that position again."

Her eyebrows sewed themselves together. "What do you mean?"

"He could have killed you." The words sucked the breath from his lungs. "And I never want you to see me do what I did again." Anger rattled his voice, and if it weren't for the gentle drift of her fingers over his shoulders, his blood would have simmered.

She secured her hands behind his neck and leaned closer. "Nash." Her lips moved luxuriously over his name. "I want you."

He weaved his hand into her hair, cupped the back of her neck, and secured his mouth over hers.

LEXI DUG HER fingertips into the corded muscles at the back of Nash's neck, pulling him closer, wanting every inch of him against her. His palm was warm against her neck, and he tilted her head, urging her back into an arch so he could delve his tongue deeper into her mouth. Her senses ricocheted against each other and her toes lifted.

She pressed her breasts against the starched

white shirt of his tuxedo. Too much material stood in her way. She lowered her hands from his neck and worked on the buttons at his chest. His tongue licked over hers and a deep throb began between her legs. His hands roamed down her back, settling on her ass. A low moan rumbled from his throat. He pulled his mouth away and her lips ached with his absence. His breath came out in heavy puffs as he ripped off his bowtie and undid the first two buttons that she'd missed.

"Upstairs," he breathed. She wiggled to the edge of the counter, but Nash gripped her thighs and pulled her legs around his waist, his palms supporting her weight. He strode to the stairs and his fingers traveled beneath her dress as he ascended. His thumb hooked into her thong and her muscles tensed. A giggle caught her throat and she squirmed.

"Nash," she wheezed.

"Mmm . . ." He nuzzled his mouth against the skin beneath her ear and kicked the bedroom door open. Moonlight shone through the open blinds into the otherwise dark room. He lowered her onto the bed and the cool cotton cover chilled her flaming skin. Nash straightened and shed the rest of his shirt. His fingers went to the button on his pants and then he eased them down. His rock-hard cock jutted under the material of his black briefs. His eyes, searing coals, bore down into hers. Her breath hitched in her chest and her fingers went to the neckline of her dress. She shrugged out of the material, exposing one breast. She trailed her finger in a circle over her nipple with her fingertip, bringing the pink flesh into a tight, hard nub.

A dark stain crept across Nash's cheekbones. He jammed his thumbs in his briefs and chucked them aside. His dick stuck out from his body, thick, long, and pulsing. *God, he's hung.* Her mouth went dry and the heat between her legs turned to moisture. Lexi ached, needing him inside her.

She stretched a hand toward him and he dropped to his knees on the bed. His hands sought the straps of her dress and he tugged the material down her chest and over her hips. His lips hardened, resembling slate. He glided his fingers from her knees and over the tops of her thighs until his thumbs joined at the apex of her legs.

"God, you're gorgeous," he growled. She burrowed her heels into the mattress to keep her legs from trembling.

"You are," she said softly. He pressed his cheek to her kneecap and chuckled, his laugh deep and rough.

"Not like what I'm seeing." The edges of his thumbs slid beneath the triangle of panty that shielded her, and his teeth sunk into the sensitive skin above her knee. "You're going to have to lose this, babe." He crept his fingertips under the waistband, and she lifted her hips. He slid the thong to her knees and then lifted each leg to peel the lace from her ankles.

Her wet, swollen lips throbbed with anticipation. Moonlight caught his olive skin, and his eyes searched hers as he eased his palms between her thighs. Her knees came apart wantonly easily. His mouth lifted with satisfaction. He pressed his lips to the inside of her thigh, his eyes never leaving her face. She twisted the blanket at her sides and watched, riveted, as he kissed his way up.

Her chest ached with the need for breath, but she couldn't force air into her mouth. He nestled his hands on the insides of her thighs and spread them further apart. She squeezed her eyes shut. Nash's hot breath on her throbbing folds stilled the air in her lungs.

"Look at me, Lex."

She finally inhaled and then lifted her eyelids.

"Don't take your eyes off me," he ordered. She swallowed and nodded vigorously. He hovered scant inches away from her sex. Need exploded inside her. She'd agree to anything to get him to continue. He smirked, and his eyes blazed into hers as he lowered his mouth to her clit. The scorching heat jerked every muscle in her body. She gasped and twisted the covers as his tongue slid lazily between her folds.

"Ah, god," she cried. Her eyes rolled back to stare at the dark ceiling, but his hands flexed on her hips.

"At me, Lex."

She sucked in one breath after another as she lowered her gaze to meet his. His tongue pressed harder against her and her knees fell farther open, her body allowing him deeper access. His fingers kneaded the flesh of her ass as he situated his hands underneath her and tilted her hips back, thrusting her sex higher in the air for his attention.

Warmth spread through her loins as his tongue trailed over her. Her blood thundered through her skull and pleasure tingled her nerve endings. On the brink of an orgasm, she gasped and her hips jerked.

"Nash, I need you—now."

His mouth left her, and he crawled up the length of her body. His cock probed her opening, and she fit her hand between his groin and hers and guided him inside her. His head entered through her folds and then pressed deep into her. Her legs spread wider, welcoming every inch of him. She cried out as he filled her. A deep, guttural groan vibrated through his chest. He braced himself on his elbow, shifting his weight so he didn't press down on her wound, and his free hand cupped her cheek. His mouth connected with hers, and his tongue sank between her lips. Her own scent filled her senses, sending her to the brink of eroticism. She dragged her hands over the unyielding muscles of his back, marveling in the thickly stacked brawn beneath his skin.

He plunged into her and her insides tightened around him. He moaned, and then his mouth moved to trail kisses down her jaw. She hooked her ankles around his waist and clung to his shoulders as he slid the length of his member in and out of her. The pleasure built, lifting her consciousness from the bed to teeter on the edge of oblivion. He rocked his hips against hers, bringing all his focus to her clit. A cry split her throat, and she thrust her hips against his, taking more and more.

An explosion of color burst behind her eyelids, and she screamed as she rode wave after wave of her orgasm. Her breath came out in sharp pants as her body jerked around his thrusts. Every ridge of his body turned to steel as he ground himself into her. His cock grew thicker against her walls.

"Lexi. Christ," he panted against her earlobe. He pumped harder and his heat filled her. His body molded to hers and his teeth caught her lip. Her senses fizzed as he grinded slowly inside her. Finally, he let her lip go, dropped his nose to her throat, and inhaled. "God, you feel so good."

She chuckled and dragged her hand through his hair. "Likewise."

He lifted his chin and met her gaze. "I didn't hurt you, did I?"

She trailed her palm down the curve of his jaw and let her thumb roam over his bottom lip. "Not at all."

"Your stitches are okay?"

She nodded, but her body still rode on gusts of ecstasy so she probably wouldn't feel if they hurt.

He nipped the pad of her thumb. "Good. Let's shower." He slid away and pulled her to her feet.

Her cheeks warmed, and she let him tug her to the bathroom. His eyes sparked at her and her belly tingled—that look meant he wasn't done. A thrill raced through her. She could get used to this.

CHAPTER 18

SUNLIGHT STREAMED THROUGH the open blinds. Nash squinted and looked at the clock on the nightstand. Nearly 7:00 a.m. Much later than he usually slept, but then, he didn't normally have sex three times a night.

He dragged his knuckles over the curve of Lexi's hip bone and arousal pulsed through him again. She squirmed and sighed then nudged her face deeper against his chest.

He grinned and stilled his hand. She needed sleep, and he'd be sure she got a little more if it killed him. Sex with Lexi had been everything he'd expected and more. He couldn't get enough of her. The way she screamed his name and her legs shook as her orgasm built. The way she stared up at him after, her mouth pink and swollen, her hair matted to her temples.

Christ, he could look at her like that every day.

Her knee inched over his thigh and her hand moved from his chest to rub her eyes. She titled her head back and looked at him. A slow blush spread across her cheekbones as she smiled.

"Morning," he said, as he laced his fingers with hers. Her chuckle jiggled her satiny breast against his side, and he dropped her hand to cup the milky silk singeing his skin. He grazed his thumb over her hardening nipple.

Her laughter turned throaty. "I hate to break this to you, but I'm going to need some time to regroup."

He nodded at the clock. "It's been four hours."

She shifted so her head lay on the pillow next to his. He kept his hand on her breast, but she didn't protest. "Give me eight more."

He tugged her nipple between his thumb and forefinger. "Get dressed then," he said teasingly. "Or I won't make it eight minutes."

She swatted his chest. He caught her hand and kissed her palm. Her fingers trailed over his scruff and her eyes darkened. A warning bell sounded in his head.

"What's wrong?"

She shook her head but kept her gaze on his jaw. When he squeezed her hand, she lifted her chin. The morning sun caught the green hue in her aqua eyes. This close, he could also see the small, yellow striations in her irises. A muscle in his chest squeezed. Of all the things that attracted him to Lexi, her eyes had been the first.

"I just keep thinking about that picture in Conrad's office." She flopped onto her back and twirled a lock of hair around her finger. "How long has he owned the group home?"

Fuck. He didn't want to talk about those days. They were so far in the past, yet every time a memory surfaced, he was back in that small, sobbing six-year-old's body.

"I think it was opened in the late seventies. Why?"

She shook her head and kept her eyes focused on the ceiling. Her mouth puckered with concentration. "Why did he adopt you?"

Nash exhaled through his nose and turned to his side, propping his head on his fist. Last night, he'd promised that he'd tell her whatever she wanted to know. Now, she was collecting. Better to get it over with.

"He doesn't have much to do with the group home now, but back then he visited often. I was always trying to run away, and I guess that put me on his radar. He decided to mentor me, and we hung out twice a week and hit it off. It wasn't long before I was spending so much time with him that it just made sense for me to move in with him. Later, he adopted me."

She turned to look at him, her gaze soft and hesitant. "He was good to you?" The vanilla scent of her hair, which fanned across the white pillowcase, flooded his nostrils, reminding him of their shower the previous night—of her wet, soapy body. She raised her eyebrows in question.

He cleared his throat. "Yeah, he was good to me. I mean, he was a good role model. At least I thought so until recently."

"What happened to your parents?"

And there was the question he'd been dreading. Fuck, he hated thinking about his childhood. Hated the feeling of helplessness that came along with being dragged back to memories of that hell. He summoned the steely armor that he'd worn for so long.

"I have no idea what happened to them. The day my dad brought us to the group home, he sat in his truck and ordered us all out. Told us to go inside because we were going to play there for the day."

Lexi's focus moved over his face, and her chest stopped its gentle rise and fall. She fit her hand into his and traced his knuckle with her thumb. "What happened?"

"My brothers ran inside and I stood there like a wimp, sobbing. Call it instinct, call it a prediction based on his parenting style, but I knew he wasn't coming back." He clenched his jaw. He'd never told the story before, but fuck, it had happened twenty-seven years ago. He shouldn't be choked up. Nothing upset him anymore.

Lexi turned on her side to face him and cupped his cheek. "I'm so sorry. You were so young . . ."

"He screamed at me to back up when I grabbed onto the window of his truck. Then he peeled away from the curb and flicked his cigarette butt out the window."

Lexi cursed and pulled his face toward her. He rubbed his cheek over the soft skin of her neck, breathing in her natural flowery fragrance.

"I'm fine, babe. It was a long time ago." He forced a tone of amusement, but the trauma still plagued him. Her fingers ran against his scalp. Their slow, constant comfort brought his breath to an even rhythm.

"I'm so glad you had your brothers with you and you didn't get split up."

He grunted. "I didn't end up at the group home until years later. We were separated a few days after my dad dropped us off. Then we were bounced around to different foster homes. Once Cole and his twin, Dallas, turned eighteen, they got their own place."

"Cole has a twin?"

"Yeah, he and Dallas are the closest. I think they carry a lot of guilt over my and Dare's childhood."

She pulled away. "How many siblings do you have?"

His lips twitched. It was no wonder they'd had a hell of a time holding down a foster home. "Three. Dare is in the middle, he's thirty-five. Cole and Dallas, the twins, are thirty-seven. I'm the youngest. He ran away and moved in with the twins, but by that time I'd met Conrad and he convinced me that an extra mouth was a lot for two eighteen-year-olds to care for. And he was right. I stayed close with them, though. Conrad always encouraged that."

"I'm glad he wasn't as terrible back then as he is now." The skin around her eyes creased, and he almost groaned. He knew another question was coming. "You never saw your parents after that? They never looked for you?"

He lifted his shoulder. "I don't think there was much remorse on their end. My dad was an alcoholic and beat the shit out of my mom. Once my brothers and I got old enough, we tried to put an end to that." He toyed with the skin on her shoulder. Another memory, the one that cut through his soul the deepest, burned his tongue.

"Nash?"

He closed his eyes. "I saw her . . . my mom . . . when I was about twelve. I was walking home from school and saw the back of her head and I just . . . I knew without a doubt it was her." Her matted dark brown hair had trailed out behind her, over the hood of the dark green winter coat she'd had since he was a kid. Six years of foster homes had hardened him, but the sight of her had kicked him in the gut and turned him back into that sobbing little boy.

"I ran after her screaming 'Mom!'" He chuckled at his naivety. She hadn't slowed down, but she'd hunched into her coat. Still, he'd chased her screaming. "She turned down an alley and I followed her."

He'd never forget the last look from her—the one image that replaced every other picture of her in his mind. "She stopped in her tracks and looked over her shoulder. A big, black bruise circled her eye. Her eyes were the same crystal-clear blue . . ." And in that moment, her emotion had flashed at him. Pain, regret—and anger. "Her cold stare crushed me, and I just dropped to my knees in the alley." His mouth twisted wryly, and he kept his gaze on the sheet, not wanting to see pity in Lexi's eyes. Despite how many years had passed, the memory was so damn vivid. Hell, he could even feel the second-hand cotton pants he'd worn soaking in the murky alley. "One tear slid over her cheek, and she turned and walked away."

He drew a breath into his tight lungs, and his chest ached with the invasion. "I guess that part hurts the most. Knowing she wasn't a complete monster. That she felt something." He shrugged. "And then she was gone." His mouth quirked. "I never told anyone that. Not even my brothers."

He finally looked at Lexi. Tears soaked her cheeks, and the tip of her nose matched the redness around her eyes. "Babe," he croaked.

She swiped a palm over her lids. "I'm fine. I just, god, it kills me. How could she?" The last word came out on a rasp, and he pulled her to him.

"She couldn't help it. Looking back on it now, I think she ran because she was ashamed of what she'd done. She didn't have answers for me and couldn't give me what I needed from her."

"But you were just a child."

He curled his fingers around a fistful of Lexi's hair, wishing he could have censored the story for her. But wouldn't have been able to. For some godforsaken reason, he couldn't hold back from her.

"Yeah, but I think in a way, she thought she was protecting me from the sick relationship she had with my dad and the conditions they were living in." That possibility made a hard ball of pain form in his chest. Never in all these years had he looked at it that way.

Lexi pulled away, and her wet, clumped-together lashes lifted. "I'm so sorry."

"Don't be. I'm not. I have good memories too. Most of them are of my brothers, but I remember things like snuggling in bed with her and the way she always pushed my hair away from my forehead. Even when she was bent out of shape from fighting with my dad, or pissed at me for not listening for the millionth time, she'd push my hair back. It's funny how things like that stick."

"She loved you."

Some of the numbness that always settled over him when he thought about his mom thawed. Dammit, he didn't want to feel. Didn't want to think about what could have been. "Yeah." The word leaked through his lips, and Lexi brushed her mouth over his. He caught the back of her head before she could pull away and locked his forehead with hers. "As difficult as it is for me to talk about this shit, thank you."

Her shoulders lifted. "I didn't do anything, but I'm glad if I was able to help."

She'd done more than help. Her gentle prying and genuine care for the young, wounded boy inside him had begun a healing journey he'd never realized he needed.

In one week, she had changed him beyond recognition.

★ ★ ★

LEXI LACED HER fingers together and stretched her hands in front of the glowing laptop screen. A ripple of excitement tingled her fingertips. She'd missed this. The months she'd been covering Lionsgate had been so stressful, and she'd been so personally invested in the story, that she'd forgotten how much she loved her work. Piecing together puzzles and unearthing criminals was not only her career, but her favorite past time. Her mind went to Nash's wandering fingers and mouth on her body. Make that second favorite pastime.

She stuck the thumb drive Brooks had given her into the computer and everything around her fell away. Except Nash, who sat slightly behind her.

His warm breath stirred the hair at the back of her neck. At any other moment she'd have been turned on, but right now, she couldn't drag her attention away from the little window that had popped up. She selected "Download Files" and sat back.

"This is what he left behind for you?"

His chest crowded her back, and she turned in her chair to face him. "Yeah. Remember I told you how he called me the night of the fire? He told me that if anything happened to him, I should go to our favorite spot when we were kids."

Nash's brows twitched. "Where's that?"

"We used to hang out in the forest near our house. There was this huge oak tree with a large knot," she said, making a circle the size of a baseball with her hands. "Inside was a ledge. We used to hide things in there and leave notes and treasures for each other." The memory hitched her lips into a smile. "I went there and found the thumb drive in a baggie. No note—he wouldn't have chanced tying me to anything that could endanger me."

The computer dinged, and she turned back around. "Now let's see what he left me."

Nash shifted closer. "You mean you haven't looked at it after all this time?"

She snorted. "Of course I have. But I don't know what a lot of it means." She brought the cursor to the first file and double-clicked. A spreadsheet opened, and she squinted at the screen.

It had been a few weeks since she last pored over the contents of the drive, waiting for something to jump out at her.

"See this," she said, pointing to the first column. "*M* and *F* must stand for *Male* and *Female*. And here"—she touched the one beside it—"looks like ages. They're all between eight and fifteen."

"Let me see that." Nash took the mouse and scrolled. There were more than three hundred cells that dated back ten years.

"If this is what you think it is, then where's the—"

She bumped his hand away from the mouse and slid the page left. "The price is right here."

Nash's breath wheezed through his teeth next to her ear. "Holy fucking shit."

"My thoughts exactly. Who has that kind of money? Look at this, the one aged nine—130 grand."

Nash shoved away. The desk rattled with the force of his movement. He paced back and forth in front of the bed. "Jesus," he muttered. She swiveled in the chair to face him. His hand rested on the back of his neck, his gaze glued to the floor.

"I know. It's disturbing. That's why we need to—"

"What part are you confused about? You said you didn't know what a lot of it means."

She gestured for him to come back to the chair next to her. He moved closer but shook his head.

"I can't sit right now, babe. Just show me." His face was dark, almost crimson. He curled his fingers around her chair and the one he'd vacated.

She brought the sleeping screen back to life. "There are two things. Here," she said, highlighting one of the middle columns. "These numbers. This one is twelve digits and I can't figure out what it means. I didn't see these numbers in your ledger, so I don't think they're assigned to any members in particular. What we're missing is buyer information. I feel like this is the clue to that, but I can't for the life of me figure out how."

"And the other thing?"

She went back to the list of files and opened another spreadsheet. "This has the same long number from the other spreadsheet, but it also has this." She highlighted the last column. "See these weird symbols? It's some kind of encryption. We need a legend to crack what this means."

"Can you email this to Cole? He's already doing some hacking. It might help if he has this and comes across any of these numbers."

She straightened and pulled up her email. "That's brilliant." She attached the file and let Nash plug in Cole's email address.

"Now what?"

Nash closed the laptop. "I've got a very important person to talk to."

"ALL RIGHT. GET into as many servers as you can. If Lexi is right about this, it won't be easy to nail." Nash dropped the phone into the cupholder between them, as they sat parked out front of Gage's school. Lexi curled her hand over his.

"How long will it take Cole and Dare to hack into Conrad's systems?" The heat of Nash's fingers penetrated her chilled flesh. She dragged her gaze up the length of his arm, and its girth made the muscles in her throat clench. Dark stubble shaded his jaw, and his eyes stayed focused on the windshield. Cold, hard, determined. Yet so sexy.

He lifted his shoulder. "Could be hours, could be days."

She nodded slowly. She knew all too well how time consuming it could be to dig for information. She'd never been able to hack, but it was probably a hell of a lot more tedious than spying and pulling information out of people. "We need to get into Conrad's house. We should go during the day while he's out."

Nash shook his head. "No way. He always has staff there during the day. Our best shot is to arrange a meeting with him."

She stretched her eyebrows. "How is that a good idea?"

"He won't expect it. I just haven't figured out how I'm going to chat with him and then sneak into his quarters to snoop."

Lexi frowned. "How is that a problem? You

meet with him and I'll do what I do best: snoop and steal."

"Absolutely not."

Lexi was about to protest, but Nash flicked his attention to the large red brick building. This was an argument to have later. "Does Gage know we're here?" Nash had told her that he needed to see the adolescent boy he mentored. If there was anything fishy going on with other mentors, Gage might be aware of it.

"No. I couldn't risk calling him. I doubt any-one would think he's helping me, but I don't want to get him on Conrad's radar. Besides, who knows what shit the brothers have told him about me."

"Has he tried to reach you?"

"Not since I texted him from Moscow. I bailed on our weekly get-together because I had to chase you halfway across the world." His forehead crinkled with annoyance but his tone rang with humor.

"You mean after I seduced and drugged you?" she said matter-of-factly.

"You're not going to let me live that down, are you?"

She stuck her tongue between her teeth. "Nope."

The school's bell pierced the air, and she turned her face toward the building. A group of middle-school-aged kids in various-colored hoodies and saggy jeans walked out of the main entrance and headed down the long, broken walkway that led from the school to the sidewalk. A flood of other students followed. Hoots and hollers filled the air as the kids escaped for lunch.

Nash laid on the horn, and a few of the kids stopped and spun around. Recognition crossed one of the boys' face, and his hard, sullen glare turned up into a wide smile. His brown hair curled around the edges of the red cap he wore backward. A cigarette dangled from his fingers, and he dropped it to the cement and crushed it beneath his black running shoes. He separated from his pack of friends, who continued down the sidewalk.

"That's him?"

Nash unbuckled his seatbelt. "Yeah. Stay here, okay? He doesn't do well meeting new people. I won't be too long, but I need to catch up with him."

Lexi leaned forward and cranked up the heat. Gray clouds hovered low, but at least it wasn't raining. "He looks happy to see you. Take your time."

Nash gave her fingers a squeeze and slipped out the door. Gage met him in front of the truck and Nash folded him into a hug then pulled away and flattened his palm on the top of the boy's head. Gage ducked, adjusted his cap, and met Lexi's gaze through the windshield. His eyes sparked with curiosity, but he followed Nash to a bench beneath a tree on the school's property.

Lexi's insides contracted with admiration. Nash had once been a dark, dangerous stranger. Now, he was fully on her side. Whatever Lionsgate was into, Nash cared.

They wouldn't get away with what they'd done.

CHAPTER 19

"WHEN DID YOU start smoking?" Nash battled to keep his cool. He'd smoked as a teen until Dallas caught him and whooped his ass. He'd never touched a cigarette again. But the same tactic wouldn't work on Gage. As close as he was with him, in situations like this, Nash struggled to reach him in ways that weren't too parental. If he started coming down on the kid, Gage might stop confiding in him. And that was the last thing he needed.

Gage stretched his legs out in front of him. The sneakers Nash had bought him for his birthday were already scuffed to shit. But Nash didn't care about that.

"I just have a drag every once in a while." Gage shoved his hands into the pockets of his hoodie and nodded toward the truck parked at the curb. "Who's the woman?"

Best to drop the smoking conversation. If there was one thing Nash learned from mentoring Gage over the past four years, it was to follow the kid's lead and pick his battles.

"That's, uh . . ." *Shit.*

Gage slid his feet closer to the bench and sat up. "Is that her? Word is she died." His brown eyes brightened with more interest than Nash had seen in him since he turned fourteen and learned somewhere that it wasn't cool to show your emotions.

"What word? What have you heard?"

"Jimmy told Mike that you ran off with some woman who was trying to ruin Conrad's reputation."

Nash rested his elbows on his knees and laced his fingers together. At least they'd censored it for the kids, but there was a hell of a lot more to the story. Shit he couldn't risk disclosing to Gage. Not with the chance of endangering him.

"Did Jimmy say anything else?" Jimmy was a fellow mentor within Lionsgate—one Nash sparred with almost every weekend at the gym. Fuck, he was losing everyone on the inside who'd once respected him. He didn't give a shit what people thought of him, but he could really use the allies right now.

Gage shook his head. "No. Just to let him know if I hear from you." He grinned. "Don't worry, I'm not stupid. I know they're lying about you. I just don't understand why."

Nash sighed. "It's complicated. There's some shit going on with Lionsgate and I'm trying to get to the bottom of it."

Gage looked at his feet and dragged his toe in the dirt. Nash's senses prickled. Whenever Gage had something going on, something he needed to talk about, he withdrew.

"What is it, Gage? Do you know something?"

The boy frowned but didn't look up. "No." His hands shifted in his pockets and he leaned closer to Nash, his gaze still riveted on his feet. Nash opened and closed his fists, waiting. "I mean, I'm not sure."

Nash inhaled a deep breath of the moist air and fought for a light tone. "How about you tell me what's on your mind and we'll go from there?"

A beat pulsed between them and Gage nodded. "Yeah, okay." He shifted to meet Nash's stare. "I've noticed some strange things at the group home."

"Like what?"

Gage lifted his shoulder and squinted toward the street. Nash didn't follow his gaze. If it landed on Lexi, he'd lose his train of thought.

"I dunno. About a month ago, a girl my age was placed with a foster home."

The angst that had built in Nash's chest eased. "Yeah? That's a good thing." Nash bumped his knee against Gage's. "But?"

Gage grimaced. "Allison was super friendly and had one of those bubbly personalities. I've talked to her a lot since she came to stay with us last summer." A hint of pink crept under Gage's eyes. Any other time, Nash would have ribbed him about having a crush, but not now.

"She was here one day and gone the next. The only explanation was that she'd been adopted but she would have told me or at least said goodbye. I asked Rene if I could stay in touch with Allison, and she said the family didn't want her in contact with anyone." Gage shrugged again.

Nash's nerve endings prickled. Rene was in charge of admittances and discharges in the group home.

"It's stupid. I shouldn't have—"

Nash gripped his knee. "No, it's not stupid. We have gut feelings for a reason."

"She just wasn't the type to not say goodbye. She must have left sometime at night, which is also weird. She and I always walked to school together."

Nash's vision closed in and pain spread across his forehead.

Gage rustled beside him. "Nash, are you okay?"

He forced his head to move in one sharp nod, but memories assailed him like a torrent of bullets.

That night, long ago, at the group home. That night he still relived in his nightmares.

Her scream . . . Summer's scream.

It was true. All of it.

★　★　★

"No. Hell no."

Lexi rolled her eyes skyward and unbuckled the seatbelt that was digging into the crook of her neck. She couldn't relax. She was too hopped up on caffeine and adrenaline. They sat in Nash's idling truck around the corner from Conrad's large stone mansion on Seattle's west side.

"Don't be ridiculous," she said. "I know these guys aren't geniuses, but it wouldn't take much for one of Leith's friends to drive by—or Conrad's men for that matter—and see me sitting here."

"And what? I'm supposed to introduce you?"

She made a sound of impatience. It was after 10:00 p.m. Nash was already late for his meeting with Conrad. She gestured at the clock in the dash. "We're setting off red flags. You should have been there by now."

"I don't want you anywhere near this."

Ever since his meeting with Gage earlier that day, Nash had been as prickly as a cactus.

"Then why did you bring me with you?" she countered. But the question was moot. He hadn't wanted to bring her, but there was no way in hell she would have stayed behind. He snorted, alerting her that he'd drawn the same conclusion.

"The closer you are to me, the better. I said I wouldn't leave you behind again and I meant it." He turned the ignition off.

"Good. Then let's go." She opened the door,

and dropped to the pavement. Nash came around the vehicle before she could take two steps.

"Where are you going?" He gripped her bicep. The rigid line of his shoulders slowed the surge of adrenaline in her veins. This wasn't one of her one-man investigations, and Nash certainly wasn't someone to leave in the dust.

She rested her hands on his waist and tilted her head back. "I'm sorry. I just get . . . anxious. I'm not used to working with someone."

His eyes softened. "Yeah, well, you're with me now." He sounded protective, like a man who had staked his territory. A little thrill raced through her and her abdominal wall softened, letting her sink farther into him. For a moment, those words promised her forever.

But they couldn't.

"Want to let me in on your plan, here?" He tugged on a lock of her hair.

A plan. Right. Normally, she did things by the seat of her pants, but that wouldn't work in this situation. This wasn't like finding informants or snitches. She lifted her fingernail to her teeth and nibbled. Jeez, she really shouldn't have had that second cup of coffee.

"When you visit him, where do you normally talk?"

"Usually we sit in the living room or the office on the main level. His personal office and bedroom are upstairs.

"Does he use a desktop or laptop at home?"

"Laptop and a tablet."

"Good. I should be able to grab that if I can't find the ledger."

Nash's hands locked on her shoulders, forcing her to focus on him. "If you go five houses down this street," he said, gesturing behind her, "you'll see a break between the houses. There's a walking path that will lead you to a small green space. On the other side of that is the back of Conrad's house." He reached behind his back and then pressed a heavy, dark object into her hand.

"No. You need—"

"I have another one." He moved her finger to the gun's safety. "Keep this on unless someone stops you."

"Nash, I know how to use a gun."

He grinned. "Yeah, I know. It's sexy as hell."

Heat scorched up her body and she shimmied her shoulders. Her cleavage jiggled in the scoop-neck black tank she wore under her unzipped leather jacket. "I know."

Nash's gaze dropped to her chest, and his hand cupped her ass. "Don't do that right now."

She chuckled, and he motioned for her to conceal the weapon underneath her jacket.

Ring, ring

She jerked her chin up and searched Nash's face. His hands moved to the lapels of her coat and his forehead wrinkled. He let go of her and fished his phone from his back pocket.

"Who is it?"

"Cole." He moved his thumb on the screen and brought the device to his ear. "Yeah?" He paused, and his gaze flicked around the street. Lexi wrapped her arms around her midsection and rocked back on her heels.

Nash's head snapped back, and his eyes branded hers as he listened. "One sec," he said into the phone. He lifted his chin away from the receiver. "Those numbers you were stuck on? They're routing and account numbers."

Lexi gripped Nash's elbow. "Does he have the account holders' names?"

Nash repeated the question to Cole and then shook his head.

Dammit! She pinched her lip between her thumb and forefinger and paced in a small circle. They had proof that money had been transferred, all they needed was to prove the spreadsheet displayed the transactions involving kids, and who the buyers and sellers were.

Conrad would have that information. Nash disconnected and slid the phone back into his pocket. "Well, it's a step closer," he said. "He's matched the numbers to wire transfers that Conrad has received in his personal accounts."

She rubbed her temple with the tips of her fingers. "We should take this to the cops. Lauren is going to have my head for getting in so deep." No.

She couldn't think about her job right now. They were onto a big fish. The last thing she needed was someone reining her in.

Nash guffawed. "We can't go to the cops. There are too many police officers who are members. It will get back to Conrad before we can blink. We need more."

"Ugh." She dropped her head back. This was the frustrating part about journalism. She knew a crime was being committed, yet if she brought the story to light too soon, without every duck in place, it would get blown to smithereens. "You're right. We still need to prove the spreadsheet is related to the kids, and find out who's involved in the exchanges."

"And we need to figure out what that encryption means. I'm hoping to hell it's a location, so we can find these kids."

Her stomach clenched. Every time she thought about what she was digging up, an iron claw wrapped itself around her.

"You okay?" Nash rubbed her arm.

She forced the image of hurt, neglected kids from her mind. If she let herself get consumed with emotion, she'd be of no help to anyone. She nodded. "We need to get into his house." The sooner she could get inside the better. They were so close to cracking this. A few missing pieces and the organization would crumble. And maybe, just maybe, she could get Conrad charged with the murder of her family, too.

"You'll have a wrought-iron fence to climb over, at the edge of the green space," Nash said. "To the west of the yard, there's a line of cedar trees. You're small, so you'll be able to squeeze between those and the fence separating his property from the neighbor's. That will keep you out of sight of the cameras."

"How do I get in?"

"There's a bathroom on the main level at the side of the house. No cameras there. I'll go to the washroom a few minutes after I get in and open the window for you. From there, you'll take the stairs down the hall to the second level. His bedroom is at the end of the hall and his office adjoins it."

"What about staff?"

Nash shook his head. "Angie, the maid, will be off duty by this time, and her suite is above the garage."

She glanced at her watch. "You need to go. It's quarter after."

Hot air hissed from Nash's lips.

"What?"

"This doesn't feel right, dammit," he said. She dropped her wrist and met his gaze. "Leaving you. It doesn't feel right after what happened with Leith."

"I'll be fine. We need to go."

His hands came to rest on either side of her

head. His dark, hooded eyes weighed hers. "Follow my instructions exactly. If anything goes wrong, call me. Scream. Anything to get my attention, all right? And if anyone corners you, shoot 'em."

She forced a mouthful of saliva down her throat and nodded. "I can handle myself. Don't forget, I handed your ass to you."

He snorted. "Don't start."

A laugh shook through her, and he pressed his mouth to hers. "Christ, I must be crazy," he said against her lips.

She grinned. "I'll take that as a compliment."

"Good."

She rose up onto her toes to get closer to Nash's face. She hated what he was going through. When he'd gotten back in the truck after talking with Gage, it seemed as if a hundred-pound boulder had fallen on his shoulders. He'd told her about the young woman, Allison. "It's not your fault, you know."

His smoky eyes softened, but a muscle at the side of his throat jumped. Lexi pressed a kiss to his chest, and he cupped the back of her head.

"Thanks, babe. But you don't know the half of it."

She yanked her head back. "What do you mean?" Her heels connected with the cement, bringing her head several inches below his chin. Nash scraped the back of his knuckles over his jaw, and the scratching sound increased her agitation. "Nash, tell me."

He let out a growl. "Allison isn't the first."

"I don't doubt it. I told you this has been—"

"No, Lex. I think this has been going on longer than even you thought."

The synapses in her brain crackled. "What do you mean?"

"When I was around Gage's age, a similar thing happened. A girl named Summer was supposedly placed with a family suddenly." His gaze swept over the road and back to her. "Except I heard her scream in the middle of the night. I ran outside and saw her face pressed against a window and then . . . she was gone. Just gone."

The dryness of Lexi's mouth rivaled that of the Sahara Desert. Words rolled over her tongue, but she couldn't piece them together.

"I remember going to the administrators, even talking to Conrad, and all I got was a dead end." His voice was raw and tight. "They convinced me I hadn't seen what I claimed, but Christ. It's haunted me for years. I just . . . I couldn't face it. That I could have done something, you know?" His mouth shifted side to side, as if it were taking him all the effort in the world not to scream.

His fingers tightened on her back. She lifted her hands and pressed them to his cheeks. Anger, fiercer than a hurricane, surged through her. "No," she hissed. "You were a kid. You did all that you were able to at that age, which was to trust your caregivers. You can't go back to that day, but we can stop them now. We have to stop them."

His ashen skin brightened. "You're right. Let's fucking do this."

CHAPTER 20

NASH PULLED INTO the triple-wide driveway and shifted into park. He'd left Lexi moments ago, and already his blood pressure had spiked through the roof. Today, he'd told Gage to trust his gut. Years ago, he'd learned to trust his instincts, and it was a skill that always served him. And now, Nash's gut was screaming at him to back out, drag Lexi's sexy, defiant ass into the vehicle, and get the hell out of the country.

Only that wouldn't do a damn thing. Running wouldn't protect either of them, it wouldn't expose the truth, and it wouldn't save those who'd been harmed. Like Summer and Allison. He stretched the collar of his T-shirt away from his neck as if it were a hungry boa constrictor and not flimsy cotton.

He got out of his truck and strode to the front door for the millionth time in the last eighteen years. When Nash had spoken with him a few hours ago, Conrad had seemed like his usual self and not at all nonplussed by the suggestion that they talk. His hand closed around the doorknob. He hadn't knocked since the first day he'd shown up to live with Conrad. He couldn't start now. Not when he needed to strive for normalcy. He pressed the latch and pushed the door open.

"Nash, my boy! I just saw your truck parked in the drive on the security camera. C'mon in." Conrad stood at the threshold of his study, his jovial tone grating Nash's nerves. Was he happy because he believed Nash had allowed Lexi to die? Or because he thought he had Nash right where he wanted him?

Nash let the door close behind him and stepped out of his loafers. His cell phone dug into his glute. His nerve endings tingled, waiting for the text from Lexi to tell him she was at the window.

Conrad disappeared into his study off the entryway, and Nash followed. His socked feet slipped over the marble floor and the hairs on his arms spiked in warning. If Conrad had any inclination what he was up to, they were fucked. One standing lamp on the floor coated the room in a yellow glow. Nash forced the tendons in his hands to relax as he swept the room corner to corner. No threat loomed.

A spark snapped Nash's attention to Conrad. With a cigar clamped between his teeth, Conrad smiled and brought the lighter to its end. The paper cracked and burned a fiery red as Conrad drew in a breath of the rich tobacco.

He gestured to the chair in front of his desk. "Sit."

Nash complied. The soft brown leather used to wrap him in warm familiarity, but now it popped beneath his weight as if to warn Conrad of his betrayal. The Beretta's warm metal heated the small of his back, and his palm throbbed to hold its weight.

"What's on your mind that couldn't wait till morning?"

Nash cleared his throat and sought a remorseful tone. It wasn't difficult. Looking at the man he'd known half his life, a man he'd respected and cared for, a river of regret flowed through him. He'd been young and vulnerable when he'd trusted Conrad. Knowing what the man was capable of only made Nash want to retract ever getting close with him. "I just want to make sure we're on the same page. That things haven't changed between us because of what happened in Moscow."

Conrad flicked his cigar. A clump of ashes fluttered into a tray. "And that is?"

Nash pressed his back into the chair, but the relaxed position did nothing to ease the tension in his muscles. *Where the hell is Lexi?* "You put a hit on Alexis, and you thought I betrayed you. That doesn't sit well with me."

Conrad's brown eyes softened. "You're like a son to me, Nash. What happened in Moscow was strictly business. I needed the job done ASAP—if you were having trouble, it was my job to send reinforcements. And look, she's dead, you're home and all that shit is behind us. Right?"

A soft buzz radiated across his tailbone. The rope of anxiety around his chest loosened. *Finally.* "Of course."

"There's just one thing," Conrad said, as he placed his cigar in the ashtray and sat forward to prop his elbows on the desk. His stare burned through Nash. "You killed Leith."

★ ★ ★

LEXI BOUNCED ON her toes in the crusher dust beneath the window. The wind picked up and found its way to every millimeter of her exposed skin, chilling her. She wet her lips but instantly regretted it when the air sucked the moisture away from her sensitive flesh, leaving an icy burn in its wake. Her legs still stung from climbing the fence and dropping to the unrelenting ground. But she'd made it to the security of the trees and stayed out of sight of the camera while making her way to the side of the house.

She'd sent the text more than five minutes ago. What the hell was taking him so long? She pulled her phone from her pocket and checked the screen for the tenth time, even though it was on vibrate. Not like he'd send a message anyway.

Was she at the right window? She squeezed her eyelids together and ran through Nash's instructions. He'd said the west side of the house. She turned and faced north. *Never eat shredded wheat* . . . yup. Right side of the house.

Light burst through the window. A squeak hissed through her lips, and she pressed her palm to her chest. The window hiked open and Nash bent through its opening.

"You scared the shit out of me," she mouthed. His lip twitched, and he stuck his hand out to her. She gripped his wrist, and his fingers locked around hers. She dug her foot into the stucco, and he pulled her off the ground. His free hand caught her armpit and he hauled her over the sill. She lowered the toes of her boots to the slick white marble and Nash released her.

She took a couple of breaths before lowering the window. "What took you so long? I was worried."

Nash reached for the sink and flipped on the pewter tap. "He accused me of killing Leith." Water gushed out of the faucet, drowning out his low voice.

Oh no. She lifted her fingertips to her forehead and massaged. Nash shrugged and caught her shoulder in his hold. "It's all right. Didn't come as much of a surprise, but I'm not sure he believed me when I denied it. He definitely tried to catch me off guard."

"What did you tell him?"

"That I was at the White Room last night—

with a date—and we left early. I told him I bumped into Leith and Drew. He would have heard that from any bystander."

Nausea flipped her stomach over. "We're getting by with the skin of our teeth. I'll get whatever I can and then we need to end this."

"I want you to go back to my truck. I don't like the feeling I'm getting." His fingers tightened on her, and strain revealed a dimple at the corner of his mouth.

She cupped his elbow and shook her head. "We can't back out now. No way. And if you don't go back now, he's going to know something's up and find us anyway."

He grunted with frustration, shook his head, and swiped his palm down his face. "All right, but we need to be quick. Ten minutes, tops."

She nodded. "Do you know where his safe is?"

He snorted. "No. Not his personal one. But I wouldn't focus on that. Even if you find it, I have no idea what the code is." He eased her behind the bathroom door, placed his hand on the back of her neck, and pressed his lips to her forehead. The heady, sandalwood scent of his aftershave tickled her taste buds, and the reminder of his mouth on her body seared through her brain. His lips were moist and firm, and his stubble grazed her flesh as he pulled away.

"Be careful, dammit," he said, his expression hard and fierce. Just seeing that hint of unease in

Nash was enough to lodge a rock of doubt into her inflated boat of confidence. She sucked her bottom lip into her mouth and nodded. As if his hand were stuck to the back of her head, he pried his fingers away slowly then slipped out the bathroom door. She circled her hand around the door handle and took one shuddering breath, then another. She couldn't let her nerves overtake her. Nash would distract Conrad if it killed him.

But that's what she was worried about the most.

She pulled the gun Nash had given her from beneath her coat and eased open the door. The hinges groaned. She winced and peeked around the corner of the doorjamb. Straight ahead, a light shone at the end of the hall, illuminating the foyer. She inched around the corner to her left and balanced her weight onto the balls of her feet. Pressing her back into the moss-green wall, she sidestepped to the doorway of the hall. She peered around the corner to see the dimly lit kitchen and main area. The solid mahogany banister soared into the hall to her right. She positioned the gun in front of her, pointed at the ground, and ascended the stairs.

Her heart thumped with each step, and a cold sweat started at her hairline. She reached the top of the stairs and scanned the hall. Dead silent. The strands of her ponytail tickled her neck, making goosebumps pucker the skin on her forearms.

She followed Nash's directions and stopped outside Conrad's bedroom door. Faint light touched the dark hardwood floors that surrounded the area rug beneath his bed, but no sound carried through the space. She slipped inside the room and edged the door shut.

Her shoulders relaxed and she dropped her head back against the wood. She'd made it. She peeled her back away from the door and crossed the bedroom to the lit doorway within the room. At the threshold of his adjoining office, she stuck her head in and swept her gaze over the room.

Empty.

She strode inside. A desk and leather chair took up the far side of the room, and a TV was mounted to the opposite wall. She tucked the weapon into the waistband of her pants and went to one of the two narrow bookshelves on either side of the flat screen.

Nash had given her ten minutes, which meant she had about seven left. She ran her fingers over the spines of the books, tugging on each of them to reveal the solid wood of the case behind. Shit, shit, shit.

Where was the safe? She couldn't leave without finding it. Even if doing so would piss Nash off. A picture in a silver frame stopped her dead in her tracks. The blood left her fingers as she reached for the frame. Her gaze was riveted to the two men with their arms around each other's shoulders. A tiny whimper leaked through her throat.

Dad.

Tears filled her eyes but acrimony burned behind them. Conrad. The sonofabitch. He'd planned her family's death, yet he kept this framed picture of him and her father on display. For what? As a damn trophy? A reminder that evil had triumphed over good?

Her vision blurred, and she dug her fingertips into the glass until it threatened to shatter. She couldn't leave the photo. It would be like leaving a piece of her father behind. She flipped the object over and quickly pulled off the back piece. Black ink stood out against the white back of the photo.

One memory among thousands—with more to come. Forever brothers, if not by blood.

—02-4728

The number blazed through her brain at warp speed. Her dad's membership number. The first two numbers stood for the level of seniority. Nash's began with 38, and her dad's had begun with 02. Conrad's, she remembered from the ledger, also began with 02.

Nash had used his as the password to his safe. With all that Conrad had to hide, he wouldn't have done the same. But he might have used someone else's. Like her father's.

She had to find the safe.

She slapped the frame to the shelf. Clutching the picture, she checked the other shelf and let out a hiss of disappointment. She moved to the desk and rummaged through the drawers. Nothing but neatly organized planners and file folders. She flipped through the pages. Nothing.

She straightened and twined her fingers through her ponytail. Dammit, she couldn't leave empty-handed. She turned in a circle. There had to be a safe. Her gaze swung to the bedroom and landed on a partially open pocket door. Conrad's closet.

She moved swiftly across the space and entered the closet. A light flicked on, triggered by a sensor. She shoved at the hanging suit jackets and dress pants and ducked to look behind the shoe rack.

Still nothing.

She closed her eyes against the raging panic that beat against her skull. She turned her wrist—three minutes. She'd never make it out in time if she didn't leave now.

No. Screw that. She'd never get the opportunity to search Conrad's house again, and she wasn't leaving until she had what she'd come for. Her focus fell to a panel of drawers. *Maybe . . .*

She dropped to her knees and pulled out the bottom drawer and set it aside. Pressing her palms into the cream-colored runner, she peered into the vacant slot. Too dark to see anything. She pulled out her phone and shone the light into the hole. The bottom seam of a gunmetal gray door covered the back. Bare white wall surrounded it.

Yes!

She pulled out two more drawers and fit her head and arms into the hole. She set the phone on the floor and pulled out the photo. Her hand shook as she held it and punched in the six-digit number with her free hand.

Beep, beep

A green light flashed. *Yes!* Her entire body sagged, and she let loose a chuckle of relief. She turned the lever and stretched her hands into the safe's mouth. Her fingers closed over a wide leather spine. Satisfaction pulled her lips into a grin as she slid out the object.

This wasn't just a ledger. It was the mother of all ledgers—easily twice the size of Nash's. Her spine tingled. She should be hightailing it out of Conrad's room, but knowing she could be holding the answers she'd been searching for, she couldn't resist parting the pages with her thumbs and flipping through the weathered paper. Two columns filled each page. The left column held the symbols Brooks had provided and the right held . . . letters. Each symbol represented a letter.

The buyers.

Fire seared her palms. She was holding the missing link. And if it contained the names of the buyers, it would have everything else. Like the locations of the kids. She clamped the book shut and hugged it to her chest. If anyone caught her on the way out, there would be no hiding this thing.

She checked her watch again.

One minute late.

She grimaced and put everything back in its place. It wouldn't serve them to have Conrad on their heels so quickly. She could only hope he wouldn't notice the missing photo tonight. It was a risk she had to take. She tucked the photo into the book, pressed the ledger against her abdomen, and pulled up the zipper of her leather coat. It didn't even go up halfway, but it would at least support the weight of the book so she could carry the gun.

She slipped into the hall. She had to get out. Nash would be waiting for her text so he could leave, and she didn't want to make him stall and seem suspicious. The muscles in her legs shook as she moved swiftly down the stairs. She kept her elbows tight to her torso, so the heavy-ass book didn't slip out, and the gun aimed at the ceiling.

Don't fall, don't fall . . .

She made it to the main level and took long strides toward the bathroom. It took every ounce of control in her body not to run. Once in the bathroom, she closed the door quietly then advanced on the window. After tucking the gun into her pants, she slid up the window and swung one leg through the hole then the other. She sat awkwardly on the edge and brought the window down as far as she could so she could pull it the rest of the way once she reached the ground. She gripped tightly to the sill and lowered herself. The ledger slipped out from the bottom of her coat and landed at her feet.

A shuffle of movement scuffed against the stones behind her. She whirled around, but a hand clamped tightly over her mouth and the end of a gun pressed against her temple.

"Don't fucking move."

CHAPTER 21

NASH SHOT BACK a sip of whiskey. The ice cubes clinked against the crystal glass. Conrad stretched back in his chair and glanced at his watch. Nash had witnessed the impatient glint in Conrad's eyes before, but it had never been directed at him.

Fuck, fuck, fuck.

"Mind if I have another?" Nash extended his glass. Conrad nodded and gestured to the wet bar across the room. Nash stood and headed for the decanter.

If he didn't get out of here ASAP, Conrad would know something was up. But there was no way in hell he was leaving until he knew Lexi was out. She'd said she would text him the second she was outside. Panic bit into his flesh. Had Conrad suspected him? Was someone else in the house now, waiting to make a move? They could have found her.

Tension lined the walls of his throat, and he coughed to clear it. If Lexi didn't message him soon, he'd have to excuse himself and go upstairs. But that would be risky as hell. The only other option was to leave and sneak back in through the bathroom window, but he'd have to park his truck a few streets away, and that would take too much time.

"Top mine up." Conrad stretched out his glass and Nash accepted it and filled it. He put the decanter back on the crystal dish and returned to his seat. He handed Conrad his drink and set his own glass on the edge of the solid desk between them. "It's getting late. I'll head out after this drink. But there's something on my mind."

Conrad jutted his chin forward. "What's that?"

"There's one thing I can't get past. Yuri Ivanov. What did he do? Why did you take him out?" He'd wanted to say, "Why did you murder him?" As it was, it had taken all his effort to keep contempt out of his tone—and he probably hadn't succeeded.

If he hadn't met Lexi, hadn't teamed up with her, he wouldn't be feeling the guilt that sucked his heart into his stomach every time he thought about the hand he'd had in her parents' death. She had changed him. The cold, distant enforcer who never asked questions and always followed through with a job was gone. Hell, he couldn't even remember who that guy had been. And he couldn't fathom how he'd been so fucking blind.

Conrad folded his arms across his chest and

frowned. "Didn't I give you the rundown on that already?" His voice held an adequate amount of uncertainty, but not enough to hold Nash's questions at bay.

"You mentioned that Yuri and his son were traitors and that they'd sold secret information." A beat passed as Nash sipped his drink. The air between them fizzled. He should back down. This whole ordeal had marked him as a traitor. But really, the traitor was Conrad. "What I'm trying to figure out is what were we hiding that was so bad we had to kill them to prevent the leak."

The temperature in the room plummeted.

"That's classified," Conrad said evenly. "'Course I would never keep anything from you. Stop by my office first thing and I'll show you everything you need to know. It's about time I pass the baton. You've long since proven yourself."

Nash's phone vibrated in his back pocket. *She's out.* Relief spread through him, but he wouldn't breathe easily until she was safe at his side. *I'll wring her neck for being late.* Nash rubbed his palms against his thighs. "I'll see you bright and early."

"I'd better head to bed then," Conrad said with a chuckle. He got to his feet, and the chair's wheels squeaked.

Nash tossed back the rest of his drink, stood, and retreated to the door. "By the way," he said, turning around, "I'll do whatever I can to get to the bottom of Leith's death. He was a good guy, and whoever killed him will pay." The lie singed his tongue, but he didn't care. If Lexi had the ledger, the game was over. If not, they'd have to get closer.

Conrad nodded sharply and his eyes darkened. "Damn right they will." The threat radiated from Conrad's tall, menacing form.

Nash lifted his hand in a wave and turned from the room. He made his way to the foyer, shoved his feet in his shoes, and opened the front door. A gust of chilly air caressed his cheek.

It took all his resolve not to check his phone. Conrad would be watching through the security camera. He pulled out his keys, hit the unlock button, and got into his truck. As soon as he was out of the driveway, he fished his phone from his pocket. He read the name across the screen and his stomach slammed into his throat. Sonofabitch! The text was from Cole—not Lexi. Ice coated his skin.

She's still inside.

LEXI STRUGGLED AGAINST the hard body that gripped her. She slammed her heels into his shins, but the steel clutches around her didn't break. Terror spiked up the back of her throat. Her gun sat firmly against her spine, but with both arms pinned, she couldn't reach it. The man shifted her in his hold and inched around the side of the house into the concealment of the cedars.

Why was he moving her away from the house? Branches slapped her unprotected face and she winced and jerked. Still, he held fast.

"Hold still and be quiet, dammit. They could be anywhere."

Her eyes flew open, and she sucked a breath through her nostrils. Who was he talking about? And why would he warn her if he was one of them? They reached the wrought-iron fence and he stopped.

"I'm going to let you go, but don't scream. I think Nash is still in there and they're onto you guys."

The death grip on her jaw loosened, and she was lowered to her feet. She spun around and a black leather jacket filled her vision. She tilted her head back and took in equally black eyes and hair.

Cole.

"W-what are you doing here?" she said, glancing at the Beretta he held loosely. His gaze swept the yard beyond the tree at her shoulder, and he pulled her under a thicker branch.

"While I was hacking into Conrad's server at the House, one of the members called and tipped me off."

She frowned. "Tipped you off? What do you mean?"

He huffed with impatience. "Conrad has hired me for the odd job, so I've made some connections with a few of the brothers over the years. One of the guys called to warn me that Conrad ordered his men to take out Nash when he leaves."

The air rushed out of her lungs, and she gripped the closest tree for support. "No," she cried, choking back a sob. "He's still in there. He's waiting for me to text him and—"

Cole's thick hand closed over her shoulder. "Don't worry. I won't let anything happen to him." He pulled out his phone, and the light from the screen illuminated his face. The determined plains of his face sent a quake through her.

His thumbs grazed over the screen and then he pocketed the device. "I sent him a text, but I need to get you out of here. Cut across the green space. You'll see my black SUV parked there." He slapped a set of keys into her palm and stepped around her.

She clamped her fingers around his jacket. "Wait!"

He stopped and turned to her.

"I dropped the ledger outside the bathroom window when you grabbed me."

He nodded. "I'll get it."

"Cole," she said. He lifted his eyebrows, impatience radiating off him. "Get him out."

"I'm on it." He retreated, and the shadows and branches swallowed him up. She wrapped her arms around her waist and squeezed her eyes tight. They'd walked right into Conrad's trap and Nash might not survive it—because of her. It couldn't end here. There was no way. They were so damn close to ending it. They had the original ledger. Now all that was left for them to do was piece together the information Brooks had supplied her with.

Nash needed to make it out of this alive. This wasn't just about the justice she sought for her family—now it was also for Nash. For the helpless, abandoned boy. The boy who'd jumped at the opportunity to have a father figure. Conrad had preyed on him. All Nash had needed was a family, and instead, he'd gotten roped up in a cult.

Her lips trembled and tears misted the corners of her eyes. She couldn't just leave. She had a gun for god's sake. Surely that was an asset. After all, she'd saved Nash's ass before. She pulled the gun from her pants and poised it in front of her.

They could be anywhere. Only the soft rustle of branches in the wind reached her ears. Would Conrad's men be scouring the perimeter of the house? Probably not. There would be no need to do that if they knew Nash was inside. The soles of her shoes scuffed over the crusher dust as she crossed the length of the deep yard to the side of the house. The still-lit bathroom light shone from the window, coating the ground below. The book was gone.

Relief relaxed her shoulders. That meant Cole had grabbed it. She kept her back glued to the side of the house. The puckered stucco scraped against the leather at her shoulder blades. She reached the corner at the front of the house and froze. She scanned the darkness. Nash's truck was gone.

He'd left without her? No way. He wouldn't have. Unless Cole's text had reached him and he'd gotten out safely before Conrad's men arrived.

Shit!

She lowered her weapon and dropped her head to the solid surface at her back. A stream of silent curses moved her lips. They were probably looking for her. She should have gone to Cole's vehicle, like he'd told her. She retraced her steps along the side of the house and returned the gun to her back.

She fished her phone from her pocket and brought the screen to life. She tapped her fingers over the glass.

I'm safe. Heading to Cole's SUV now.

She grimaced as she reread the words, anticipating Nash's anger at her impulsiveness. Her finger hovered over the Send button. A slew of stones scattered at her feet and she whipped around, her lips parted in a scream. An object swung at her. She dodged out of its reach.

Her phone dropped to the ground and she reached for her gun, but fear made her movements clumsy. The shadowed man let out a growl and advanced on her. She whipped out her gun and fired. His shoulder jerked back violently, and he howled.

"You fucking bitch!" he wailed into the night. Her breath hissed through her throat. She turned and ran—and slammed into a hard chest. Fingers gripped her shoulder, and something hard cracked against her skull.

Her head snapped to the side and she staggered. Another blow sent her careening to the earth. White flashes sparked behind her closed lids and pain scorched through her scalp. Darkness stretched out its greedy fingers, pulling her into oblivion.

CHAPTER 22

It's a trap, the text message read. *Get out now.*

Nash slammed his fist into the dash and growled. He dropped his phone in the vacant seat next to him and gripped his hair. Raindrops misted the windshield as his truck idled around the corner from Conrad's. He ran his palm down his face. Shit. He couldn't just sit here. He'd been stupid to think Conrad wouldn't move first. Shifting his truck into gear, he settled his hands on the wheel and checked his rearview mirror.

Bang!

Nash jerked his head in the direction of the sound and reached for his gun A dark form stood at the passenger window. His chest bloomed with hope then quickly deflated. Cole. He removed his hand from the weapon at the small of his back.

"Open the door," his brother mouthed, knocking on the glass again. Nash punched the unlock button and pinched his eyebrows together.

"What the hell are you doing here? I thought you were Lexi."

Cole moved Nash's phone to the cupholder and dropped into the seat, shutting the door. "She's safe. I grabbed her when she climbed out the window." He buckled his seatbelt. "I got a tip from a guy on the inside. He warned me that Conrad was going to have you killed when you left his place tonight."

"Fuck." Conrad had been one step ahead of them. But there was a chance they didn't know she was still alive, or that they were after anything. His insides twisted. Conrad would have killed him without batting an eye. That fact stung. Whatever Conrad was hiding, it was worth killing his adopted son over.

Cole unzipped his coat and pulled out a dark, thickly woven book. "Pretty sure Conrad is going to lose his shit when he realizes this is missing."

"She found it." Goddamn, she was good. Pride lifted the corners of his mouth, and he ran his fingertips over the book he hadn't known existed. He snatched his hand away as if the leather had caught fire. "We need to find her. We're running out of time. Where is she?"

Headlights came around the corner, illuminating his rearview mirror. He squinted but didn't take his gaze off the vehicle. Nash gripped the steering wheel as the maroon pickup truck revved past him.

"That's Drew's truck." The words came out on a whisper. Cole followed his line of vision and made a sound under his breath. Nash pulled away from the curb. "Where is she?" he growled.

If Drew's orders had been to take out Nash, they wouldn't leave empty-handed.

"Hang a left up here," Cole directed him. "I told her to wait at my vehicle." The taillights of the truck grew small as it accelerated out of the subdivision. Warning bells screeched in Nash's head. Every instinct shouted at him to follow the truck, but he couldn't until they had Lexi. He followed Cole's directions and slowed alongside the sleek black SUV. His blood turned to thick sludge and crawled through his arteries. The vehicle was empty.

"Shit!" Cole thumped his hand against his thigh.

Sweat moistened his hairline. "They have her, Cole. Sonofabitch." The last part came out rough and haggard. Nash whipped the truck into a U-turn and stomped his foot against the pedal.

"They couldn't have gotten far." Cole's hand stretched toward the window. "Hang a right here. They would have got on the interstate, and this way will be quicker."

Cole was right. They wouldn't chance killing her so close to Conrad's residence. They'd take her to a place where her death wouldn't be tied to Lionsgate. Nash ground his teeth and nodded. It was a damn good thing Cole had shown up because panic had made Nash's brainwaves flat.

He never should have brought her along, never should have endangered her. It didn't matter that she was hell-bent and headstrong. He should have foreseen the dangers and kept her hidden. Dammit to hell and back, why hadn't they come after him instead?

Because Lexi was right. It had always been Conrad's goal to kill her. To silence the leak that had started with her family. If they had her, they were going to kill her and likely dispose of her body where it wouldn't be found. If they hadn't killed her already . . .

"There." Cole pointed to the maroon truck three cars up in the left lane. Nash pressed his foot to the floor and they shot forward. He swerved in and out of the lanes until he got directly behind the truck.

"I'll keep it steady," Nash said. Cole pulled out his gun and rolled down the window. A pang of fear made Nash tighten his hold on the wheel.

Cole glanced around the busy interstate. "Fuck, I can't shoot."

Nash dragged his gaze from the road to stare at him. "Are you insane? You have a clear shot."

"It's too dangerous. There's other people on the road." Cole shook his head and checked the gage of the gun.

"You're getting soft. What do you suggest we do? Wait for them to dump her body?"

"C'mon, Nash. They won't kill her yet. Think

about it."

Cole was right, but that didn't stop the sweat from rolling down Nash's spine. If Drew spotted them, they were screwed. "I'm going to fall behind a little. As soon as they get off the interstate, take them out."

Five minutes later, the maroon truck changed lanes. "Where are they going?" He hadn't been paying the least bit of attention to where they were. All that mattered was that he was hot on their heels. It would take nothing short of hell freezing over to separate his truck from theirs.

The truck signaled at the approaching exit and turned off. "Industrial district," Cole mumbled.

Nash's neck muscles clenched. That didn't bode well. Old warehouses, little to no people or traffic at this time of night. Screams would go unheard. And there were many ways to kill a person with industrial equipment. "We need to stop them now. If they reach their destination, they could have backup and we'll be outnumbered."

Before the words were out of Nash's mouth, Cole had his seatbelt off and the window down. Nash held the wheel steady and kept his eyes on the slowing truck. His brother was a damn good shot. There was no one he trusted more with a gun, other than himself. Nash didn't have to tell Cole that a bullet to Lexi's head was equivalent to one to his.

Crack! Crack!

Drew's truck swerved, bumped over the shoulder, and then got back on the road.

"Sonofabitch!" Cole hissed. He adjusted himself at the window.

Crack! Crack! Crack!

Glass from the rear window pelted the back of Nash's head. A bullet sailed past his ear and into the windshield, splitting it into a kaleidoscope. He whipped around in his seat—a black suburban closed in on his bumper.

"Fuck! There's two of them now." The maroon truck peeled through the intersection at the end of the off-ramp. Nash accelerated. He couldn't lose them.

Blood galloped through his skull with the force of a herd of elephants. He flicked his gaze to the rearview mirror. Two men hung out either side of the SUV, their faces hidden behind the butts of their guns.

"Nash, look out!"

Nash craned his neck around the web that had torn apart the windshield. A man leaned out the passenger side of Drew's truck and fired.

Pop!

Nash's front tire blew, and the weight of the truck shifted. The flat tire flapped against the road, and the deafening screech of metal against pavement split the air. Cole hung out the window and fired behind him. The suburban slammed into their bumper. Nash's chest collided with the steering wheel, and Cole fell back into his seat. The flat tire pulled them toward the side of the road. Nash gritted his teeth.

He might not be able to kill every single one of them—yet—but if they were going down, the assholes in the suburban were coming with them. Nash pounded his foot down on the brake.

"Christ!" Cole screamed, grabbing the dashboard.

The suburban swerved around them and into the next lane. Bullets rained down on the truck, hitting the hood, roof, and tires like hail before a tornado. Cole shoved him below the dash. As tires squealed, Nash tore away from his brother.

He shoved open the door and leaped from the vehicle. Gun drawn, he chased the retreating suburban. The weapon cocked back in his hand with each fire until he emptied the clip.

The maroon truck whipped around a street corner—*gone*.

Nash cried out. They'd taken her. They'd gotten away. He stomped back to the truck and shot his foot out to kick the side panel. Cole paced with a phone to his ear, but Nash couldn't make out his words through the thick mist that had fallen around him. Then his brother's firm hands gripped his shoulders.

"We'll find her."

Nash shoved Cole's chest, making him drop his arms. "How the fuck are we going to do that?"

For once, Cole's hard, unemotional face creased with strain. His brother's eyes, so much darker than his own, filled with sympathy. "I don't know." He took another step closer. "But we will. I give you my word."

Nash snorted and paced the road. The glow from the streetlamp over his head and the brightly lit storefront of the nearby convenience store stung his senses. "We don't even have a fucking car."

"I called a cab. We'll go back to Conrad's house. If the bastard is there, we'll slit him to pieces until he gives her up." Cole grabbed his shoulder again.

Nash shook his head. "He won't be there."

"Why not? He's a fucking coward. He sends men to do his dirty work while he sits on his ass."

"I'm telling you, Cole. He won't be there. He wouldn't chance us sending someone to kill him."

Cole strode to the passenger side of the truck, reached into the footwell, and then lifted the ledger into the air. Nash's instinct was to shout at him to conceal the book, to protect the same fucking organization that had Lexi and would kill him in a heartbeat if given the chance. Not anymore. His ties to the brotherhood had been irreparably severed. Every single one of them.

Cole smiled. "I think Conrad will listen to us now."

"KEEP MOVING." A calloused palm shoved her shoulder. Her foot caught the edge of the stair and she stumbled. Behind her back, her hands jerked against the restraint at her wrists. Fingers gripped her bicep, preventing her from tumbling headfirst down the stairs.

She closed her eyes and swallowed. A thick gray fog had lined her vision since she gained consciousness in the back of the truck.

"I said, keep moving." He enunciated each word.

"Maybe if you hadn't given me a damn concussion I could walk normally," she hissed. She lowered her toe to the last step and her muscles shook as she balanced out her weight. Her temples throbbed in a synchronized rhythm. Her vision dithered with every beat.

His sharp fingertips closed on her shoulders and propelled her into the dark basement. If her hands had been free, she would have stretched them in front of her. She dug her feet into the solid floor. The soles of her boots scraped against the broken concrete, and the sound echoed through the space. The sharp scent of bleach hit her nose, burning her palate and then the back of her throat. She coughed.

Why does it smell like bleach?

"You won't have to worry about the concussion anymore." His hand bumped against the wall next to her face. Bright fluorescent lights snapped on. She winced and turned her face away. He shoved her farther into the room. The toe of her boot caught the edge of something, and she fell to her knees. But she didn't land directly on the concrete.

Clear plastic crinkled beneath her jeans. Her blood swelled in her veins. She jerked up her head and took in her surroundings. Plastic sheeting lined the walls, ceiling, and floor. She couldn't blink. Couldn't breathe. Her lungs ached for air.

A metal chair sat next to her. Leather shackles hung from its arms and front legs. She shook her head.

No. No, no, no, no!

The man behind her laughed. She whipped her head around to put a face to the brute who'd grabbed her.

Drew smiled and stepped onto the plastic. She fell to her butt and scooted backward. But there was no way out. She couldn't run. Couldn't overpower him. And with her hands tied, she didn't stand a chance. Her gaze fell to his shoes. A small pool of black dotted the concrete outside the plastic.

Blood.

And soon, it would be hers.

CHAPTER 23

THIS IS CONRAD. Leave a message and I'll get back to you.

The gruff greeting resounded through Nash's ear for the fifth time. He growled as he hung up.

Cole entered the kitchen, his gun drawn but lowered. "Basement is clear."

Nash pressed his closed fist to the gray-quartz counter. "He's gone," he said through clenched teeth. "That motherfucker." They'd turned Conrad's house upside down. Even though the Tesla that should have taken up the second bay of the garage was gone, Cole had insisted they search the house.

"I can't threaten him with the ledger if he doesn't answer." Nash lowered his gaze to the flecks of rock in the counter. His body vibrated with the need to keep moving, to not stop until they found her, but if he pried himself away from the counter he'd walk in aimless circles. Cole stopped on the opposite side of the island and lowered his forearms to the stone. Nash lifted his head to stare at his brother's hard face. "We need a plan."

Cole nodded. "If I hadn't given Lexi my—"

He snapped up. The frown lines on his forehead smoothed as a smile touched his eyes. Smiles were such a rare sight on his brother's face that even at a time like this Nash warmed. "She has my keys," Cole said.

Nash didn't return the grin. "I don't see how that's a good thing."

Cole moved around the island and snatched a set of keys from the shelf next to the garage-access door. "Let's go."

Nash followed him into the garage and punched the button to open the metal door. It rattled as it parted from the concrete. Cole hopped into Conrad's Range Rover.

"Would you tell me what the hell you're so excited about?" Nash said, as he climbed into the passenger seat and buckled his seatbelt. Cole backed down the driveway and peeled out of the subdivision.

"Don't you remember what you got me for Christmas two years ago?"

"No, and I don't care. Where the fuck are we going, bro?" He couldn't even attempt patience anymore.

"You got me a key finder." Cole slapped his cell phone on the console. "Pull up the app and locate them."

Hope opened Nash's airways, and he sucked in a deep breath. "I forgot about that." He lifted Cole's phone, opened the app, selected the key icon, and hit Find.

Please wait . . .

Nash balled his free hand into a fist and didn't take his gaze from the screen. *C'mon, c'mon . . .*

Item not found.

"Fuck. It can't pick it up. We're probably too far away." He dropped his head back. He should have known it wouldn't be that damn easy. He'd purchased the gift for Cole mostly as a gag because he lost his keys on a daily basis.

Cole guffawed "That's right, I forgot. The range is just over 300 feet. We know they went to the industrial district, so we'll start there."

"And if we can't locate them?"

As Cole took the on-ramp to the interstate, the glow from a streetlamp illuminated his face before it was washed in shadows again. Cole's jaw clenched. His gaze flicked to Nash and then back to the road. "We will."

Nash massaged his temples. That wasn't enough. Goddammit, he'd been on the other side before. He'd never hurt women, but he'd given many men a beatdown. It wouldn't take long for them to take her somewhere, tie her up, and . . .

Fuck.

Sweat collected at the neckline of his shirt, but his skin was cold.

"I know you're going through hell right now, but you need to think," Cole said. "You were an enforcer. Where would they take her?"

He snorted. "We normally met people at their houses or in parking garages, roughed 'em up, and that was enough."

"But that's not what they're going to do to Lexi," Cole said.

Nash didn't need the fucking reminder. The cords in his neck tightened until they threatened to snap. No. They weren't going to scare her off. Conrad wanted her gone. Just like he'd wanted her family gone six months ago. The gentle vibration of the tires against the pavement turned his stomach. Acid bubbled up his esophagus and his eyes burned with the effort it took to swallow.

"You all right?"

Nash grunted. He lowered his elbows to his knees and sucked a few breaths through his nose. He couldn't fall apart. Couldn't think about how quickly they could—would—kill her. And what they would do first. A white streak flashed across his vision.

"Sonofabitch!" He slammed his fist against the passenger window and the glass shook beneath his skin. Nash pinched the bridge of his nose, but it didn't slow the force of blood rushing through his skull. The interior of the SUV closed in around him with every breath. He needed to get out, to be moving.

"Try the app again." Cole's voice pierced the darkness that wanted to suffocate him. The vehicle crawled off the ramp toward the industrial district. Large, unlit buildings inched past his window. Nash nodded, pulled his hand away from his face and hit the key icon.

Please wait . . .

Nash scraped his teeth against his tongue and stared at the screen. Cole was right, there had to be a location. Something he was too distraught to think about. Shit, he'd been with Lionsgate for almost two decades. There wasn't much that went on without him knowing.

Except child trafficking.

The screen blinked. *Item not found.*

He dropped the phone in the cupholder. Cole growled next to him and tightened his hands on the steering wheel.

He had to come up with something.

"Stop," he barked.

Cole halted in the deserted street. "What is it?"

Nash harrumphed. "We can't just drive around aimlessly. The least we can do is check out some of these warehouses." He nodded at an old building with boards on the windows jumping against the brick with every breeze.

"If you say so," Cole's uncertain tone didn't sway Nash.

"Park in the alley over here," Nash said, gesturing to the dark gap between two buildings. "We don't need someone to notice Conrad's Range Rover."

If they're even here.

Cole turned down the alley then cut the lights. Nash swung open the door and stepped out. The crisp air bit at his skin, and he tucked his chin. He rubbed his thumb over his index finger inside his jacket pockets then pulled his face from the protection of his coat.

Lexi could be cold right now, too.

Cole rounded the hood of the SUV and advanced on the building's side door. Plywood hung on other windows, though more securely in the protection the alley offered from the wind. Nash moved closer to the door and lifted the heavy, rusted padlock.

"Have you been to any of these warehouses before?" Cole asked.

Nash tucked the corner of his mouth in. "I've been to a lot of rundown warehouses." He pulled out his Beretta. "Stand back."

Cole complied, and Nash pointed the mouth of the gun at the padlock and pulled the trigger. Metal shot out and connected with an old tin dumpster. The lock bounced at his feet. He kept his gun up and opened the door. A light flicked on from behind him—the flashlight of Cole's phone. Its beam swept across the floor, illuminating their way.

Dirt and dust covered every surface and hung

in the air. The small particles kicked up by their movements stirred the hairs inside his nostrils. He burrowed his mouth in his sleeve. When he inhaled again, the eye-watering scent of piss hit him in the face.

Cole retched. "Ah, gross. Looks like squatters have been using old paint cans as fucking toilets." He choked on another gag.

Nash pressed his arm tighter against his face. His gaze landed on a set of stairs. "Let's check upstairs and then get the hell out of here."

Nash took the steps two at a time and balanced his weight on the balls of his feet. The light from Cole's phone stayed low enough to brighten their path but not alert anyone they were inside. When he reached the top floor, Nash crouched and scanned the wide-open room. Forgotten supplies, tarps, and more paint cans littered the plywood subfloor.

"It's empty, let's go." Cole nudged him in the back. The board on the window flapped, scraping against the windowsill.

"One sec." Nash pocketed his gun and strode farther into the room. He stopped at one of the boarded up windows and moved the loose plywood to gaze out at the dark, partially abandoned district as if he expected some kind of clue to reach out and thump him in the face. He was losing his edge. He couldn't think straight with the constant reminder that Conrad had Lexi and he didn't want her alive.

"Hey, Nash. Come check this out."

He pulled himself away from the window. On the other side of the room, Cole stood in the shadows, his body rigid, the light from his phone now off.

"What is it?" His shoulder brushed against Cole's as he approached, and he followed his steely gaze out the window that overlooked the alley. At first glance, a brick wall filled his vision. Cole pointed to a building adjacent to the one they stood in. A double garage with an empty parking pad in front of it sat two hundred feet or so away.

"That garage is lit up. Can't see if there's a vehicle in there, but we should check it out." The three small windows at the top of the garage door glowed. Cole pulled out his phone. "I'll use the key—"

Nash closed his hand around his brother's elbow. "We need to get closer." He charged to the staircase, not paying attention to the litter that scattered across the floor in his wake. Cole's footsteps pounded behind him.

He hit the main level and the scent of shit hit him like a wall. He coughed and charged through, his stomach lurching. He welcomed the chilly air in the alley with a deep inhalation but didn't pause. He kept his eyes trained on the garage off the alley. The windows were still lit, but the building beyond it was as dark as the rest on the street. He tightened his hold on his Beretta and the muscles in his forearms jumped with tension. What were the chances someone other than the guys who had Lexi would be in this area at this time of night?

"Nash, hold up." Cole's hand caught his bicep.

Nash's body hummed with adrenaline. They couldn't stop. Taking even a second could cost Lexi her life . . . it would cost *him* her life. Lexi meant something to him. Hell, she meant a lot.

If she dies because of me . . .

No. He couldn't go there. He couldn't lose her. Another innocent life wouldn't be taken because of his stupidity. He'd find her if it meant him dying in the process.

"What?" He wheezed the word through his tightening windpipe.

Cole turned his phone to face Nash. Everything around him slowed. The steady whir of the streetlamps amplified, and the slapping of the plywood against brick synced with the galloping of his heart against his breastbone. A red dot pulsed on the map.

Item found.

★   ★   ★

"LET ME GO, you sonofabitch!" Lexi kicked out her boot, and the heel connected with the brute's shin. He grunted, but his fingers chomped down harder on her biceps. He dragged her toward the chair, scraping her hip against the plastic-covered cement. Her chest spasmed with each shallow puff of air. She couldn't for the life of her slow her heart rate enough to draw in a proper breath.

She couldn't die here.

His talons released her, and blood rushed to the abused area.

Click

The clink of metal against metal turned the sweat on her skin to acid. She licked her lips and turned her head over her shoulder. Her eye met the black mouth of a gun. Her bones turned to jelly and sharp tremors attacked her muscles. She ran her gaze all the way up the length of his arm to meet his sharp green eyes. Drew's thick stubble had grown since the previous night—had he taken her to avenge his murdered friend? The other man from the truck stood a few paces behind Drew, sneering at her.

"Get in the chair." Drew gestured to the metal chair beside her with the gun and then trained the weapon back on her. "If I have to put you in it, you're going to get a bullet in the foot first."

She lifted her hands and nodded. Compliance was the only way to stay alive. If she continued to fight, things would get ugly. She had to stall. Had to come up with a plan. She pressed the sole of her foot into the ground and forced her weight to steady. She inched toward the chair and slid herself into it. The cold steel bit through the thin denim of her pants. Her gaze fell to the leather straps on the armrests. Dark crimson stained the material. Vomit crawled up her throat. She closed her eyes and forced the image of what the chair's previous occupant had suffered from her mind.

Drew's low, gruff chuckle broke the silence. He dropped his arm. The gun pointed at the ground. He stepped back until his shoes moved off the plastic.

"Don't worry, I won't use the restraints until the boss gets here." He glanced at his watch. "Any minute."

Lexi's muscles jumped with the need to catapult out of the chair and run the twenty feet to the stairs. But she'd never make it. He'd stop her with a bullet. She swept her gaze around the room. Five gallons of bleach lined the wall behind Drew. There was also a dinette table and chairs, and what looked like a toolbox on wheels. Other than that, it was bare.

The driver stepped forward. "I'm going to the bathroom," he said to Drew. "Don't start the fun without me." He winked at Lexi and then turned for the stairs.

A small pile of items on the table caught her eye—her gun, her phone, and Cole's keys. Drew's phone rang, and he dug it out of his coat pocket. Keeping his eyes trained on Lexi, he answered.

"Yup." A beat passed, and he backed away from her. "What the hell are you talking about? Jimmy said he arranged for the pickup at nine."

He checked his watch. "They're still here? Jesus, you should have told me that."

Lexi froze. *They're still here.* Who were "they"?

Drew paced away from her toward the stairs. She shifted her attention to the table across the room from her. If she could grab her gun, she could get off a shot that might just buy her time to run. She scooted her butt to the edge of the chair and looked in Drew's direction. She counted his steps as he argued with the person on the other end of the phone.

One, two, three, four, five, six, seven.

He turned around and walked back toward her and then retraced his movements.

Seven paces.

The table was a good fifteen feet away. But she could make it. Drew's voice rose a notch, and he sliced his hand through the air. "It's not my fucking fault you can't arrange shit!"

She pressed her boot into the floor and kept her eyes on him. As soon as he turned his back she would—

The staircase creaked. *No!* The driver was back already. Heavy footsteps shook the rickety stairs and then wide shoulders—much wider than the driver's—filled her vision. She clenched her fingers around the chair's seat and locked eyes with the newcomer. Gray streaks highlighted his hair and beard, accentuating the deep tan of his skin. His brown eyes warmed when they landed on her, and his laugh lines crinkled like scrunched tissue paper.

Conrad.

He strode toward her, his hands tucked in his brown leather coat, his movements slow and lazy.

"Ms. Ivanov. So nice to finally see you in person again. You've only gotten more beautiful. I can see why Nash is so consumed."

She sucked the insides of her cheeks over the ridges of her teeth. Her fingernails dug into the bottom of the chair and clawed into something sticky. She didn't want to explore its identity. Conrad looped his hand under the backrest of a chair at the table she'd been ready to dart for and dropped it in front of her. He lowered himself into it, sat back, and rested his ankle on his knee.

It had been almost a year since she laid eyes on him. Her dad had been hosting poker night. She'd passed Conrad on her way out of the house after dinner. That had been a few months before he'd plotted and carried out the murder of her family. And her. Though he hadn't succeeded at killing her, part of her had died that night in the fire.

Millions of words singed her tongue, but she couldn't form a single one. His mouth split into a grin, and her body pulsed with the need to lunge at his thick throat.

"It's been years since you've been in my house. What'd you think of the remodel?"

Acid burned her veins. "It's shit. Just like you."

The remark sprung from her mouth but fell flat in comparison to what she really wanted to say to him. Some of the amusement in his eyes faded, and he rolled his tongue along the inside of his bottom lip.

"You've always been a little bitch," he said, his cool exterior finally cracking.

"I'd rather be that than a murderer."

He folded his arms across his chest. The air between them crackled. If she had her gun, she'd shoot him in the face without a second thought. Then he laughed. The sound echoed through the space. "Trust me, Alexis. It's not my favorite method. I had no choice, just like I don't with you." He made a *tsk-tsk* sound. "Shame to kill someone so pretty." He shifted and pulled a metal lighter from his pocket and then lifted a cigar from inside his jacket. He sparked the end, inhaled, and puffed a ring of smoke at her. Not wanting to breathe the sweet cloud, she turned her head.

Rage pulsated through her, followed by disgust. She wouldn't die at the hands of this monster. Conrad deserved a bullet between his eyes, but she'd never make it to her gun. A bullet wouldn't save her life right now. But her mind could.

"Drew, come over here," Conrad barked, not taking his eyes off her. The man snapped something at whoever was on the other end of the call and disconnected. He strode toward them, and Conrad leaned forward in his chair. "Why don't you tell me what you know, Alexis?"

From the corner of her eye, she saw Drew raise his gun. She lifted her hand, keeping her eyes trained on Conrad. "There's no need for that. I know you're trafficking kids. I have the spreadsheets of orders, the account numbers of the buyers who've sent you money, and"—she leaned forward, mimicking his posture—"I have the ledger. The real one. The one from your safe."

The hard exterior of Conrad's face crumbled, and he shot forward. His hands closed around her throat. She gasped and clawed at his wrists, but he didn't loosen his hold. Fear took hold, and she kicked frantically as heat filled her face.

"You fucking cunt," he hissed. Spit sputtered between his teeth and landed on her cheek. Her chest convulsed. Blackness touched the corners of her vision. Drew muttered something that didn't penetrate her fog, and a beat later Conrad released his grip and tossed her back into the chair. She leaned forward, resting her elbows on her knees. She sucked in a breath, but it stopped at her throat. Her shoulders slumped until they touched her knees. Nausea knocked against her belly. She massaged the area his hands had vacated and focused on slow breaths until the blockage in her airway cleared.

Conrad's shiny loafers filled her vision. "I had no idea they'd gotten so much information," he said to Drew. "Send some guys out to find Nash. I want him dead tonight."

She snapped her head up, and her knees jerked on a tremor. They couldn't kill Nash. She wouldn't let them. She had to think of something.

"If anything happens to Nash and me, my colleagues have access to a safety deposit box. All the information we have on you and the sources will be leaked."

His lips spread into a smirk. "If that's true, you're going to be sorry you told me that." He turned to Drew. "Get your tools."

Drew disappeared behind Conrad momentarily, and she heard metal rattle over the concrete floor. He pushed the red toolbox beside her. Ice coated her skin and her blood turned solid. Drew lifted a small object, and the overhead lights illuminated the razor-sharp edge of a scalpel.

A low buzz sounded in her ears, drowning out their voices. Her mind revolted, but her body didn't respond.

"Let's get started, Ms. Ivanov."

CHAPTER 24

NASH TURNED TOWARD the garage but Cole's hands locked on his shoulders and propelled him against the back of the building they'd just left. As his shoulder blades connected with the brick, Nash shoved his brother's hands away.

"What the fuck are you doing?" He moved toward the garage again, but Cole blocked his path.

"You can't go in there yet."

Nash scoffed. Like hell he couldn't. Lexi was in there. Nothing short of an army would stop him. He closed his hands into fists. "Move."

Cole pressed his palms into Nash's chest. He brushed them away. "Look," Cole said. "We don't know how many men are inside. There were two in the vehicle when they took her, but there's likely more. If we go in without a plan or backup, none of us will make it out alive." Cole relaxed his stance. "It's your call, but you know if it were any other circumstance, you'd say the same."

Adrenaline pulsed through his muscles and

down to his feet. He shifted his gaze past Cole to the warehouse next to the garage. If Lex was in there, the guys wouldn't waste time. She was smart—she'd stall them—but there was a lot of shit they could do to make her suffer. Depending on who the guys were, things could get ugly fast. Cole took the momentary pause as an opportunity to punch a contact on his phone.

"Let me call Dare and Dallas. If one of them can come, we'll—"

Nash pushed past him. "Do that. In the meantime, I need to find out who's there." He moved to the side of the garage and gripped the door handle. He swung it open and faced Conrad's red Tesla. The sheen of sweat on his forehead rolled over his brow. He broke away from the door and wiped his eyes with his jacket sleeve. Of all the men who could be inside with Lexi, the last person he wanted was Conrad. At least some of the dudes had consciences and wouldn't volunteer to hurt a woman. But with Conrad overseeing things directly . . .

Fear slammed into Nash's palate and his throat closed. He had to get inside. If he was too outnumbered, he'd wait for his brothers before going in—if Lexi was safe. One thing was for certain: Lexi was getting out alive.

Even if he didn't.

He gestured to the warehouse. Cole's brusque voice telling him to stop didn't slow him. He'd deal with his brother later. But a tiny finger of relief wrapped around his heart. Seeing Cole's stony face reminded him that his brother was deadly. There wasn't a better man he could have on his side if shit went south. He tightened his fingers around the Beretta and stopped at the warehouse's main door. He tried the handle: locked.

He reached into the inside pocket of his jacket and pulled out his lock-pick set. If he shot the lock off, he'd alert the guys inside. If they were torturing Lexi, he sure as hell didn't want to accelerate things.

He inserted the tiny tools into the keyhole. Metal clanked against metal and the knob released. He gripped the Beretta tighter as the door creaked open. He closed the door quietly behind him and blinked until his eyes adjusted to the darkness. Not a chance he'd turn on the flashlight on his phone. Hearing a voice coming down the hall toward him, he darted for a set of stairs leading to the second level. He ascended to the third step, out of view from the hall.

"I don't know where the hell I'm going to get a van at this hour. Call me back if you find something."

Drew.

Nash shifted his gun so he held the mouth of it, the butt poised to slam into the motherfucker's head as soon as he stepped outside.

Achoo, achoo, achoo!

Nash snapped his head back and narrowed his eyes at the floor above his head. What the hell? The front door clicked shut. He wanted to follow Drew and question him, but the sound of that tiny sneeze ate at him. Drew had come from the other end of the main level, meaning he'd likely been in the basement, judging by the layout of the stairs.

The sneeze had been too child-like to have been Lexi's. But he couldn't ignore it. He moved up one step at a time. The wood groaned beneath his weight. Near the top of the stairs, he pressed his back to the wall and stalked sideways, his gun pointed in front of him.

"But, Allison . . ." a tiny voice wailed.

"*Shhh*, we need to do this now," an older female voice hissed. Nash pulled his phone from his pocket and turned the flashlight on. Hushed squeaks met the glare as he moved across the top floor. Nash froze.

Nearly a dozen sets of wide, terrorized eyes landed on him.

The children.

UH, CONRAD, WE have a problem," Drew said, his voice low and hesitant. Conrad's brown orbs fixated on him. Lexi watched their exchange, but her gaze kept jerking to the scalpel in Drew's hand. Footsteps sounded on the stairs—the driver was back.

She rubbed her thumb over the pad of her index finger. She had to keep the knife at bay and get Conrad talking.

"What kind of problem?"

Drew looked at her and then back to Conrad. "Uh—"

Conrad waved the air in front of him as if he were shooing a fly. "Don't worry about her. She won't be talking to anyone."

"The kids are still here."

Lexi wheezed in a breath. *The kids?* Her blood hammered through her veins. If the children were here, under the same roof, she could save them. No, she *had* to save them. Conrad's face morphed. Red lines cracked the whites of his eyes, and a vein down the center of his forehead protruded.

"How is that possible? They should be halfway to Texas by now!" His voice boomed in the small space.

Drew dragged his teeth across his bottom lip. "Jimmy called before you got here. He said the van broke down and we need to arrange for another mode of transportation."

Conrad huffed with annoyance, dropped his foot to the ground, and stood. "I told you to make sure this exchange was fucking seamless."

Drew's hand, still holding the scalpel, shook, and the driver stayed near the table and out of Conrad's line of vision, as if doing so would save him from the man's wrath.

"I-I know. When Leith died I—"

Conrad jabbed his forefinger toward Drew's chest. "Enough about Leith," he snarled. "Fix this. Now."

Drew nodded, resembling a bobblehead. "I can get a van and be back here in less than an hour."

Conrad jerked his head toward the stairs. "Then get the hell out of here." He flicked his cigar, and a chunk of ashes fell from the end of the paper and fluttered to the floor. Conrad lowered his gaze to her, and his lips melted into a smile. He whistled. "Boyd, get over here."

The driver stepped forward and shoved his hands into the pocket of his navy-blue hoodie. Drew passed Boyd the scalpel and ran for the stairs. Boyd gripped it, holding it away from his body.

"Take off her pinky," Conrad ordered. He returned to the chair in front of her and sucked on the end of his cigar. Lexi balled her hands into fists and lifted her chin, not daring to look at Boyd and the knife. If she did, she'd cave to the rush of panic. She couldn't give in to the terror. Somewhere in this building were cold, terrified children. Her heart wrenched against her breastbone. She was their only hope. When Drew came back, they'd be gone for good.

She leaned forward in her chair and fixed her stare on Conrad's weathered face. "You're not going to get away with this. We have too much information. Nash will—"

Conrad's chest shook on a laugh. "Nash will be dead within the hour."

She smiled. "You know as well as I do he's not easy to kill." She lifted her shoulder and crossed her legs. "Besides. He's not working alone."

Conrad's smirk faltered.

Time to go in for the kill. "We've been very careful to cover our bases. If you kill us, you will be exposed."

Conrad snorted. "Let me guess, if I don't kill you both, you won't rat me out if I let the kids go?"

She shook her head. "Oh no. You're going to jail for sure. It's your choice if you want to add two more murders to your charges."

"Killing you is long overdue." He motioned at Boyd.

The guy sauntered forward and stopped beside her. A thick wall of cologne hit her, burning her nasal passages like alcohol. She wrinkled her nose. Heat radiated from his thin body, and his hand knotted into her leather coat. Every muscle in her body tensed, but she didn't pull away. If she did, he might slice her.

"Is that why you killed my family? Because they knew about what you were doing with the group home?"

"Of course. Your dad was too goody-good. Always on the straight and narrow. He came to me a few months before I had them killed. I tried to pacify him, but he was like a dog with a bone. If he'd just turned a blind eye like everyone else, he'd still be alive today. And your mom too."

"And Brooks?"

Conrad shifted. "And him."

"What did you do with him, Conrad?" Her voice hit a high pitch. She didn't want to beg, but if she was going to die right here and now, she needed to know what he'd done to her brother.

Conrad flicked the end of the cigar again and then brought it to his lips. His eyes narrowed behind the haze of smoke. He rocked the chair back on its rear legs and smiled. "We were a bit more creative with him."

The air seeped from her lungs and tears burned her eyelids. She pressed her tongue to the roof of her mouth. Conrad deserved to die. Her family had been too good, too soft.

She wasn't.

She leaped from the seat and charged at Conrad. She shoved his shoulders and he toppled backward, the chair slid out from under him, and his head connected with the cement with a *whack!*

"Get her!" Conrad reached for her ankle. She jumped over his arm and lunged for the table. Footsteps scuffed across the floor behind her as she closed her hand around her gun and whirled around. Conrad knelt on the ground, his top lip arched into a snarl. Boyd held up the scalpel, his fingers devoid of color. She widened her stance and moved her thumb over the safety switch.

Click

Both men jumped. She smiled. "Don't fucking move."

CHAPTER 25

"**I**'M NOT GOING to hurt you," Nash said. The words came out on a croak as the enormity of what he'd stumbled upon sank in. Hell, after all he'd been through with Lionsgate this past week, plus the evidence Lexi had, it was futile to deny the organization's crimes. But a part of him had hoped they were wrong.

They hadn't been.

Numbness crept over his body, and he drew one slow breath after another. How the hell could he reassure these children?

A small girl, no more than eight years old, snuggled into the arms of the oldest girl. She turned her dirt-smudged face and peeked through her fingers at him. His heart ached. He'd been that small, terrified child once, and the scars hovered close to the surface. Then red-hot rage burned through him and he clamped his mouth to keep from roaring.

He dropped to his knees, placed the Beretta on the ground, and stripped off his sweater jacket. A boy, no older than ten, whimpered, "He's one of them, Ally. He has a gun." The boy scurried to a corner and cowered behind two pails. Nash shook his head and held out the sweater to the oldest girl, the one the boy had called Ally.

Ally . . .

After the sneeze, someone had said "Allison." Gage's shadowed face crossed his mind. His mentee had been worried about a girl who'd been suspiciously placed with a family . . . a girl named Allison. She had her arms curled protectively around the child.

She swept her gaze over him. Her eyes were sharp and hesitant. She was the oldest here, the defender of the younger ones.

He cleared his throat. "Yeah, I have a gun. But I'm after the guys who took you. You're safe now." A beat passed. No one moved. "I promise. My name is Nash. Allison, is it?"

She nodded. He forced his lips into a small smile in an attempt to put the kids at ease, but the way the corners of his mouth protested undoubtedly scared the shit out of them.

"My name is Nash. I think we have a friend in common—Gage Hunt."

Her bottom lip loosened and her jaw moved, but no words came out. She nodded and sniffled. Tears rolled over her cheeks, and she brought her knuckles to the tip of her nose. The kids all turned their faces to her and then back to him. Allison reached out and accepted the jacket then bundled it around the young girl's shoulders.

"You're Gage's mentor, right? He always talked about you."

This time the corner of his mouth twitched for real. "Don't believe everything he says."

She chuckled but didn't break away from the group of kids. Admiration swelled in his chest. God only knew what she'd been through the last couple of weeks, yet here she was, putting on a brave face and protecting the younger ones till the end.

"I'm going to make a quick phone call and get you guys out of here. How does that sound?"

One of the boys shuffled across the floor from the corner of the room. "Can you get us food? We haven't eaten since yesterday."

Fresh anger washed over Nash. Hell yeah he'd get them food. And warm clothes too.

"You bet, bud. We'll have you out of here in a few minutes and I'll get you a buffet of food."

The boy's eyes lit up. "Okay. Can I hold your gun?"

Nash snorted. Damn, kids were resilient. "No can do." He swiped up the gun and concealed it at the small of his back. "But you can pick out what food to order."

"I want pizza!"

Allison brought her finger to her lips. "Eli, please. We need to stay quiet until we're out of here."

Nash nodded his agreement and stood. He brought out his phone. With any luck, Cole had gotten a hold of backup and the kids wouldn't have to wait long. His insides spasmed. He needed to find Lexi, but he sure as hell couldn't leave the kids.

Cole answered on the first ring. "Yo."

"I need your help. I found a group of kids inside but haven't gotten to look for Lexi yet."

Cole hissed. "You found the kids?"

"Some." He didn't want to think about the kids who had come before this group. No, he couldn't. If he started to think along those lines, he'd go on a fucking killing spree. He'd have no problem doing that, but not until the kids and Lexi were safe. Then he'd release the beast. He stalked toward the window that overlooked the alley and out of earshot of the kids.

"I'm coming in," Cole said. "I have Drew knocked out and tied up in the Rover. He won't be any trouble."

"And Dallas?"

"He'll be here with a couple guys soon. I'm at the door. Where are you?" His voice dropped to a whisper.

Nash told him where they were and disconnected. He turned back to the kids huddled on the floor. "Hey," he said, crouching so as not to set them on edge any more than they were. "My brother is coming upstairs right now. We're going to get you guys outside, and a ride will be here in a few minutes."

The little girl lifted her head from Allison's shoulder. "We can go home now?"

Nash's throat clenched. The backs of his eyes burned, and he didn't trust himself to speak. He nodded. As the floorboards creaked beneath them, Nash stood.

Cole approached them slowly and quietly. He cleared his throat. "I'm Cole," he whispered. "I'm going to help get you guys out of here, but we need to hurry."

Eli stood and caught Cole's hand, and Nash accepted the little girl from Allison. Her small arms circled around his neck, and a fierce wave of protectiveness washed through him. If anyone tried to stop them, he'd annihilate them.

"She's sick," Allison said. "I think she's weak from not enough food and water."

Nash nodded and fought against the onslaught of emotion simmering inside him. "I need to carry my gun, okay?" he said to the young girl.

She tensed. "Okay."

"What's your name, sweetheart?"

"Lacey." Her small voice entwined itself into the fibers of his heart.

"Hang on tight to me, Lacey," he said, as they moved toward the stairs. She locked her hands at the back of his neck and burrowed her face into his throat. Nash followed Cole. Eli and two other kids walked between them. Allison and the rest of the kids stuck close to his back. Allison's fingers held the material at his spine.

"Watch your step," he said behind him, as they moved down the stairs. Near the bottom of the stairs, Cole stopped and held out his hand. Nash nodded and stopped as well.

Cole moved the few paces to the front door, cracked it open, and leaned outside. A couple of breaths later, he waved to them. Nash stepped off the bottom stair and held the door open as Cole disappeared outside. He ushered all the children out in front of him. Outside, a dark shadow stepped forward, and his pulse kicked up. Then the man's face caught the glow of the moon and Nash's shoulders relaxed a fraction.

Dallas.

Crack! Crack!

Nash jerked his head and met Cole's eyes for a beat. *Gunshots.*

From downstairs.

Lexi!

His stomach dropped to his abdomen with the weight of a lead ball. He thrust Lacey to Cole and stormed to the back of the warehouse. The subfloor shook under his feet. Blood hammered against his temples and adrenaline burned through his veins. He closed in on the staircase and silence met him, sending a river of sweat down his spine.

No. Please, God, no.

★   ★   ★

NOW WHAT?

Lexi's breath came out in short puffs, tearing at her dry lips with the force of a sandstorm. Her eyeballs strained as she jerked her gaze from one man to the next and back again, but she couldn't leave one of them unwatched for more than a millisecond. Conrad knelt on the concrete in the age-old pose of a proposal. Boyd stood a few paces to the left of Conrad, the scalpel clenched in his hand, both hands raised to shoulder height.

If she allowed them to move, they'd jump her. She'd be able to get off one shot, but not one that could take them both out. And any second, they could accept that risk—unless she thought of a way to get to the set of stairs that lay behind them.

Her hand burned to lower the gun and grab her phone, but she couldn't chance it. If she pulled her eyes away for even a moment, they'd cross the ten feet of distance and overpower her. She needed a plan, and she had nothing. Boyd shifted his gaze to Conrad, and her blood pressure spiked.

"Look at me!" she cried, bouncing on her toes. Boyd snapped his head back in her direction. "Lower the knife to the ground and slide it across the floor." Boyd's face hardened. "Do it," she growled.

His face crumpled into a scowl, but he did as

he was told. The knife skittered across the floor, but only a few feet away from where he stood. Bastard. She shifted her attention to Conrad. His hands hovered by his hips, his focus intent on her face. She should just kill him and be done with it. But as much as she wanted to, as much as he deserved it, she wouldn't give him that gift. Conrad would pay for what he'd done in prison. She could, however, shoot and injure him so she could escape. But what would Boyd do if she did? Could she take out Conrad and get off a second shot in time to stop Boyd?

No more indecision. She had to act fast. "You." She gestured to Boyd. "Take out your phone and call Nash."

He lifted his shoulders. "I can't. I don't have his number."

She narrowed her eyes into slits at him. "Fine. Take Conrad's phone, dial Nash, and put it on speaker. If you try anything funny, I'll shoot you both."

"No need to do anything rash, Lexi," Conrad said. "I'm reaching for my phone." He lowered his hand to the pocket at his thigh. Boyd inched closer to Conrad, and she shifted her gaze to him for a flicker of a second.

Conrad moved, and she snapped her attention back to him. In his hand was a steel object: a gun.

Shit, shit, shit.

"I think you can drop that now," Boyd said

with a snicker. She tightened her hold on her weapon. No way in hell she was backing down.

"Last chance, Ms. Ivanov. Drop the gun." Conrad pushed to his feet, stretching to his full height. She took a step back. She needed justice. Justice for her family, justice for the children, justice for Nash. She couldn't get that if he killed her. Her chances shrunk by the second.

She had no choice. Her shoulders stiffened in preparation of the kickback, and she locked her hands tighter around the handle. Conrad moved his finger on the trigger.

Crack!

She ducked. A bullet whizzed by her head. She pulled the trigger.

Crack!

Concrete dust exploded across the room. She'd missed.

Crack!

The gun careened out of her hand and pain exploded across her knuckles. She gripped her injured fingers with her free hand. Blood oozed down her wrist. Spotting her weapon under the table, she dropped to her knees. She stretched for the piece, and pain seared across her side as her stitches pulled at her skin.

Boots scuffed across the floor and a meaty hand knotted into the hair at her scalp. Her skull lit with fire as Conrad dragged her to her feet. His balled fist connected with her injured midsection, and the air leaped out of her lungs. She gasped as pain ripped across her abdomen. She twisted in his hold. Strands of hair ripped away from her delicate flesh. He wound his fist up again—

"Let her go!"

Conrad froze but didn't loosen his grip. Footsteps rushed across the rough ground. Conrad's arm looped around her neck, flattening her back against his chest. The hard metal of a gun ground into her cheekbone. Her gaze swung to Nash. His dark eyes met hers, slamming into her soul. Fear, sharp and raw, creased his face. His Beretta was trained on Conrad . . . and her.

"I should have done this a long time ago," Conrad spat next to her ear. Nash was screaming. His voice reverberated around the room, but it didn't penetrate the fog of terror suffocating her. Conrad's rough cheek worked up into a smile against hers, and he lowed his lips to her earlobe. "Say hi to your dad for me."

Click

Her legs gave out and a blood-red haze crept over her vision. Her pulse tapped against her temples, and the ice that had settled on her skin slowly warmed. Conrad cursed.

The gun didn't go off.

The feeling came back to her limbs, one cell at a time. Her lungs moved of their own volition. She was alive. Nash filled her vision. His arms and legs pumped as he sprinted across the room. Conrad pulled the trigger again, and it clicked in her ear. The clip was empty. Nash's fist split the air and connected with Conrad's face. His head snapped away from hers, releasing his hold. Nash pulled her into his arms and backed them toward the stairs, his Beretta pointed at Boyd and Conrad. His woodsy scent touched her nostrils, and her muscles relaxed as if reacting to a sauna. His lips brushed her cheek and his arm snaked around her ribs almost too tightly, but there wasn't a chance in hell she'd ask him to let her go.

"You're safe, baby." The words came out gritty with emotion. She grasped her hands around his forearm and let him continue to move them away from Conrad. Nash's solid strength pulsed against her back and his arm that held the gun didn't waver from its target.

Boyd's skin tone was flaky gray. He dropped the knife and lifted his hands. "I wasn't going to go along with anything, bro. I swear to god. Ask your brother—I tipped him off about Conrad's plan to trap you."

"You traitor!" Conrad got to his hands and knees and dove for the gun that still lay beneath the table.

"Don't move, you sonofabitch," Nash barked. Conrad didn't slow. Nash fired. The bullet slammed into the concrete wall above Conrad's head. Conrad stopped advancing and raised his hands in surrender.

"Get to your feet and face the wall." The no-nonsense timbre of Nash's voice brought the strength back to her muscles as the men complied. He inched her out of his arms and took a step toward the two men. The bottom stair brushed her leg, and Nash ushered her onto it while keeping his gaze on Conrad and Boyd. "Go upstairs, honey. Cole is right outside and—"

She gripped his shoulder, preventing him from boosting her further up the stairs. "There are kids here, Nash. We have to find them."

The deep crease in his brow flattened, and the hard corners of his mouth softened. "One step ahead of you."

She gasped. "You found—"

Footsteps roared across the floor overhead. She turned her head to the top of the stairs and three beams of light assaulted her vision. She raised her hand to block the glare and squinted. Several people in uniform crowded the opening, guns drawn.

"Police! Drop your weapons!"

CHAPTER 26

B ODIES RUSHED DOWN the stairs and circled Conrad and Boyd. Nash allowed an officer to disarm him and search him for weapons. Dallas showed up a second later to clear his name with the cops—Dallas was the only one in the family with close connections to the police department.

The second the officers backed away from Nash, he dropped to his knees in front of Lexi. She sat on a crusted orange pail, her hands shoved back into her hair, her eyes wide and riveted on the plastic sheeting only feet away. Blood rolled down the back of her left hand, covering her wrist. She'd need to get the wound looked at as soon as possible.

He smoothed his hands down her arms. Ice chilled his palms even through the leather of her jacket. If he hadn't given his jacket to the kids, he'd have wrapped it around her shoulders.

"Lexi, honey," he said. His voice shook as his gaze took in her mascara-smudged eyes. Her lashes lifted. Her eyes were pained.

"Did they touch you?" he rasped. He'd kill them. Fuck, he'd do more than kill them. He'd tear them apart. He'd wrap his hands around their worthless necks and—

She shook her head. The tight bundle of tension in his chest released just enough to allow him to breathe.

"He was going to. Conrad ordered Boyd to cut off my pinky finger, but I . . . I . . ."

Nash cupped the back of her head and brought her face to his throat. "Shhh. Baby. It's all over." Her fingernails bit through his shirt, piercing his sides, but he didn't care. He massaged the back of her neck until her rigid muscles loosened in his grip. He lightly lifted her injured hand. "What happened to your hand?"

"Conrad shot at me. It's just a graze." She inhaled, and her chest expanded against him. She pulled away and looked into his eyes. "I'm so glad you're here."

He pressed his forehead to hers and chuckled. The thought of being anywhere else, of not moving mountains to find her, was inconceivable.

"What's funny?" Her breath puffed from her lips, and all the chaos around them fell away.

"Nothing is funny. But honey, I've been out of my goddamn mind these last few hours. I'm never letting you go on a mission like this again."

She snapped away from him. "Never letting me? What the hell is that supposed to mean?"

He smiled and tugged a lock of her hair. "Going into Conrad's house was risky as hell and you know it."

She snarled, and he had to suppress the smile that tickled his mouth. "Yeah, and look what we accomplished," she said, gesturing to Conrad's back as he ascended the stairs in handcuffs. "If we hadn't done this tonight, he'd have gotten away with it. And the kids," she said, practically wailing. "How can you say it was too risky?"

He stroked his knuckles along her jawline. "Because I'm in love with you, Lexi." The words scraped out of his throat, and he touched her full bottom lip with his thumb.

Her eyes rounded, and she sucked her breath in through her teeth. She searched his face, and some of the color she'd lost returned to her cheeks. But she didn't say anything.

He cleared his throat. Had he scared her? His mind worked at the speed of light. He needed to explain the pit of devastation that had taken residence in his heart since the second he found out she was missing. "I was really close to losing you tonight. The thought of that makes me insane. When I heard those shots, I thought you were dead." Pain spread through him at the memory. Had she died, it would have been his fault. His fault for not protecting her, for not finding her quicker, for not doing things differently. But he had found her. And he'd never let her go again.

She reached up and dragged her hand through his hair. Her teeth nipped the very tip of his thumb and her eyes sparked. "I love you too, Nash." She connected her mouth to his and her words fell around him, reverberating through his soul and marking her claim on his heart. She loved him. It had been years since anyone had said that to him, and even longer since he'd believed them.

But he believed Lexi. He didn't need anyone else for the rest of his life. He welcomed her sweet, intoxicating flavor as her tongue touched his and then pulled away. He opened his eyes. The sweet-as-sugar sparkle that had lit her face turned sour, and she pursed her lips.

"But I can't give up my work. Please, don't ask me to." She spoke it as a request, but her tone teetered on shrill. He blew a breath through his lips. She was crazy, headstrong, driven, and so damn cocky it turned him on like nothing else.

"I should have known you wouldn't make this easy."

The crease between her eyes deepened.

"I wouldn't change you for the world, babe. Even your job."

"Good. You couldn't anyway."

He laughed and helped her to her feet. "Let's give our statement and get the hell out of here."

"Ms. Ivanov?" Nash turned to face the woman addressing Lexi. "I'm Detective Aldridge. May I have a word with you?" The woman's light brown eyes sharpened on Nash. She studied his face and then pulled her attention back to Lexi and gave her a tight smile.

Nash planted his arm around Lexi's shoulders. "We're happy to provide any information we can, but first we'd like to know where the kids are."

She nodded. "It was lucky you stumbled upon the missing children. I hate to think about what would have happened had you not found them. They're being taken to the hospital, and their families will be notified immediately. They're dehydrated and weak, and surely their trauma will need to be addressed." She bounced her eyebrows at Lexi. "Ms. Ivanov, can you explain what happened?"

Lexi nodded and straightened her shoulders. As if she'd given thousands of statements, she offered precise details of the events. At one point, Detective Aldridge held up her hand. "Wait, I'm not following you. You were kidnapped outside Conrad's house? Why were you there to begin with?"

Lexi squirmed against him. He didn't need to read her mind to know she was afraid of handing over the ledger and the files her brother had given her. High-profile cases like this tended to disappear. When Lexi didn't respond, the detective lowered her pad and pursed her full lips. Nash tightened his hold on Lexi. Detective Aldridge was too damn sharp and observant.

Could she be trusted with this information? He wouldn't know for sure until he spoke with Dallas. Her eyes, the color of milk chocolate, zeroed in on him.

"One of the other officers mentioned your name is Nash Holmes. Correct?" She flipped her notepad open again and Nash nodded.

"The children said there was another man who helped them leave, but only you and Dallas were here when we arrived. Who was the other man?"

Nash tucked the corner of his mouth in. "It was just Dallas and me. The kids must be confused." He shoved his free hand in his pocket. Heat from Lexi's glare ate through his cheek, but mercifully, she stayed quiet.

The detective frowned and snapped to a previous sheet of paper. "Really? Because they were all certain there was a third man. One child said the man had introduced himself as Cole, and he gave a physical description."

Lexi took a step forward, and his arm fell away from her. "I'm sorry, Detective. We're really exhausted, and I think I'm in a bit of shock. If there aren't any other pressing questions, can we meet you tomorrow? We'll give you more details then?"

Detective Aldridge's sniper-like stare scanned Lexi. Then she shrugged. "We have no grounds to keep you here." She smiled, but the corners of her mouth pierced her cheeks with tension. "But I would appreciate a visit tomorrow." She pulled out two business cards and handed one to each of them. "Call me if anything else comes to mind before then."

The detective turned and climbed the stairs. Lexi spun around to face him, her eyebrows sewed together and her turquoise blues riveted to him. "Why—"

"Shhh. We'll talk when we're alone." He led her up the stairs and outside. The chilly air had dropped several degrees to damn cold. He bundled Lexi under his arm and led her to Conrad's Range Rover.

"Whose vehicle is this?"

Nash ushered her into the passenger seat and then rounded the vehicle and hopped in. "Conrad's," he said, as he buckled his seatbelt. He shifted into drive.

"I'm surprised the cops didn't confiscate it. So why did you lie about Cole being there?"

Nash rolled through a stop sign and got onto the main road leading toward the interstate. He massaged the steering wheel's firm leather, and it crackled under the pressure. "Because he'd be arrested." He checked the sideview mirror and merged onto the interstate. He glanced at her. She sat with her knees pressed together and her hands tangled in her lap. She didn't acknowledge his reasoning, but her mouth was tense. Dammit, he hated asking her to lie, but there was no help for it.

He had to protect his brother. "Check the glove box."

She leaned forward and pulled the handle. "Oh my god," she said with a gasp. "You have it!" Her thumbs smoothed over the book.

"Yeah, and we need to get home and get as much information decoded as we can before we talk to that detective again."

★　★　★

LEXI RUBBED HER eyes, but it only made the graininess stick to her lids like chalky eyeliner. The laptop's blue light penetrated her vision, making the headache that had started an hour ago pound even more. She needed sleep, a shower, and copious amounts of caffeine or wine. Either would do.

Nash's thick fingers slid around the nape of her neck and massaged. She moaned and rested her forehead on her balled fists.

"Rest, babe. We'll be a hell of a lot more productive after a few hours of sleep."

She snorted. "You don't seem at all fazed by fatigue."

He laughed, and his breath tickled her neck. "I'm used to this. You're not."

She grunted. "I can't stop though. We need to get these names together and figure out the best way to expose them. Maybe email is the safest option. We can CC the FBI and Congress." She moaned again. "Just don't stop what you're doing."

"I love it when you say that." He joked, his voice soft but his hands gently kneading.

"If you don't stop, I'll fall asleep." Her body rebelled against her words, needing his connection as much as the easing of her tension. His palms continued to work, and she forced her eyes open to stare at the screen. She ignored the part of her that wanted to relax into his strength and close her eyes. She had twenty names of buyers decoded, and there were dozens more. Nash had been on the phone since they got in. He'd ordered ten pizzas, and Dallas was delivering them to the kids in the hospital. Then he'd talked to Cole. His voice had dropped low as he explained that the cops had been given his name and description. "You'll need to lay low for a while," Nash had cautioned him.

He leaned past her and hit the Print Screen button. "I can help decode now. We'll get this done in no time."

TWO HOURS LATER, Lexi dropped the pen to the desk and massaged the ache in her wrist. It had been years since she wrote so much by hand—and neatly enough that she could take a picture of it and convert it to a JPEG file. She'd be lucky if she didn't develop carpal tunnel syndrome.

Eighty-seven names. A dozen of which were high profile. One, she was certain, was a well-known judge. She'd make several copies of the list and email it to her boss and colleagues—and she'd even be early on the deadline Lauren had given her. Having a large group of people in strategic positions would be key to getting this story out and the criminals prosecuted.

Nash rolled his chair closer and placed his hand around her right wrist. His thumb smoothed over the tendons on the back of her hand. A thick white bandage surrounded where the bullet had grazed her left hand.

"How the hell did you get through those so fast with an injured hand? I still have ten left." The heat of his palm warmed her skin to the bone. God, she loved how he could do that. One touch from him raised her body temperature in seconds. But it wasn't always need that had that effect on her. It was just him. He was in tune with her, connected by an invisible channel to her inner needs and fears.

"My right hand is fine."

"Luckily, but I'm sure the other one hurts like a beast." He brushed her hair away from her shoulder and his lips, soft and firm, touched her bare skin. "You need to sleep, honey. We can do more in the morning."

She turned over her hand to tangle it in the one that still caressed her wrist. "And you're going to let me sleep, are you?" She cocked her eyebrow at him. He lifted his fingertip and tapped the arch of her brow.

"Is that a challenge?"

She laughed and dropped her head back. "It would be if I weren't so exhausted."

He brushed his lips over her forehead. "Let's go to bed."

★   ★   ★

DETECTIVE ALDRIDGE SPREAD her honey-toned hands over the pages of names. Her eyes skimmed the information as if she were mentally download-ing it. Nash rested his palm on Lexi's thigh and gave it a tight squeeze. Comfort emanated from his skin and she ached to sink closer to his side. She covered Nash's rough knuckles with her hand but didn't take her eyes off the detective.

Nash had called Dallas first thing that morning, and Dallas had said Detective Aldridge was one of the few people on the force he knew for certain wasn't corrupt. If they were wrong about trusting her with this, they were screwed. Lexi had done her due diligence by sending their findings to the proper chains, but with something this big and with the influential names they'd decoded, it was hard to say who—if anyone—could be trusted.

Lexi reached across the desk and pointed to a name. "You've probably heard about—"

Detective Aldridge shoved her chair back and stood. She crossed the room to the open door of her office and shut it. The blinds on the window swayed back and forth and rattled with the force of it.

She strode back to the chair behind the desk. Her light-gray dress pants outlined her toned legs, and her white button-down shirt brought out the rich tone of her skin. She sat, flung her straight, dark hair over her shoulder, and folded her arms on the table.

"You can't speak about these names to anyone," she said, her voice firm but barely above a whisper. Lexi shuffled to sit on the edge of the seat. Nash had been quiet the whole time, present under duress. But Lauren had given her no choice. If she wanted the story to run—which was a must—she had to play by her boss's rules. Sending the email to the FBI and congress first had been sneaky, and the move would probably come back to bite her in the ass, when Lauren found out, but she had to protect her own life, not just her job.

Lexi slid her gaze to Nash. He was leaning back in the chair beside her. His ankle rested on his knee and his jaw was set in a hard, sharp line. She licked her lips and brought her attention back to the detective.

"You should know that this story will be published tomorrow," Lexi said. "I sent this list to the FBI and Congress—"

Detective Aldridge held out her hand. "I'm not sure I would have done that, Ms. Ivanov."

Nash sat forward and pinned the detective with

his glare. "Why not?"

Her dark eyes shifted to the desk and then back up. "A lot of these people are high profile. But there are a few who are more concerning than others."

She knows something.

Was it possible Conrad and Lionsgate were already under investigation and Lexi and Nash had beat them to it? Lexi bounced in her seat. "Who?"

Detective Aldridge tapped her index finger against one of the pages and rolled her lips in and out. Her eyes crinkled with indecision and she took a deep breath. One side of her mouth lifted. "Well, all of them. I'd say with the information collected, you're in a good position. We'll have a team on this immediately, and I don't see any reason why there isn't enough proof to hold the people involved. I mean, you even have wire transfers. This would have taken our team a year, and you did it in a fraction of the time." It should have been a compliment, but something about the woman's tense shoulders and unrelenting gaze said otherwise.

Lexi forced a smile. "I'm damn good at my job, Detective."

She leaned forward. "And you didn't have any other help?"

Nash's fingers flexed on her knee. She resisted the urge to elbow him. She wasn't stupid enough to throw Cole into the mix. "Nope. Just my run-of-the-mill sources that every journalist has." She lifted her brown leather messenger bag from the floor. "If you need anything else, please don't hesitate to contact me."

Nash dropped his feet to the floor. Detective Aldridge stretched her arm across the desk to shake Nash's hand, and then Lexi's. "I'm impressed with your work. We'll be in touch."

"Thank you," Lexi said, smiling.

She followed Nash through the police station and outside. Rays of sunlight broke through the cloudy sky. He walked her to the passenger side of his truck, but instead of opening the door, he rested his hand on the window beside her.

"You okay?" He laced his fingers with hers. She nodded and pressed her back to the door, not caring about the droplets of water that would stick to her coat.

"I'm fine. I hope she's right and they get everyone involved into custody." She tucked her hair behind her ear, and his hand moved from her fingers to her waist.

"You're safe. I'm glad you're taking time off after this."

Lauren had insisted she take her three weeks' vacation, plus additional time without pay for stress leave. Lexi would have been more than happy to just take her regular vacation, but Nash had been adamant—she needed the time away from work.

She pushed her fingers through her hair. "I might go crazy not working."

Nash laughed and lowered his mouth to hers. His tongue slipped through her teeth and her insides melted. She rose up on her toes and gripped his coat. Fire spread through her and she bent her head back, wanting more. He smiled against her mouth and pulled back.

"I have something that will help your separation anxiety."

"Mmm," she said. "I don't need to take time off from work to enjoy you."

Nash squinted, looked up at the sky, and raised one shoulder. "You do if you want to enjoy me in the Maldives."

She dropped back onto her heels. "What are you talking about?"

He grinned. "We need to get away." Some of the spark left his dark eyes, and he traced her jaw with his thumb. "It'll be safer if we're out of the country until the dust settles and we're certain who's being charged. Our flight leaves at 6:00 a.m. tomorrow. You in?"

She pinched the inside of her bottom lip between her teeth. The fact that Nash didn't feel safe set her nerves on edge. But there wasn't much else she could do. They'd handed over all the evidence to the right people and covered their bases. The story would run first thing in the morning and by that time, they'd be on a plane. A few weeks in paradise with the man she loved would be heaven.

She rose onto her toes again and slipped her hand around his neck. She closed her mouth over his and his arms snaked around her waist, pulling her closer. She leaned back and nipped his bottom lip. "Hell yeah. There's nowhere else I'd rather be."

EPILOGUE

L EXI LIFTED THE edge of her white bikini bottom, revealing pale skin. Almost time to roll over. Her gaze skimmed the spot on her side where the bullet had grazed her, now fully healed. She wiggled her shoulders on the lounger, settling deeper into the stiff material. Warmth radiated over her skin and only partially because of the vibrant sun that beat down through the cloudless sky. The other reason for her warmth slid his knuckles over her hip. Tremors raced over her skin. God, they'd had sex twice today and it was just past noon.

"You need to stop that," she said, rolling to her side to face him. All that did was shift his fingers to the lip of her bikini bottoms covering her butt. The last two weeks had been perfection. The turquoise waters of the South Pacific surrounded their overwater bungalow and lapped around them in a gentle, constant symphony.

Nash's lazy, lopsided grin sent throbbing need through her thighs. "You won't be saying that when your legs are shaking."

She laughed and swatted his chest. He caught her hand and brought her knuckles to his mouth. The rough scrape of his whiskers made her turn her hand over and palm his jaw. He caught her wrist and kissed the old wound on her hand that was now a fresh scar.

"I love you." And god, did she ever. Being on the island had shown her a side of Nash she hadn't seen before. He was relaxed. Happy. He didn't stalk around with purpose but waded slowly in the water or stood still on the sand absorbing the sunset and holding her in front of his chest.

He'd said she needed this trip, but *he* had too.

"Have you checked your email today?" she asked.

The smile slid from his face and she wished she could take back the words—sort of. Life was perfect on the island, but at home turmoil roared in their wake. Conrad faced human trafficking and forced labor charges. The FBI had gone to great depths and discovered that he'd been exploiting children for two decades. He'd been using the group home as a front. Rene, the administrator, and Jimmy, another enforcer and mentor, had also been arrested.

But it was all so much bigger than she and Nash had expected. Conrad had been paying social workers to bring him children of certain ages and physical descriptions before selling them off to the highest bidder. Conrad also had a niche—selling teenaged boys for forced labor. All in all, he'd been raking in nearly a million a year in human-trafficking deals. The good news was that so far, more than twenty kids who'd been sent to the US, Mexico, and Asia in recent months had been rescued.

Nash lifted his phone and brought the screen to life. "Oh shit." His thumb moved over the screen as he read. Lexi pushed herself up on her elbow and leaned onto his chair. It was too bright outside to see at her angle.

"What?"

"Well, they have Congressman Anthony Greer in for questioning." Nash whistled through his teeth. "And Judge Tim Olsen."

Thank god. She'd been worried about those big names slipping through the cracks. "You know, I wasn't sure about Detective Aldridge, but she's been a pit bull with this case."

Nash's free hand fell to her forearm, and he toyed with her lightly oiled skin. "Well, you dropped a bomb with that article. It would have been next to impossible for anyone to bribe their way out after that."

She smiled and stretched back out on the chair. Her cheeks tingled with delight. Lauren had congratulated her on a seamless case. She'd been pissed as hell that Lexi had gone straight to the paper with the story, but despite that, she'd promised her a raise. And according to one of her colleagues, there was buzz about her being nominated for an IRE Award.

"How's Gage doing?"

Nash sat up, his body tense. Lexi turned to see a waiter approaching with a tray. She lay back down while Nash stood and approached the man. They exchanged a few words and Nash returned with a plate of fruit.

"He's good," he said. "I think he'll be really happy in the new foster home. It also helps that we were able to place him with Allison.

"You know, we could take them both in," she said softly.

Nash beamed. His eyes watered, and he turned his head toward the ocean. "I've been considering the same thing. We'll let the dust settle first and see how Gage and Allison feel about that. I don't want them too close to this until we know it's over." He cleared his throat. "Hungry?"

"Ugh, I'm starving." She sat up and accepted one of the plates then scooted over so Nash could sit beside her on the lounger. He pulled up one of the side tables, which held two iced beverages. She picked up the light blue one and sipped. Coconut rum and other delicious island liquors puckered her taste buds and instantly took the edge off the heat that bore down on them.

"He said the papaya is to die for."

"Mmm." She lifted a wedge lying on a large

purple flower and popped it in her mouth. As the slippery fruit's flavor exploded on her tongue, her eyes fell to the petals it had sat on. A large pear-shaped diamond ring composed the white kaleidoscope at the center of the flower. She sucked in her breath, by some miracle managing not to take the fruit along with it.

"Nash . . ."

She reached for the ring, and her fingers shook as she lifted the heavy piece of jewelry. If she had to guess its weight, she'd say three carats. She dragged her eyes away from the sparkling beauty pinched between her fingers and turned to face Nash. He'd propped his sunglasses on top of his head, and his teeth gleamed in the sunlight. He gently took the ring from her.

"I knew you were different when you drugged me on our first date." A rough chuckle broke through his lips as he picked up her left hand. "I can't say it was love at first sight, but even when I wanted to throttle you, I admired you. You're stronger than anyone I know and have taught me how to love. And more importantly, how to trust someone."

Her chest swelled with happiness. A wall of tears filled her eyes, and Nash became a hazy form. She laughed, took off her sunglasses, and swept them away. Nash leaned forward and kissed her beneath each eye, and then on her mouth. She licked her lips, tasting her own saltiness. Just when she parted her lips for more, he leaned away.

"Hold that thought, babe." He plucked up her ring finger and held the ring at her manicured fingernail. "Alexis, will you continue to make me the happiest man . . . forever?"

The water balloon of happiness in her chest burst and she threw her arms around his neck. He should have staggered or even toppled off the chair, but he didn't budge. Instead, he closed his arms around her and kissed her hair.

"Yes, yes, yes!" She bounced in his arms on a teeter-totter of giddiness. His chest rumbled with a chuckle. She pulled away and held out her trembling hand. He slipped the ring on her finger, and the dazzling diamond ate up the bottom part of her appendage. "It's incredible," she whispered.

He squeezed her hand, forcing her to look up into his eyes. It was hard to imagine that she'd once interpreted his onyx orbs as evil. She now knew them to be raw, honest, and protective. His heat dampened her palm, and she squeezed his hand back.

"God I love you," she said.

He rested a hand on her cheek. His forehead hovered an inch from hers. The depth of his eyes crashed through her aura and sucked her in. "Not nearly as much as I love you."

She dipped her head as more tears swam toward her lashes. She sniffed and dashed them away, but the hole of devastation that had been in her heart for months grew tenfold. Nash's brows met over his nose.

"What's wrong, honey?"

Shit. This was supposed to be the happiest moment of her life and yet all she could think about was Brooks. How could she get married without having him apart of her day? With their parents gone, he'd want to walk her down the aisle. Her stomach clenched. Detective Aldridge and the FBI had promised to search for him, but he'd disappeared without a trace—or in this circumstance, a paper trail.

"I'm fine." She laughed through her tears.

He shook his head. "We'll find him, honey. I promise you." She sucked back a sob, and he wrapped his arms around her. Some of the pain ebbed away. If Brooks was alive, Nash would find him. But what she feared most was that instead of finding him, they'd find out what had happened to him.

She rested her head on Nash's shoulder and stared out at the clear, shallow ocean around them. As soon as they were back home, she'd focus all her energy on finding Brooks. But for now, she was going to enjoy the bright ray of happiness who engulfed her. Nash. The man who made her laugh, who made her feel safe, and who drove her crazy— all at the same time.

And he was all hers. Forever.

Turn the page for an excerpt from
TRACED . . .

Excerpt from Traced

CHAPTER 1

A *SSHOLE.*

Tess jangled the keys in her palm as she took the last few steps to her apartment door. Three damn hours she'd waited in the bar and he hadn't shown. As if she had time for this nonsense. Okay, so maybe it wasn't the enigmatic, elusive black-market-dealer's fault—perhaps the bartender hadn't passed along her message, or maybe she'd gotten the instructions wrong.

No, no, no. She'd delivered the words exactly how Alexis had instructed, and the young bartender's wide-eyed stare had proven he'd correctly translated her meaning when she'd asked for "a side of fairy dust" with her cosmopolitan. What a bust. Now she had to find someone else to sell half a dozen bricks of solid gold to. God. She needed a glass of wine. Once she got out of the too-snug red dress, which she'd worn for the sake of the club's dress code, she'd relax.

She inserted the key into the lock. It didn't snap.

She froze and glanced down at the door handle wrapped in her hand. She'd locked her door. She *always* locked her door. She swallowed and retracted the key then pushed the door open. She'd been busy fuming over being stood up—maybe she simply hadn't felt the lock's resistance because of that?

Darkness met her at the threshold.

Warning skittered up the back of her neck.

The living room lamp she always left on was off. She shook her head and moved into her apartment. She was losing her mind. No one was after her—at least not yet. Her father had given her his assets only hours earlier, before leaving the country. His warning had been clear: she had three days, tops, before the organization realized he was gone. She needed her hands clean of the gold, but there was no way Lionsgate Kinship could know about her involvement yet—her father had made sure of that.

The spring-loaded door swung shut behind her. She didn't bother groping for the light switch. The kitchen bulb had burned out two days ago and she hadn't made it a priority to pull out the ladder and change it. She blinked rapidly, trying to adjust her eyes to the eerie darkness of her one-bedroom apartment.

She made her way past the kitchen island and into the open-concept living room. Thankfully, light streamed through the large sliding glass doors at the far end of the room. This time she reached for the light switch next to her bedroom door that jutted off from the living room. Her knuckles bumped over the smooth drywall.

A rush of movement sounded.

She whirled around just before a solid body slammed her against the wall. Panic drove her senses into a frenzy. Fight versus flight clashed behind her eyelids like two trains hitting head-on. Fight won. She opened her mouth to scream, but a large, hot palm clamped over her lips, cutting off the sound. Her back connected with the blasted switch she'd been searching for, poking her in the spine.

She jerked her knee in the vicinity of her attacker's crotch, but the thick muscle of his thigh blocked her. Her arms lay crushed between her chest and his.

Immobilized.

Her breath came in fast pants, and the thick odor of his cologne—citrus and tree bark—hit her nose. A serene forest certainly wasn't the first image to come into her mind.

He's going to kill me.

"Don't fucking scream." The command lacked bite, but the cool monotone rattled her core.

Tess tried to nod but couldn't make her head move. She stared into the face that hovered less than an inch from hers. The glow from the streetlamp outside her patio doors created a large rectangle of light on her living room floor. Dark hair waved back over the top of his head, and the sides were smoothed down in some kind of fade. Shadows shielded the true color of his eyes, leaving only onyx-looking irises staring at her.

Part of her ached to see the rest of his face. To know what her killer looked like. But she didn't dare move.

"Understand?" His growl shattered the steel that had taken over her muscles. She jerked her head successfully this time. He peeled away his hand.

Instinctively, she licked her lips. Salt from his sweaty palm hit her taste buds. Revulsion filled her. "Who are you?"

He placed his hands on either side of her head, boxing her into his space. "You know exactly who I am."

Saliva swarmed her mouth and she forced it down. It couldn't be. She'd waited at the table the bartender had guided her to and hadn't moved until last call had been announced. She'd given the bartender her name—a requirement when making the request to see the dealer—but that was it. She didn't even know *his* name. "How did you find me?"

He snorted and drew his head back an inch. "I know everything about you, Tessa George. I know you own Hit the Mat yoga studio, downtown. I know you have over a hundred grand in the bank.

I know your daddy paid cash for this condo. I know you use the same password for all of your social media accounts as well as your online banking—didn't anyone tell you that's stupid? I also know you're single. What I don't know is why the fuck you came looking for *me*."

The muscles in her throat pulled down another gulp of moisture. She didn't—couldn't—tear her gaze from the hot, angry-as-all-get-out eyes that bore into hers.

She opened her mouth. And snapped it shut. She should've listened to Alexis. This was a damn bad idea. Lexi was always right. From the moment she'd shown up at her yoga studio two months prior, they'd become fast friends. She told Lexi almost everything, and her friend's job as an investigative journalist made her even more of a kick-ass know-it-all who always had her back.

He harrumphed. His arms straightened, but he didn't push away from the wall. Instead, he raked his gaze down the length of her and back up, lingering at her thighs, before meeting her eyes again. "Usually women find me for a booty call— but that doesn't fit. Even in that dress." His fingers grazed her hip.

She jumped. Fire scorched the skin beneath her dress, heating her stomach. It wasn't arousal. Well, maybe a hint of arousal. But only because she hadn't had sex in months. His hand fell away. The air between them thickened.

"No, that's not it. Shame."

Questions swirled through her mind. If Alexis knew the black-market dealer was a bloody gigolo and had given her the instructions anyway, Tess might just kill her.

"What is it you want, Tess? Your friends call you that, right?"

She didn't bother asking what friends he'd spoken to. If he'd been on her social media accounts, he'd likely read every comment and message and would know that no one called her Tessa.

She wouldn't be afraid of him. After all, Lexi hadn't said he was a killer. Surely that would be the first thing she'd tell her. Instead, she'd said he was dangerous. That was fitting. And if he decided to kill her, well, his fingerprints were now on her dress and the wall.

Lifting her chin, she unglued her tongue from the roof of her mouth. "I have a proposition for you. One you won't be able to pass up."

One dark eyebrow climbed with interest. "That so? Well, the only thing I never pass up is money and pussy, so cut to the chase."

More Books by Samantha Wilde

Dangerous Distractions series
Abducted
Bait
Exposed

Pretty Thieves series
The Last Heist
Fully Loaded
Straight Shooter

Blood Brothers series
Bound
Traced
Unchained
Extracted (coming 2022)
Marked (coming 2022)

About the Author

Samantha Wilde resides in Saskatchewan Canada with her husband and two daughters. Ragnar, their red heeler, completes her family. Samantha writes steamy, fast-paced romantic suspense novels in the rare moments she has uninterrupted—even interrupted, she manages to apply words to paper. Aside from her love of writing, her other interests include cooking, fantasizing about working out, and eating far too much chocolate.

Want to hear more from Samantha?
Website: samanthakeith.co
Newsletter: eepurl.com/dPyJI5
Facebook: facebook.com/authorsamanthakeith
Goodreads:
goodreads.com/author/show/17716819.Samantha_Keith
Twitter: twitter.com/authorsamantha
Instagram: instagram.com/authorsamanthakeith
BookBub: bookbub.com/profile/samantha-keith
facebook.com/groups/375343326689529